Goodbye to
Tenth Street

Goodbye to Tenth Street

A novel
by Irving Sandler

Pleasure Boat Studio: A Literary Press
Seattle, Washington

ISBN 978-0-912887-72-2
Library of Congress Control Number 018941389

Editors: Jack Estes, Sara Karrabashlieva, Jeff Welker
Cover design by Catherine Sandler
Book design by Lauren Grosskopf

Pleasure Boat Studio books are available through your favorite bookstore
and through the following:
SPD (Small Press Distribution) 800-869-7553
Baker & Taylor 800-775-1100
Ingram 615-793-5000
amazon.com and bn.com

and through
PLEASURE BOAT STUDIO: A LITERARY PRESS
www.pleasureboatstudio.com
Seattle, Washington

Contact Lauren Grosskopf, Publisher
Email: pleasboatpublishing@gmail.com

Dedicated to

my wife Lucy

my daughter Catherine

my grandson Jackson

PREFACE

I cannot say that any similarity to actual persons or events in this novel is coincidental. My subjects are fictitious, but they and the situations in which I have put them hopefully possess a sense of reality. So do the recognizable characters despite the imagined events in which I have involved them. In short, Peter Burgh, Neil Johnson, Diane Knight, Herbert Stein, Celia Loeb, Morton Nichols, Marshall Hill, and Joseph Sawyer never existed, and yet I have met the likes of them in my more than six decades in the art world. However, I could make them "real" only by inventing them.

PROLOGUE
(September 30, 1963)

On the morning of September 30, 1963, Michael Pearson (or Little Mike, as he was nicknamed), walked south from the Fourteenth Street subway on Fourth Avenue and turned left on Tenth Street. He noted the seedy tenements lining both sides of the street, which looked even drabber in New York City's slate blue light. He stopped at number 86, the studio of Peter Burgh. He climbed up the cast iron steps in front of the building, let himself in with a key the artist had given him, and looked down on Burgh's body sprawled on the floor in front of one of his canvases, his chest covered in drying blood, a revolver in his hand. Sadly, he addressed Burgh's corpse. "I knew I couldn't stop you killing yourself, but I tried, maybe not hard enough." Pearson glanced at a book next to Burgh's body. Balzac's *The Unknown Masterpiece*. "So you've aped Frenhofer's suicide in the end. You should have junked that fucking book years ago."

Pearson phoned the police, and when they arrived told them that he was Burgh's best friend, and yes he would be available for further questioning. After the police were finished examining Burgh's body and had left, Pearson phoned the artist's lawyer, Gilbert Truson, who said he would make funeral arrangements. Pearson then called the *New York Times, Herald Tribune,* and *New York Post.*

The following day, the three newspapers ran front-page news stories. So did the *Daily News,* whose headline read "BIG-TIME ARTIST SUICIDE." The *Times* obituary was written by Mark Wall, its senior art critic, and spread over a third of a page with a photograph of the artist and one of his canvases. It read in part:

> Even a movement such as Abstract Expressionism, despite its growing worldwide recognition, is polluted by mediocrity. It does, however, include a few genuine artists, indeed, painters of sterling achievements. One such was Peter Burgh, justly renowned for his lyrical paintings of the early 1950s. They were heavily influenced by Impressionism, perhaps too heavily, but as abstractions, were nonetheless highly original and exhibited a masterful command of painting rare among his fellow artists. Unfortunately, Burgh's last paintings, exhibited at the Sandy Jones Gallery, were failures, the issue of an artist in decline, but this should not detract from the superb work that preceded them.

In the *New York Post,* Joseph Sawyer wrote, "Had Burgh been a School of Paris painter, his obituaries would have hailed him as a 'Jewel in the Diadem of French Culture.' Americans are uncomfortable with such encomiums, but Burgh's contribution to modern painting in the global arena deserves just this sort of tribute. Indeed, Abstract Expressionism is the triumph of American painting, and in large measure, its stature depends on Burgh's paintings."

CHAPTER 1: Peter Burgh
(July 22, 1956)

Eyes to the floor, Peter Burgh paced from the rack of paintings on one wall of his loft to the window on the opposite wall. He watched his shadow change as he moved. Sweating, he glanced into the glare of overhead floodlights. *It's hot enough for July without you. This frigging heat wave's gonna give me jungle rot.* Burgh stopped and stared at the painting. It consisted of an image of toned down red, yellow, and orange softly brushed areas in the center of the picture that stretched close to the edges but left a border of bare canvas. Colors that generally evoked pleasure looked depressed. *I keep turning beautiful pigment into shit—death. That phony art critic Marshall Hill asked in his crappy review, why don't I get the painting to the picture edges? He added that I paint like a girl, arrogant asshole. Like I can't get it up. But I may damp down the colors even more and leave more canvas to show America's top dog critic that my image has to be its own world. That new critic—what's his name, Sawyer?— understands it. But he still turns me into a latter-day*

Monet, an Abstract Impressionist, like I'm painting hay stacks, or big tits like Renoir. God help us. Screw critics.

Burgh looked down on the newspapers he had spread across the studio floor in front of the painting wall and grimaced at the heaps of drying pigment scattered about. A clump of cadmium red partly covered a headline, "...Miller Admits Helping Communist Front Group." *And the scribbler marries Marilyn Monroe, lucky guy. Three frigging weeks of painting, and nada. How depressing can it get?* He was suddenly aware of the jarring scratch of a needle spinning on his record player's turntable. He walked to the corner of the loft, moved the needle back to the beginning. Louis Armstrong. He stood for a moment listening, relaxing. Then, tensing up, he returned to his canvas. He glanced at his watch. *Past midnight already.*

His eyes again focused on the canvas; he lowered himself onto a wooden folding chair in the middle of the room and lit a Lucky Strike. He picked up a bottle of scotch, which was sitting next to an empty glass near the edge of a glass-topped table covered with mounds of pigment and brushes. He poured an inch into the glass, and as he did, noted that the bottle was half empty. He glanced at two crumpled cigarette packs on the floor and an ashtray full of butts. He shook his head in disgust. *Got to cut down on the drinking and smoking.*

Burgh addressed the painting wearily. "You're frigging hopeless." Picking up a palette knife, he scraped pigment from the canvas onto the pile on the floor. *Three weeks of painting shot to hell.* Burgh suddenly felt exhausted. *Fourteen hours in the studio.* Eyes heavy, he shut them.

Opening them, he shook off his drowsiness, downed the drink on the table, walked unsteadily to the phonograph, flipped it off, and continued on toward the back of the studio, past a dilapidated armchair, a Formica table covered with old art magazines and a radio, past a clothes closet and an unmade bed, which doubled as a couch, above which he had tacked a color reproduction of Piero della Francesca's fresco in Arezzo, a postcard of Jackson Pollock's *Lucifer*, and a small geometric-abstract oil painting by Michael Pearson. Stumbling on a book on the floor, he picked it up, glanced at the title, *Ulysses*, and flipped it toward a bookcase full of books surrounded by stacks of more books on the floor. He looked around his studio. *How shabby can you get? Got to clean this shithouse, straighten it up, like Neil Johnson's loft. Got to talk some babe who stays here for more than a one-night stand into picking up a broom.* He himself did so only when a collector, critic, or curator arranged to drop by.

Burgh felt hungry and recalled that he had not eaten since breakfast. He looked into a small adjoining room, at a sink full of food-encrusted dishes and a pan on a hotplate coated with acrid fat, some of it oozing. Turning away in disgust, he walked to a small refrigerator, opened it, looked inside, and closed it with a frown. He decided to go to the Cedar Street Tavern for whatever food was still available. Perhaps the bar scene would brighten his mood. Burgh washed his hands, removed his paint-spattered overalls, and tossed them on the couch. He removed a pair of corduroy pants and a khaki shirt from the closet and put them on. He reached for a knit tie but changed his mind.

Not in this heat. He glanced at a small mirror on the wall in the bathroom and ran his fingers through his thinning hair. His reflection reminded him of Delacroix's portrait of Chopin, but his face was not as long or thin as the composer's. *Where had I seen it? Can't remember.*

Burgh looked back at his unfinished canvas and shook his head dejectedly, flicked the light switch, walked out of his studio into the hall, and climbed down a flight of uneven steps. The studio odor of oil paint and turpentine faded as he registered the urine smell of bums who had figured out how to jimmy open the front door and, in inclement weather, slept in the hallway. Downstairs, Burgh opened his mailbox, removed an envelope, glanced at the return address—the Whitney Museum—and slipped it into his jacket pocket. Out in the street, the heat intensified the stench of rotting garbage, automobile fumes, and stale liquor that wafted from a cellar bar, a favorite of East Side derelicts. The face of his former wife, Eileen, involuntarily came to mind, but he quickly suppressed it and thought he could use a woman, but shrugged it away.

From beneath the stairs leading from the street to the bar came a muffled voice. "Dime, Mack?"

"Is that you, Red?" Burgh responded.

"Yeah." He threw down two quarters.

"Thanks, sport."

Kicking an empty wine bottle in a brown paper bag out of the way, Burgh walked west to University Place and then south toward Eighth Street and the Cedar's store-front window, which, like a beacon, lit up the deserted street without dispelling its forlorn aspect.

Burgh entered the air-conditioned tavern, sat down on a stool at the bar close to the door and relaxed. Just being there calmed him. He never could figure out why. Perhaps because the bar was frequented by fellow artists. The Cedar's appearance itself had little charm—a nondescript place, no different from thousands of lower-middle class American taverns, a long bar in the front and booths in the rear. Perhaps it was the Cedar's anonymity that Burgh liked. And it served a purpose. Colorlessness became protective coloration. The lack of arty decorations—chianti bottles, driftwood, travel posters, or far-out paintings—kept away the local bohemians who lived the life of art without creating any. And the bar's lack of television made it unattractive to neighborhood folk. Its ordinary appearance also discouraged Madison Avenue types who posed as bohemians after five o'clock, the chic of all varieties who came slumming, and tourists from Brooklyn and the Bronx who came to Greenwich Village to gape at the weirdos. Burgh recalled Willem de Kooning's description of the Cedar as a "no-environment." No picturesqueness, no romance, no nostalgia—just the right hangout for avant-garde artists in New York who wanted to be left to themselves. However, there *was* "art" on the walls—run-of-the-mill 19th century English sporting prints. Burgh found them oddly restful. While studying one in which racehorses jumped over a hurdle, he thought that the trees in the background were nicely handled.

John, the Cedar's owner, who was tending bar, greeted Burgh cordially. John was a former army sergeant. Seeing him always reminded Burgh of his stint as an officer in the Marine Corps during World War II, and he involuntarily stiffened his posture. The two veterans rarely talked about the War, but in an unspoken way, they seemed to recognize their mutual experience and take pride in it. Burgh ordered a scotch and soda and a sandwich or whatever was still available in the kitchen. John said, "You're in luck. Cook's still in the kitchen cleaning up and he'll make you something, not predicting what though."

Drink in hand, Burgh stood up and walked along the length of the bar toward the booths in the rear to see who was there. He heard a drunken bellow, "Burgh, you sad-sack son of a bitch." Jackson Pollock was seated in a booth, and next to him, Marshall Hill, the critic.

"Hi Jack," Burgh sighed.

"Get the fuck over here, asshole."

"Not tonight Jack. Too beat." He felt a twinge of distaste and regret. Wheeling around he retreated back to the far end of the bar. He was joined by Neil Johnson who had emerged from the men's room in the rear. Burgh brightened and said, "Hey, Neil, how's the second-generation hotshot doing?"

"Not as well as I should be what with you old farts, pardon me, old masters, hogging the limelight and shoveling in the dough. Are Jackson and his conniving mouthpiece over there giving you a hard time?"

"Just the expected. But that fat-assed Hill really pisses me off. Did you read what he wrote about me in *Art News*? That I'm arguably the best lady painter around. The asshole said *arguably*, imagine that, arguably. That frigging pen-pusher could really use a seeing-eye dog."

"The beast would probably write better prose than he does. It could be worse. Hill might have had orgasms over your work. After all, he comes all over Pollock's dribbling. All-America's primo art critic and All-America's former supremo painter and current world-class boozer. All hail."

Burgh said gruffly, "Don't talk like that! You owe Jackson. We all owe him. Europe is finally waking up to the fact that we're number one. Jackson did that. The literati are always searching for some novelist who has written the great American novel. But Jackson may have painted the great American picture. He had his brush on this country's pulse, its space, its drama."

"Yeah, that was Jackson then, not now."

Burgh shook his head sadly. "He may still surprise us. Jack was my comrade in the thirties and most of the forties, I mean like a best friend. Looking at him now, it's hard to imagine what he was like before *Life* magazine made him a household name. Before the hard muscles we admired in the 1930s turned to flab. I was painting noble strikers getting clubbed by vicious cops and bloated capitalists sitting on bags of dollars. Jack was into the Mexican muralists. Sounds corny now, but then, God, how exciting it was to argue with him about painting and politics. Before rotgut corroded his brain."

Pollock stared at Burgh and, sensing that he was being talked about, lurched up and started to move out of the booth, knocking over a glass, which shattered on the floor. He shouted, "I'm gonna kick that fucking wimp's ass." John raised a cautioning finger, and Hill waved it away. As big as Pollock and heavier, Hill reached over and held him back.

"Nah, nah, Jackson, let the loser be. It's late. How about finishing our drinks? Let's pay up and go."

Pollock slouched back in the booth, "Second-rate son of a bitch." John came over with a dustpan, swept up the glass shards, and handed the bill to Hill. "Glass is on the house, this one time only."

Burgh looked back at Johnson and continued, "When Jack made his first drip paintings—when was it? 1948? No, 1947—he invited me to his studio on Long Island to look at them. A huge canvas was spread out on the floor, you know, it stretched from where we're at to where John's standing, just like a rug. It was covered all over with streaks of paint, dripped, poured, and splattered. It was titled *Jupiter*, I think. Jack was cold sober that day. He said nothing, just stood there, head bowed, shoulders hunched, not sure of what he'd done or afraid of what I might say. I was amazed. The canvas looked like a holy mess and yet it hung together. It was brand new, never saw anything like it. It was unbelievable the way Jack was both spontaneous and in control. No one who wasn't around at the time can imagine how way-out there Jack's painting looked. We had been schooled to look for structure, any kind of design. But what in hell was Jackson's composition? It looked like chaos. I can still recall the shock. Whatever Jack had made, I felt it, really *felt* it. I told him this and that his pictures had some kind of presence that was really new and important and to keep at it. Some time later, he thanked me and told me how much my encouragement had meant to him in that moment. That was some confession for Jack to have made, even then. I was as surprised as I was touched."

Burgh stopped and looked down, caught up in his thoughts. Johnson began to speak, but in deference to Burgh's reverie, kept quiet.

Burgh went on, "Then, two years later, I had a show of my World War II pictures, my bloody war nightmares that I had translated into Greek myths. That was before your time. They made a big splash. Jack showed up stinko at my opening, looked around, grabbed me, and shouted, 'It's crap, phony Surrealist crap, academic crap, yellow-bellied crap. Fucking bad dreams crap. It's all old hat, dead-end crap. When the fuck are you going to paint something modern, something risky, something real and relevant?' I shoved him away and said, 'Why don't you bugger off, you pathetic drunk.' He swung at me, missed and pitched to the floor. Muttering incoherently, he struggled up and staggered out of the gallery. Everybody looked shocked. I said, 'Forget it. That's Jackson doing his Jackson number. Forget it.' But that night he did me a big, big favor. Sure, he made me furious, but I saw my painting through his eyes and he was right. I knew there and then that they were no longer believable and I couldn't keep knocking them out. A bleeding Hercules wearing sergeant stripes in a foxhole or a beautifully painted rigor mortis. All the 'C's'—critics, curators, collectors—ate it up. Yeah, my pathetic mythic sagas were hailed as the hope of American painting."

Burgh seemed to forget that Johnson was there, and looking into the distance, talked as if to himself. "I would cheer everything I painted, in my head I would cheer it, bravo, bravo, Burgh, *cher maître*. And I'd take my bows. Not after that bout with Jackson. I knew I had to change. I said to myself, 'You paint about society, hurrah for you. But what the fuck does a Greek hero in khaki *mean* today after Hiroshima? And where the fuck are *you* in your painting?' So I stopped painting. This led to months of do-nothing depression. Then I took my cue from Jackson and began to use the improvisational process of painting itself to find out what I ought to be about. I no longer began with an idea of what I ought to paint or what it meant. Nothing satisfied me. Painting became hell. I hated the agony of the not knowing. But I kept on smearing and scraping pigment, until I found something that I felt was authentic. Painting was torture—still is—except in those rare moments, those 'eureka' moments—when a canvas all comes together. They are worth the frigging struggle. And that's how I became a *painter*. Jack, that arrogant son of a bitch, did it."

Burgh looked back at Johnson, "Jack and I would meet again at openings or at parties and chit-chat if he was sober, or, if he was drunk, he would curse and accuse me of hating his work and being in de Kooning's camp, but we would never really chew the fat again. It was a sad ending to our comradeship."

Hill paid the bill and left change on the table. As they passed Burgh on the way to the door, Pollock thrust his gross face aggressively at him. "Think you can paint better than I can? Bullshit." Burgh waved limply at him.

Hill held back and said, "I meant everything I wrote in my review of your show. Why would a big man like you want to paint like a sissy? And your shitty gray isn't color. I don't get it."

Burgh looked directly at Hill and responded quietly, "If you ever did get it, Marshall, I'd worry. It isn't decoration, old buddy, or what you would call 'Apollonian,' whatever the fuck that is, and I hope it never will be." Burgh continued to stare at Hill.

Hill stared back, then hunched forward as if about to throw a punch. Face flushed and fat jowls trembling, he clenched his fists in front of him and began to answer, but instead turned and caught up with Pollock.

Burgh and Johnson watched Pollock and Hill as they walked across the Cedar's window, Pollock stumbling, Hill still hunched up, steadying his companion.

Johnson laughed, "How to make friends and influence people!"

Burgh said, "Him or me?" He shook his head. "Did you see that? The asshole was about to slug me. He's supposed to be good with his fists, but I bet I could whip his frigging ass. That phony, with his humongous reputation of being an 'eye.' All he ever sees when he looks at a picture is whether it apes his stupid idea of what painting ought to be. And he's out to screw me, the power-hungry creep. Neil, young buddy, I think scotch and paranoia are creeping up on me. Watch out for booze and paranoia. They're the occupational diseases of the art world. Nobody can tell you why one picture is better than another, not Hill, not Rosenberg, not Greenberg, not Hess, and certainly not those young punks clawing their way up, like that Sawyer guy. Not anybody. There are no rules for judging what's good or bad. But Hill is able to convince people that he has some special kind of eye for quality. Yeah, a third occupational sickness, crying in your beer."

Burgh smiled and took Johnson by the arm. "Be careful, paranoia can fuck up your mind. End of today's lesson. And watch the booze and yeah, the smoking too."

Johnson said, "Thanks for the sermon, I mean warning, *cher maître*. Hey, what's that paper sticking out of your pocket?"

"Oh, almost forgot about it. It just came." Burgh tore open the envelope, shook out the letter, and glanced at it. "I'm in the Whitney Annual. Big deal."

"I should be so lucky." Neil sighed.

"You will be. I should really turn the frigging bureaucrats down." Burgh hesitated. "But I won't, not yet. The painting will probably sell, and I can use the dough. But how I hate that show, surrounded by all that third-rate crap."

"Your pain gets me right here." Johnson tapped his chest with his thumb. Turning, he said, "But I've got to go now. Got a broad to wake up. See you soon."

"Sure, have a ball. Adios."

Burgh looked around. There were a half-dozen artists left in the bar, none of whom he wanted to talk to. Luckily, no one approached him. John brought him a ham and cheese sandwich with a sliced tomato and a sour pickle on the side and said, "Sorry, that's the best Cook could rustle up."

"It's fine, and I'll have another scotch."

Burgh finished the food and drink, told John to add the bill to his tab, said goodbye, and left unsteadily. The night air set off Burgh's smoker's hack. His eyes teared, and not seeing where he was going, he bumped into someone.

"Excuse me, I'm sorry. Oh, it's you Lewitin. You're out past your curfew tonight." Landes Lewitin, a stout figure dressed in a black suit and black tie, with a black beret, the emblem of his sojourn in Paris, said dejectedly, "I couldn't sleep in this heat." Then, sternly, "You look terrible. If you don't stop boozing, you'll end up a drunk like Pollock and de Kooning and then you'll paint *really* crappy pictures."

"Thanks for the good word, Lewitin old friend. You may be right and now I'm off to bed."

As he passed Lewitin, Burgh called back, "Lucky you don't drink, but paranoia is also bad, worse than booze. Take care."

* * *

The next morning, Burgh stared gloomily at the canvas. He picked up tubes of cadmium red medium, titanium white, and mars yellow, and squeezed a mound of each with smaller piles of orange, blue, and black on the glass-topped table. He was struck by how appealing the pigment in the raw looked and he smiled as he recalled that he always thought of this every time he began to paint. *Who was it that said that the mission of the artist was to make his painting more expressive than pigment squeezed out of a tube? Lewitin? Yes, it was Lewitin on one of his better days.*

Ruffling his fingers through an inch-wide brush, Burgh dipped it in the red, moved close to the surface of the canvas, looked over the remains of the image he had knifed out, hesitated for a moment, took a deep breath, and gently made a single red mark. The aggressiveness of the red made him shudder. He quickly mixed the white and black into gray and darkened the red, wiping and scraping away what didn't feel right. He continued applying red and gray, now with touches of grayed orange and yellow, using different brushes and his palette knife. Stepping back, the picture felt too decorative, despite the dark cast of the colors. He began to paint more quickly, growing more assured as he did. Then suddenly, the shaded colored marks began to emanate a somber light that he had been aiming for. He didn't know how to create it, but knew that when he encountered it, his picture would be finished.

Burgh suddenly stopped, stood back, contemplated the painting, and lit a cigarette. His hand was shaking. *Anxiety? Alcohol? Nicotine? All three? Anxiety.* He felt a tightening in his chest and a shortness of breath. He sat down still staring at the canvas. *No, the image is not there yet, but what more can I do?*

Burgh tried to steady his hand. Then, he spun around and walked out of the studio, not bothering to lock the door. *Which way to go? Toward Fourteenth Street or Houston?* He stood rigid for a moment and headed north on Fourth Avenue to Union Square. He stopped to listen to a soapbox orator bad-mouth President Eisenhower as the tool of American imperialism. The text was hackneyed, but delivered with passion. *Passionate enough to shoot a Trotskyite in the back of his head but not smart enough to be a Soviet spy.* Burgh returned to the studio. *Back in the thirties, we used to call any anti-communist or even non-communist "a running dog of American imperi-*

alism." We actually said things like that, and believed them, or did we? The walk calmed Burgh. Back in the studio, he studied the canvas close-up, moving first to one side, then to the other. He backed away. It was coming along.

Burgh lit a cigarette, took two puffs, and pressed the butt into a bucket of sand. He picked up a brush to begin again, thought better of it, and stopped. He would let the canvas rest for now.

* * *

Burgh continued working on the painting for another two weeks to the day. That morning, as he looked at the canvas, he suddenly began to sweat and felt a panic attack coming on. *Snap out of it. You can finish this picture. You always have.* Staring at the canvas, he dipped his brush into the yellow mound as the doorbell rang. It both startled and disturbed him. *Not now! Who could it be? Don't answer it.*

He looked out the window. It was Stanley Jones, his dealer. Burgh shouted down, "What are you doing downtown? Why aren't you minding the store?'

"I was visiting de Kooning. Thought I'd look in on you, if you weren't busy."

"Of course I'm busy—painting masterpieces. But it's okay. Come on up. Here's the key."

Burgh dropped it. Jones caught it, let himself into the building, and walked up to Burgh's studio. He stood before the canvas. "So that's what an unfinished Burgh looks like."

"You may be the first to see one, and I don't know why I didn't turn it to the wall. It's still nowhere."

"Looks pretty good to me. What's wrong with it?"

"Well, that grayed red area looks good. But that off-yellow next to it is still dead, deader than the proverbial doornail. And that bitch of an orange, even that small area, kills the light. Wrong orange. It all needs changing, but how? Change what? Why? The colors? The brushwork? The interval between the colors? Why? Change them? Like I said to Kline the other night, 'It's the intervals between the colors that count.' Look there in the lower right corner. Mark Rothko snuck in while I wasn't looking. I love Mark, but he's gotta go. Why?"

Burgh paused and peered at the canvas and said more to himself than to Jones, "It's still that frigging orange and yellow. I've diggled those frigging colors more than a hundred times, at least a hundred, and I still haven't got them right." He turned to his dealer, "Now you know what the romantic life of the painter is, Stan, old man, diggling orange and yellow. I think I'll cut my ear off. What's it for? Why am I breaking my balls? Nobody asked me. Still, why and what for?"

"Go ask Piero or Pablo. Their names start with 'P' like yours. I wonder what they'd say?"

"They'd probably empathize. They're not like the money-bags you peddle my art to."

"Bite your tongue. Don't bad-mouth the golden geese."

Burgh smiled. "You know Stan, once when I was asked 'what's-it-mean' by one of your fat-ass collectors, I rolled my eyes heavenward and then looked him straight in the eye and said, sensitive-like, 'It has my light.' He seemed to want more, so I floated three inches off the floor and intoned, 'It's also the light of our time, a kind of *zeitlicht*, as the Germans would say.' *Zeitlicht*, pretty impressive. And the funny thing is that, pretentious though it sounds, I think I meant it."

Jones looked up. "The light of our time, the *zeitlicht*, I like it. I'm going to use it. Make you a fortune."

"Lotsa luck. Do you think Morton Nichols would buy that rap?"

"You bet. That vulgar money-grubber is in the dog house after he flipped the Kline he bought from me and sold it at auction for a big profit, the one I sold him less than a year ago. I told him if he wants to be a dealer to take his business elsewhere. But if you want to sell him something, be my guest."

"He asked to see me."

"Double your prices, triple them. And remember I get my cut. By the way, I need some young blood in the gallery. Grapevine has it that Joan Mitchell is an up-and-coming painter. Do you know her work?"

"Yeah, she's the real thing. Check her out."

"Well, it's time for you to return to your glamorous misery."

"Thanks for your condolences."

Burgh accompanied Jones to the door and returned to his canvas. He reached for a tube of white and brushed it into the yellow. He said out loud, "It's there—or almost there." *Just like that. But like* Maître *Lewitin said, "No matter how light the painting is, it's not light enough."*

Burgh lightened the orange. He stood back and lit a cigarette. *That's it.* Then, dejectedly, he stared at the canvas and shrugged. *It looks too pat, just like my painting is supposed to look. It's like a Peter Burgh knock-off.*

Burgh shifted the brush from his right to his left hand. The anxiety began to build up in him again. *The yellow's not working, it's like piss, goddamn piss.* He was suddenly exhausted. He backed away from the canvas and stared at it. *It's really not bad; the light's looking good.* He felt better and decided to stop for the day.

* * *

Before going to sleep that night, Burgh removed his journal from the drawer of the night table near his bed and wrote, "Stanley Jones asked what would Piero or Picasso think about my work? That's not the issue. The question is, why am I painting differently from them?"

In the middle of the night, Burgh bolted up, eyes open, just as he had once or twice a week since the battle of Guadalcanal. Sweating and groggy, he fumbled for a cigarette and lit it. He was awoken by the Dream—a skirmish in the jungle during World War II. As his head cleared, Burgh recalled every detail. A squad in the platoon he commanded was on patrol, working its way out of swampy vegetation in a ditch. A flare. Then a burst of machine-gun fire. A cry, "I'm hit, I'm hit." It was Corporal Jim Ryan who had been sent out to scout. Burgh and the rest of his men pitched to the ground. Then Ryan cried out, "They got me in the gut. God it hurts. Help me, it hurts."

Burgh whispered to the men on his right and left, "Pass it along. Move back into the ditch. Hug the ground. Don't fire back. Pass it along."

Frankie Smyth, his sergeant, said, "I'm going out there to help him."

"No, stay put. That's an order." But Smyth had already begun to crawl out.

In a few minutes, he crawled back and said, "Jim's guts are all over the place. He's bought it." Another flare. A burst of machine-gun fire. Before he could take cover, Smyth rolled over dead on top of Burgh, blood spurting over both of them.

Ryan kept moaning, "Help...hurt." Then a shot—and silence. The Japanese machine gun opened up.

Burgh began to fire his carbine in the direction of the sound and shouted, "Commence fire!" His men opened up. Then, a few minutes later, "Cease fire!" Silence. Burgh said, "I think we got the bastards or they've shoved off. We'll wait here till dawn." When he and his men were convinced that the Japanese had retreated, they retrieved Ryan's body. Burgh suspected that his corporal had been shot by one of his own men. Was it necessary? It was clear that the man was dying. Why let him suffer? Burgh asked no questions and did not include the mercy killing, if it was that, in his report.

Fully awake, Burgh stubbed his cigarette in the ashtray, lit another one, lay back, and wiped the sweat from his face with his pillow. He was suddenly overcome with fear and hate, like the fear he felt that night on Guadalcanal but hadn't shown, and the hatred of the enemy whose brutality he had not forgiven and never would. Burgh recalled that, in the Dream, the image of Smyth's face was that of his father with a bullet hole in his right temple. He later wondered what Siggy Freud would make of that.

Burgh never talked about the skirmish, except once to Eileen. One night, after waking up shaking and wet with sweat, he blurted out the Dream. He then confessed, "I was scared in Guadalcanal. Scared shitless. Sure, back at company headquarters, I acted the cool cat my men admired. If they only knew the truth! I told my captain that Smyth deserved a medal, even though he disobeyed my order to stay put. Still, I couldn't help feeling I should have gone instead of Frankie. Dammit, he was younger than me. He was battle-savvy and his know-how carried me through the frigging campaign. I loved that son of a bitch. I looked down on him the next morning, crumpled on the ground, brains and blood spattered on his blonde hair. What a great-looking guy, what a waste, almost as handsome as my old buddy, Little Mike. What helped get me through the war? It was Captain Carson. He was a shoot-from-the-hip career Marine who had seen more than his share of combat, but he understood my anguish. He said, 'You did right out there. Your sergeant should have obeyed orders. You gotta forget it.' But I couldn't. The nightmares kept recurring and so did the guilt. And the question I kept stewing over was could I have done something different that night on patrol? That goddamn Dream is sucking my lifeblood. It's my Dracula. Well, I did become a hero later, knocked out a machine-gun nest in Saipan; was awarded a Silver Star for bravery. Big frigging warrior. What did that prove? We all knew that we could have been killed at any moment, and it mostly depended on luck. Frankie's death hit me like no other death I had ever witnessed except my father's, and I had seen a hell of a lot of dying. Maybe if I had time to mourn when Frankie bought it, I wouldn't have these panic attacks, but there was no time. The goddamn war didn't stop."

Eileen had cradled his head in her arms and wiped his face dry with the end of the sheet. Burgh began to shiver. Eileen held him tighter. He looked up at her face, classic features, a mass of blonde curls, and for an instant, it reminded him of Smyth dead on the ground, then of Pearson. She reached down and kissed him. "Like what's-her-name said in *Don Giovanni*, I know what'll make bad dreams go away."

* * *

Burgh looked at his canvas the next morning with great expectations. From a distance, he addressed it, "Sensational." But as he approached, he was overcome with feelings of inadequacy. *Of course it looks good, so pretty, so frigging pretty. I've copped out again.*

For years, Burgh had been debating with himself, Rothko, Guston, Pearson, and other artist acquaintances of his, as to whether art ought to focus on the artist's traumas, fears, rage, and depression and, by extension, the awareness of death and of the world's senseless bestiality and violence—the Holocaust—or whether it should provide a release from anxiety and anger, and even convey something of the beauty and joy of life.

Rothko said to him, "You want optimism? In your grave?"

Pearson countered, "Sure, life under capitalism is shitty, but do we have to make it worse? Society has gotta get better. Can't our art speak to that future?"

But Burgh asked, "How can we avoid lapsing into decoration?" Or, with a scornful edge in his voice, "designer art?" He quipped to Pearson, "It's either angst or self-indulgence." But Burgh knew that he had no choice and that he had to paint from his "inner necessity" as Kandinsky said, without sentimentality—ruthlessly. He was often surprised that what he considered his tragic paintings sold and he felt somewhat guilty about it. One of his collectors, Morton Nichols, told him that they were "lyrical." Maybe his pictures were more decorative than he thought.

Burgh picked up a brush and put it down. *That frigging orange!* Reaching for a rag, without looking, he whipped it across the orange. He said aloud, "holy shit." Rather than depress him, the smear elated him. It presented fresh options. He suddenly *recognized* the image. Burgh weighed a tube of orange in his hand, squeezed two inches out on the glass table top, then added small piles of yellow, white, and black. He placed three brushes within reach of one hand and a palette knife in the other, moved close to the canvas, and began to paint without backing up—barely thinking, barely looking—literally with his nerve ends. The cerebral phase was over; it had only been preparation, prelude to this moment. He mixed pigment and brushed it quickly, using his palette knife to cut away what looked unfelt. Caught up in the intensity of the flow, he pivoted from the canvas to the glass tabletop. He painted as if by instinct, his eyes barely scanning the surface. His eyes ricocheted to and from its four sides as he brushed and scraped, bonding the strokes and searching for his light.

As Burgh painted, the shapes became weightier, darker, and massed in the center of the canvas. To contain them, the space became more three-dimensional. He suddenly stopped and stood back, surprised. He hadn't painted shapes like those before. They were new. Then it struck him that the ones in the middle looked like figures, blurry figures. He reached for his palette knife to scrape them out. He stopped in mid-air. The forms were at once strange and oddly familiar. He would leave them as is. Burgh stepped back in order to take in the entire canvas. Sweating and exhausted, he lit a cigarette, took a gulp of scotch, and looked at what he had done. Then dragging himself to his feet he examined the surface of the canvas inch by inch. It looked better. He stood straight up and studied the canvas. *Now what to do? Nothing. It has my light, even with those peculiar heavy shapes in the middle. It's done.* Burgh felt an upsurge of elation tinged with fatigue, a momentary sense of conquest.

* * *

Burgh slept late the following morning. He then examined his canvas closely. It was indeed finished. As he dressed, the phone rang. He picked it up. "Little Mike here. Just checking in on you, old comrade. How are you?"

"Couldn't be better. Just finished a painting. I'm looking at it now, and you know, the image reminds me of some pictures I made in the 1930s, you may remember, like the one of striking workers grouped around a union organizer with a clenched fist on a soap box haranguing them. Would you believe this? It's got bulky shapes that look like figures, one even has a brush stroke for a face, and they're in a kind of circle. But don't tell anyone. I'm an abstract artist, aren't I?"

"How should I know? Am I an art critic? I called to say that I'm going out of town for a few weeks. I have a teaching gig at the Oklahoma School of Art. They never heard of my commie past or don't care."

"Great, phone as soon as you return."

Burgh hung up. He continued to mull over the remark he made to Pearson. If the forms in the new picture resembled those he painted two decades ago, was there some underlying connection? Maybe even something in his psyche? He had repudiated his earlier Social Realist works, even told a collector not to exhibit the one he owned. Burgh would rethink the issue of figuration versus abstraction, but not now.

Suddenly, Burgh didn't want to look at the painting anymore and turned it to the wall. He remembered that he had promised Johnson to meet him at the Cedar. But that was later. He would shower, get a decent meal, maybe take in a movie. As he walked out of his building, head erect, rays of the setting sun broke though a bank of leaden clouds. *Even the Good Lord rewards a good painting.* Burgh looked up into the glow, and raising his hand to his temple, saluted it. Even Tenth Street—polluted, desolate Tenth Street—looked agreeable in God's light. He caught himself. *Come now, don't get sentimental. It doesn't suit you.*

Johnson was waiting for Burgh at the Cedar nursing a beer. Burgh joined him and, after the how-are-you's, lit a cigarette, ordered a scotch, and announced, "I just finished a painting, and I'm still on a high. Weeks of thinking this and thinking that, pushing this, pushing that, and then, bingo, the moment you stop thinking and just do it. You know that feeling. What a moment, like a world-class ejaculation. No, truly, truly—it's better than sex."

"Whoa, don't get carried away."

"And then it's over, and you want the damned picture to go away. Like some broad you've had a one-nighter with but don't know what to say to her the next morning. You want the picture out. OUT! Maybe it's because you're out of it. Who said it, de Kooning? When you begin a painting, the whole art world—artists, critics, curators, dealers, collectors—are in the studio with you, trying to get your attention, ordering you around. Then they leave by one until only you're left, and then you leave."

Burgh added quietly, "Funny, I never know whether I can finish another picture, find my light, whatever that is, but I know when I have it. I wish I could figure out how to produce it. But what do I know? Let's celebrate. Your next drink is on me."

"Thanks, last-of-the-big-time-spenders."

They ordered their drinks and Burgh said, "I read your statement in the new *Art News*. You called yourself a professional artist. Did you really mean that?"

"Sure do. I've got an MFA, certified by Yale even. I would hang it in my studio, like some dentist's diploma, but you old farts would sneer at me."

"More likely laugh."

Johnson stated, "You can get a good art education, make honest art in your studio, and have a career in the art world, and even make some dough. It may help to kiss some col-lector-curator-critic ass, but you don't have to jump on any bandwagon."

Burgh interjected, "I'm also interested in fame and money, but it bugs me that I am. It doesn't seem to bother you."

"I take what I can get, but I won't sell out."

Burgh shrugged.

Johnson added, "Not starving may make it easier to paint but it doesn't make painting any easier."

"I'll buy that. But I don't feel like a professional. I once thought I knew what that meant but no longer."

Johnson downed his drink and tipped the empty glass at Burgh. "Thank you for your charity, old sport. You won't mind if I run out on you. I've arranged to visit the studio of a lady artist. Maybe get laid, if I tell her how great her art is and seem to mean it."

"Don't tell her she paints as good as a man."

"Not until after."

Burgh watched Johnson stride to the door and admired his slim young body. *The question remains, do you really believe what you just told me? Can you, young friend, make honest art?*

* * *

Burgh returned to his studio, flicked on the lights, and turned the picture around. He was suddenly overcome by doubt. Pacing up and down in the back of the room, he could no longer fathom why he thought it was finished. On the other hand, he could think of nothing more that he could do. *Is it any good? What would Piero or Pablo say? Is this the latest word in the grand tradition of Western art? Or the best I can do in the aftermath of Stalin, Hitler, Mussolini, and Hirohito? Millions butchered—Frankie. Was Piero's time any better? Did he have any doubts? Is it like Rothko said, "you can't avoid doubt, not if you're for real?" Why can't I, after a quarter century of painting, just make a Burgh picture, fabricate it? Why the anguish, the pain? Be a professional, like Neil says he is. Turn it out. Who would know the difference? The few that count. That's who.*

Burgh lit a cigarette. *Does the world need this picture, a picture of my private feelings, my existential anxiety? Meyer Schapiro says that today's kitsch culture needs authentic art to combat it. In the thirties, Meyer would have asked if it was good for the proletariat. I would have too.* Burgh snickered at the thought. *Enough beating myself. I'll never get it right, get it all. That's what the hero in Balzac's novel, Frenhofer, tried to do—paint pure passion, and he ended up killing himself. Could I ever do myself in? Nah, no future in it. Go out, take a walk. Look at some chess players in Washington Square.*

As Burgh was about to open the door, he turned and looked again at his canvas. *Should I dig into it once more or begin another? It is finished! Start a new one.* But why did he feel depressed? *Is it the painting's depressed look, its tragic cast, or what it's still missing? The Beyond!*

* * *

Two days later, Burgh sat at the Cedar bar making water circles with his scotch glass. John stood nearby looking over some bills. Burgh glanced at the clock in the rear and said to John, "Two A.M. Ought to go home." John grunted. Burgh remained where he was. He watched Joseph Sawyer enter and walk towards him.

Burgh spoke first. "It's kinda late. Don't baby art critics have a curfew? So, what's the word from *Art News*? Does Tom Hess still not love me?"

Sawyer looked distraught, "I don't think you've heard."

"Heard what?"

"Jackson Pollock is dead, killed in a car crash."

"What? When?"

"I heard it from Joan Mitchell. It happened several hours ago. Out on Long Island. Smashed his car into a tree. A lady friend was also killed."

Burgh's stomach knotted up. "Son of a bitch. Bet he was drunk. Son of a bitch. Car crash. Hit a tree. Dead."

He sat silent, looking at the floor. Then he ordered Sawyer a scotch and himself a double. "They should have confiscated his driver's license years ago and impounded that goddamn Ford of his. Was it suicide? Did they say? Where was Lee?"

"No, no word about him killing himself. I thought you and Pollock didn't get along."

"What does that mean? That we didn't hold hands? He was a great painter—and my comrade—until he became a household name and a drunk. I owe him my life as an artist, more than I can say."

Burgh beckoned to John for a refill. Sawyer refused a

second drink and said, "You're heading for a world-class hangover."

Burgh wanted to get drunk but the liquor was having no effect. "The son of a bitch was younger than me. August the eleventh, 1956, mark this day, August the eleventh, a milestone in American art. I gotta get out of here."

"Let me walk with you."

"Thanks. But I'll be okay. Need to be alone."

Burgh staggered out into the dark and began to wander the streets aimlessly.

* * *

Weeks after Pollock died, Burgh could not paint. *Why am I chained to the brush?* He would pore over his collection of art postcards. *Was any painting worth a life?*

CHAPTER 2: Michael Pearson & Celia Loeb
(September 1, 1956)

Burgh was caught up in painting when the phone rang. It was Michael Pearson. "Hi Pablo. Are you free? Can I come over?"

"Oh, sure Little Mike."

"You're not working?"

"It's okay. Give me a couple of hours."

Burgh lit a Lucky Strike, downed the dregs of a drink, and poured another. *What can I do? Little Mike is my burden. Now that I have money, I have to look after him.*

Pearson came in with a painting under his arm.

Burgh said, "I've told you a hundred times that you don't have to bring me anything. How many of your canvases do I already have, at least two dozen?"

"It's a good one from the 1930s, I haven't sold you many of those."

Pearson propped the picture against the glass table, settled himself in a chair, accepted a scotch and said, "I just built stretchers for that jerk, Neil Johnson. He says you recommended me. What a pretentious asshole. Just because he's making it, he thinks he can lord it over me. He even tried to lecture me on art. Can you imagine that? I can paint rings around that punk. I took my work around to galleries again last week. There's always a hoity-toity skinny broad with dark glasses sitting at the front desk looking down her nose at me. Me! With my more than twenty-five years as a painter. One looked me up and down and said that the gallery wasn't taking any new artists, wasn't even looking at new work. I said, 'Do I look new?' Then I asked her if I could use the toilet and she looked at me as if I might contaminate it and said, 'It's not a public facility but okay, use it this once.' As I left, I told her not to worry, my syphilis was in remission. I know my work doesn't fit what the art world wants, but I get so fucking mad."

Pearson continued, "Sometimes I think I was better off when I was dirt poor, I mean not just me, but all of us. I ran into that dealer, Celia Loeb, on the street yesterday. The Park Avenue slut made believe she didn't see me. But I know she did."

"You shouldn't let people like that get you down." *You look like a bum. Smell of cheap rye, need a bath and a shave. Your faded denim jacket is dirty, your heavy boots are cracked. You look more unemployed than you were during the Great Depression.*

Pearson said, "And the love of my life, Julia, that bitch, is after me again for money I don't have. I can't imagine why I ever married her. Shit. I can't blame her for leaving me. I was a real fuck up. Even after that bastard McCarthy shot down my teaching career, I coulda done carpentry, owned my own business by now, and painted on the side. She's sucking my blood."

Pearson's complaint triggered Burgh's memory of his own marriage. "Yeah, I know what you mean. I keep trying to forget Eileen, but I can't. She was so in love with me and my art. She wanted to be my muse and my wife and I denied her that. When she told me she was pregnant, her face was all lit up, she was so happy. I said, 'Eileen, how could you do this to me? Think of my art. How can I paint with some brat hanging around?' I'm still haunted by the hurt in Eileen's eyes. There was worse to come. I told her that as an artist I had to be free. What baloney. Free to sleep around. Wiggle a fanny in my direction and I dropped my pants. At first, Eileen tried to look the other way. But it got too much for her. The end came when one of my 'conquests,' a teenage blonde, whom I can hardly remember, accosted her. 'Peter loves me,' she said, 'and you're standing in our way.' Then Eileen packed up and left. And only then did I recognize how much I needed her, loved her—too late, too late. And I never saw the daughter I didn't want. But I've told you that a hundred times."

Pearson said, "Five hundred. Peter, you've got to stop beating yourself up about Eileen."

Burgh responded, "That sore will never heal. I can't stop picking at it and wallowing in self-pity. You cry on my shoulder, I'll cry on yours. What sad sacks we are. Aw, fuck it. It's funny Little Mike, you're the only one I can confide in about my life. I wonder why?"

"Must be because we grew up together during the good old Depression and the War, when we were young, promising, and cute."

"And the Holocaust."

"Yes, the Holocaust. That too."

Pearson looked down at the floor and mumbled, "I'm a little short of cash. Buy this painting? Like for a hundred and fifty. Can you spare it?"

Burgh answered, "Look, Little Mike, don't bring me any more paintings. You know I'll give you money when I have it, and I have some now."

"I'm making believe it's not a handout. I know it's nuts. But indulge me. Make believe you're a bona fide collector and that I'm selling my work to you. Like I keep telling you, one day, believe me, one day, there will be a revival of my work, all of it, and I'll be art history. And when they discover me, they'll discover you, as the major collector of Little Mike's masterpieces. If you're still alive, you'll be in the clover, a rich bastard, like the ones we always hated. So put my masterpieces in your storage and wait."

"You're going to make me a bona fide bourgeois. Thanks."

Burgh picked up the picture Pearson had brought and studied it. "It is one of your best. It's terrific."

"You didn't think I would sell you anything less?"

"The sad thing is, Little Mike, all I can spare is a hundred."

Pearson said with a small smile, "That'll be more than enough."

Burgh felt a pang of guilt. *It's the Great Depression talking.*

"No, come to think of it, I can swing a hundred and fifty, and I'll let you buy me dinner at the Cedar."

"For a hundred and fifty, the treat's on me."

Burgh sat in Pearson's loft looking at a canvas. Pearson, slumped in a chair next to him, said, "A goddamn washy Mondrian. Ten years of fucking up Piet's edges by smearing pigment. Liquidating them, no pun intended. And the upshot: goddamn decoration."

"You're being too hard on yourself. It looks really good to me."

"Big deal. I don't know why I keep churning this stuff out."

"Sure you do. You want to make work that's both free and in control, like you want your life to be. Geometric abstraction enables you to do that. It's what you need to make. Maybe we all need your message."

"Collectors sure as hell don't. I keep asking, 'Is this canvas what humanity needs?'"

"In our frigging world, I say yes. And so do you, more than you think."

"Do you really think humanity needs pretty colors? I used to be a longshoreman and an infantryman. Now I paint like an old lady. It's decoration. I should title it, *Explosion in a Posh Boutique.* It ain't enough. And if I can't come up with anything more I keep asking myself, why go on painting? I don't know. I just keep doing it. But I don't know why anymore."

"The day you stop doing it, you'll be in deep shit."

They heard a noise and looked toward it. A rat had nested in a pile of old yellow newspapers.

Burgh shook his head and said, "Little Mike, when you're

not whining, put a broom to this floor every now and then and get rid of the junk. It'll change your mood."

"Thanks for the advice, old comrade."

* * *

After Burgh left, Pearson turned to the canvas. The dirt and the filth he was living in, his stomach raw from cheap food and cheaper rye, his nagging ex-wife no longer mattered. He suddenly saw how he could fix an edge that had been bothering him for days. A touch to the right. But what does it matter? It mattered to Mondrian. Pearson turned to a postcard of a Mondrian painting tacked to the wall, tipped his brush to it, and said, "Okay Piet, I'll do it for you."

Pearson shifted the edge an eighth of an inch and got that old frisson of elation, but just for a moment and then the doubts returned. He reached for a bottle of rye and poured three inches into a dirty glass, not only to blot out his thoughts, but also the sight of the dark and dirty studio in which he had been reduced to living and working. *Peter keeps saying, "Little Mike, you're a master painter." Does that justify my shitty life?*

* * *

Burgh phoned Celia Loeb at her gallery, "I want to talk to you about my old buddy Mike Pearson. He's a terrific artist. I know he's difficult, but he's really had a tough time, tougher than you can imagine. I'll tell you about it sometime. Mike's good, a damn fine painter. It's time for the art world to take another look. What can you do for him?"

She replied, "Pearson's a creep and a loser. He showed me his paintings once, and I said I couldn't take him on. He kept bringing more, hounding me. I told my receptionist to put him off. But if you recommend him, what can I say? Why don't we meet at the bar at the Pierre and kick it around?"

'You're on."

'Better still. Let's have a cocktail at my place."

'Around six?" *This is an invitation to a bout of fucking. Well, it's a good deed for a friend.*

* * *

Loeb poured scotches for Burgh and herself and looked at him smoking and studying a painting by Diebenkorn on the wall across from them.

He nodded, "Not bad, not bad at all. Who is he?"

"Diebenkorn's his name. Young California artist. But let's talk about you. You look yummy." *I couldn't lure you into my den before, but now I gotcha. Mike Pearson must mean a lot to you. Business first or sex? Sex. Then love? God, how I hope so. But how to start? Lay it on the line. Peter Burgh, you are about to be fucked like you've never been fucked before.*

"You do know Peter, I'm going to seduce you, or try to. Now, don't resist."

She began to undress, wiggling her body provocatively as she did, and the sight of her nakedness excited him. When he removed his pants and shorts, she pushed him on the bed and clamped her mouth around his penis. She looked up at him, "Let me have it?" He came quickly. She held him in her mouth until he softened. "You taste delicious. Let's celebrate my conquest with a bottle of champagne. I've got one on ice." After two glasses, he reached over, caressed her vagina, and mounted her. Pressing his hard penis into her, it felt like the old days for him. Even the thought of Eileen didn't curb his sense of macho power. She moaned, "The earth is moving. Oh, Peter, don't stop."

As they rested, Loeb said, "You know Peter, it was never this good. How was it for you?"

"Great."

"You seemed to really enjoy the fellatio. I don't suck cock, but you're special, so you get a special treat. Any time you want an encore, just whistle."

"I'll keep your invitation in mind." *I wonder why this time I performed so well. What was it about Celia? She's good looking but nothing special. She's passionate and great at sex, but that doesn't matter. That's it. It doesn't really matter.* Peter felt a pang of remorse. *Was she just a convenient piece of ass? Could there be more than that?*

Loeb said, "Okay Peter. I've been thinking about Pearson. Here's what I'll do. I'll buy ten of his paintings—I get to choose—at four thousand dollars for the lot, to be paid in installments of four hundred dollars a month. That'll leave me free to develop a campaign for him. And I'll give him a show, of course."

"It's so little money."

"That's where you come in. You've got to convince him that it's to his advantage. If I succeed, the paintings he has left will be worth much more. If I fail, then Pearson will have eighty bucks a week for a year, that's a year free to paint. All he might lose are ten works nobody wants, and most important to me, I won't lose too much. I'll even return the paintings I can't sell, gratis. That's my offer."

"Won't you sweeten it a bit?"

"Okay, anything I sell above four thousand, he gets fifty percent. That's my limit. What I'm doing isn't business. It's charity. And I'm doing it for the love of you."

"I'll run with it. I think I ought to go with you when you visit him. Mike is unpredictable. One moment he's a pussycat, the next moment, a crazed tiger. Look, I'll add on a thousand to your four, but keep it between us. That'll give him a hundred a week."

Loeb said, "Suit yourself. Our business is done? I'm not one for fancy talk, but I have had this thing for you, had it a long time. It might even be love. It's surely infatuation. You must have sensed that."

He nodded. She went on, "Any feelings on your part?"

"I'll be frank. I'm still recovering from the breakup of my marriage. It's still got me all shook up. I just can't commit now."

"Didn't that happen so long ago? Isn't it time to let go?"

"I know. I keep trying to get it out of my system."

She said breathily, "I want you Peter, and I'm going to get you. But for now, anytime you could use another cuddle, I'll be here for you."

"I don't know. Celia, I don't want to use you. If you feel about me as you say you do, you could get hurt."

"I'm a big girl. I can take care of myself."

As Burgh was about to leave, Loeb said, "Please don't

take what I'm about to ask you as a quid pro quo for helping your friend, but I would kill to have a drawing show of yours in my gallery."

"I'll talk to Jones. I think he'll go for it."

* * *

When Burgh told Pearson about Loeb's proposal, he said, "Five thousand for ten canvases? It's not much."

"No, but it's enough to keep you going for a year, a whole year, and if she succeeds, the rest of your work will be worth a bundle. Besides, you'll get a show. Put the work out in the world after all these years, and who knows what can happen. But what's really important is you'll get a hundred bucks a week, which will leave you free to paint. It's been a long time, Little Mike. This could be your break."

"Okay, I'll go along with it. Pablo, I know you've put yourself out for me, and I can't thank you enough. I mean it. You've been my friend, in capital letters. What more can I say? I'm going to cry."

"No sentimentality, please. Enough now. I'll call Loeb and set up a time. I'll come along to ease things. It's important that I remind you that she's your class enemy, a rich bitch. Her father was a killer in the clothing trade. His factory is now union, but he fought it with all his might. Celia went to Vassar. One of the few Jews they let in. She hated the shiksas but copied them and learned their act better than they did. She still plays at being a high-class Wasp. Can you cope with that? If not, let's not go there. You'll have to behave yourself. But it's for your art. Are you reading me?"

"Sure, Peter. Loud and clear. I'll behave."

* * *

Little Mike managed to straighten out his loft, got rid of the piles of old newspaper, put out some rat traps, cleaned the toilet, washed the dishes, swept and mopped the floor, changed the bedding, even ran a damp rag over the windows. He bought a bottle of decent scotch, just in case, and some peanuts. Burgh and Loeb arrived and, after hellos, Pearson began to show them his paintings and Loeb began to make her selection. At the seventh picture, Pearson said, "I'd hate to give you that one for the pittance you're paying. I worked on that baby for more than a year."

"I know it's not much. But there may be a lot more in the offing."

At the ninth picture, he said, "The money's not enough."

"That's all I'm able to afford now."

"This is my life, you know."

She remained silent. He began to redden. He rasped, "You're sucking my blood."

"Look, Peter explained the deal to you."

He began to shout, "Fucking bloodsucker. She's offering me peanuts. It's an insult to my work."

Burgh interjected, "Cool it, Little Mike, please cool it. Turn down the deal if you want to, but don't insult your guest."

"Who the fuck does she think she is?"

Loeb said, "I'm out of here."

Before Pearson or Burgh could say anything, she swept out of the studio.

Pearson quickly subsided and said miserably, "I screwed up, didn't I? After all you've done for me, I screwed up. Can you talk to her Pablo, can you tell her I'm sorry, and get her to come back? I'll do whatever she says."

"I'll see what I can do. But meanwhile, you ought to phone her and try to patch things up yourself."

* * *

Pearson called Burgh, "I've been phoning Loeb. Phoned her a dozen times. Her secretary says she'll call back, but she doesn't."

"Look, Little Mike. Write her a note. Tell her how sorry you are and that the deal is on. That may work. I'll also give her call."

Burgh phoned Loeb. Before he could say a word, she shouted, "No way, Peter, I'm not going to deal with that fucking lunatic again. You tell him that. It's over. Finito."

"Come on, Celia, poor Mike is mortified. You know how crazy artists are."

"Okay, I'll calm down. I'll tell you what. If you run interference, I'll take on Pearson's work. But I want to see that maniac as little as I can. I mean it. You choose one more canvas, that'll make ten. I'll have 'em picked up, and see what I can do with them. We'll discuss the details of a show later. How about tonight? Let me take you out to dinner. Celebrate our deal. Come at seven. I'll reserve for eight-thirty. Give us some time for a drink and…"

***

That would be the first of many dinners, then openings of shows, concerts, and plays. Loeb did not hide her love for Burgh. How did he feel about her? He found her attractive and neither interesting nor boring, but pleasant enough. At first, she talked about sales and collectors, but she soon stopped when she sensed Burgh's disinterest. She had a heartfelt feeling for art. Most important, she was convenient, and he felt free—sexually free—with her but he recognized that his freedom issued from a feeling of detachment on his part, and an undemanding attitude on hers. He sensed that his apathy was a symptom of his underlying depression. But he had to help Pearson and why not get a blowjob and a lay doing so?

One night she said, "Tell me about your marriage."

"I don't want to go there."

"Please, who was she?"

"Oh, what the hell. Eileen was a social worker who worked with ghetto kids, helping them cope with their miserable lives and writing a book about her successes and failures. She loved her work, much as it often depressed her. She would tell me about a nine-year-old boy who tried to commit suicide. I listened patiently, but would wonder whether it was worth her life. I once said, 'So what if you save Betty? What'll happen to her? Drugs? Prostitution?' She looked shocked and said quietly. 'It doesn't matter. The future doesn't matter. I can't predict it. It's a child's life today.' I was a smug, callous bastard. She did more for the masses than I ever did. Enough of this."

Burgh thought that Pearson had learned his lesson and would behave with Loeb, even show her his genial side. He invited Loeb and Pearson to dinner. He knew immediately that he had misjudged. Pearson, the proletarian, and Loeb, the petit-bourgeois, recognized each other as class enemies and showed it, but at least they were civil.

Pearson led off. "I'm curious. How do you figure out how many dollars and cents a work of art is worth?"

"The market tells me."

"Does that have anything to do with how good the work is?"

"Of course. Collectors are interested in quality."

"So, what Rockefeller will shell out determines quality? Is a work that sells for two hundred dollars better than one that sells for one hundred dollars?"

"Many collectors think so."

"Do you?"

"Price does count."

"Money talks."

"Not to you obviously."

"Does selling a work make you happy?"

"It most certainly does. That's why I'm a dealer. If I sell one of yours, wouldn't it make you happy?"

"I have to pay the rent. But I hate the idea of relating art to money."

"You don't have to. That's my job. You're free to just paint."

"Free to starve, you mean. I want my work to reach people."

"That's where I also come in. My gallery is free."

"And you show what sells to the money bags. In the end, they decide what you show."

"No, I decide."

"I guess I ought to be thankful for the money you'll make me."

"It would help. You may meet a Rockefeller at your show. He may even like your work and buy it. Take you out to lunch. You may even like him."

Pearson turned away. Burgh spoke up jovially. "The upshot of this class struggle is a draw. Now let's eat up, comrades, and make merry. Praise Mammon like we used to worship Stalin."

* * *

Pearson later said to Burgh, "She's an ugly money-grubbing bitch, see her eat her soup with her little pinkie stuck out, stuck up. How can you fuck a phony broad like her?"

"I know you hate her, but remember, she's your dealer. She's on your side. Now what's in it for me? I don't rightly know. I guess I need some stability, some normality. Like a steady woman. Maybe I can get it from Celia."

"Well, if you need her, I'll do my best to be friendly. But I can't help hating that snooty bitch, her and those fucking fat-cat collectors and curators. They used to be our enemies. They're still mine."

Burgh had always admired his friend's working-class pride, but he also recognized his friend's envy of wealth, power, and social ease, although Pearson would rarely admit it.

As if reading Burgh's mind, Pearson continued, "Those fucking art snobs are always looking down on me. They know I'm not one of them. I'd go to one of those dinners after an opening of a buddy, and I would always say the wrong thing. You never did, Peter. I shoulda gone to college like you instead of marching on picket lines. Shit, even when I try to dress right, I end up with a button missing or a frayed collar or something. And the eyebrows go up. They make believe they don't notice, but I know that they do, the bastards."

"Yeah, and then you begin to boil inside, like the prole that you are. You intentionally say the wrong thing or make clumsy gestures or even lose your temper."

"And that makes me feel guilty. I know I need them, those filthy rich assholes. But I'll never stop hating them. And that goes double for your slut."

* * *

Burgh and Loeb were in a booth at the Cedar. She was complaining, "That buddy of yours is a boor, see him slurp his soup. He's worse than my janitor. Or those union loafers who made life a living hell for daddy. Never doing their jobs but always grabbing for more money." *If it wouldn't get you mad, the bum would never show in my gallery.*

Pearson walked in and joined them. He and Burgh started to talk about Senator McCarthy and his two sidekicks, Roy Cohn and David Schine. Burgh said, "The creeps are three of the ugliest assholes in American history."

"Yeah, and their witch-hunting is slopping over into the

arts. When I appeared before McCarthy's committee, that drunken bully asked me to name names and I told him to go fuck himself."

"Yeah, but that got you fired from your teaching job. That jerk McCarthy nailed you, old buddy, but didn't finger a single Soviet spy. I think part of the reason you were subpoenaed was because you're an abstract painter."

"Sure was. Those asshole congressmen think abstract artists are commies."

"Face it, Little Mike, your paintings are subversive weapons to undermine our American way of life."

Pearson guffawed and raised his glass, "Yeah, I hope so. Here's to the revolution, Pablo."

"But not to those fucking commies, not after what Stalin did with our dream."

"Okay, Pablo, the commies are shit, but that doesn't make capitalism smell sweet."

Loeb suddenly spoke up, "Hasn't what you term 'capitalist exploitation' produced a standard of living—automobiles, television sets—for what you call 'wage slaves' way beyond the dreams of the masses in Russia or anywhere else? Why would American workers want to make revolution?"

That Loeb should have a political opinion stunned Burgh momentarily, but he replied, "They obviously don't, but do they really need all the crap they buy? And the kitsch that Madison Avenue feeds them? Does that satisfy their real needs?"

Burgh and Pearson again ignored Loeb. It wasn't just the conversation that shut her out, but their familiarity, their camaraderie. She was suddenly overcome with pangs of jealousy and began to wish that Burgh would bond with her as he had with Pearson.

* * *

Loeb had scheduled a show for Pearson, but two months before the opening, postponed it, and substituted Milton Silverman. Burgh complained to her, "Why show that second-rater? He can't compare to Little Mike."

"It's business, Peter. There's a market for Milton, and I have to take advantage of it, you know. Besides, he's my entry into the de Kooning circle."

"Okay, but when will you show Little Mike?"

"Oh, the next slot I have."

"That might not be for months."

"We'll see. Don't worry, when I do it, I'll do it right, you'll see."

The show was planned for a few months later, but Loeb postponed again.

That night, at dinner, Burgh said to her, "Are you really going to give Little Mike a show, or are you just giving him the runaround? I know he's not your cup of tea, but what you're doing to him is brutal."

"Let's not talk about it now. We're both a little soused."

"What's that got to do with it? Yes or no?"

"The time isn't right for a Pearson show. I've been showing his work to collectors in the back room. No response, not even a nibble. It'll take more time to build him up."

"Why not let a show do it? Look, you promised him a show. When will you deliver?"

"When I think it's time."

"No, Celia, now's the time."

"Okay. Let's say three months from now. I think that's the first opening I have."

"And I think that's a lot of bullshit."

"I know my business."

"Yeah, lucre over art."

Loeb gulped her wine, "Yeah, I'm a dealer not a social worker. What's this with you and Pearson? Sometimes it really sounds queer."

"Queer?"

"No, no, I didn't mean it that way. I meant strange."

"I think that Little Mike got it right when he called you a blood sucker."

Loeb began to cry. "That's not fair, Peter. I deserve better than that. And I didn't mean what I just said."

Burgh stood, took out his wallet, put four twenties on the table and walked out.

* * *

Early the next morning, Burgh phoned Pearson to tell him that the show was off, that it had never been on, and that Loeb had been stringing him along. Moments later, she called.

"Okay Peter, I apologize. I'm really sorry. It's going to cost me, but I revised my calendar. Can Pearson be ready to show in two months?"

Burgh phoned Pearson. "The show's on again, in two months."

"Fuck it. There's a limit to my ass kissing. I'm way past it with Miss Celia Loeb. Tell her to go fuck herself."

Burgh phoned Loeb, "Little Mike asked me to tell you to go fuck yourself. That goes for me too."

* * *

Pearson phoned Burgh. "Hey Pablo, it's Mike. Could you possibly come to the loft? I've got something amazing to show you."

The loft was dark when Burgh entered. Pearson said dramatically, "And now. *Voila*."

He turned on the light. Six recent geometric abstractions had been placed stretcher to stretcher along two walls. They had all been slashed. Burgh was visibly stunned.

"Some surprise, huh," said Pearson. "What do you think?"

"I don't know what to say."

"Don't you get it? I've introduced violence into my painting. Construction and destruction. That speaks to our time. It's a major breakthrough."

"But you've destroyed your wonderful paintings."

"No, I've added a new dimension to them."

Burgh stood silently.

Pearson said with an edge in his voice, "You don't get it, do you?"

"It's too much of a shock. I need more time to sort out my feelings, Little Mike. You say it's about order and disorder. But slashing canvases will be viewed as a nihilistic act. Vandalism."

"Remember in the 1930s, the Reds kicked me out and I

became a modernist. I still had a vision of art in the brave new future. The working class would take power and would get rid of that crappy, reactionary bourgeois art and embrace abstract art. That's why geometry appealed to me. A rational art for a rational utopia. I was stupid. At the same time, I—and you too—thought that the bourgeoisie would never accept our art because they were fucking philistines, but that didn't bother us. They ended up loving us, at least the likes of you. Did our art make society better? No. Our dreams got turned into commodities—expensive dry goods. Look around you, Peter, if anything, things have gotten worse in the world. I don't have to spell it out for you. It's really hopeless. Can you imagine me, the eternal idealist, saying that? What you call nihilism is actually realism, and in this work, I've really summed it up."

Burgh responded softly, "You're right, our utopian visions were bullshit. In the old days, when we used to talk about things being hopeless, we meant that the public would never understand our work. Or it meant that we would never paint *the* picture, you know, anything as great as Picasso or Matisse or Mondrian. Or Frenhofer's masterpiece. But we would try. Hey, those were the good old days when we were young and foolish yet."

Pearson smiled at Burgh's pun.

Burgh went on, "You say the world today is hopeless. I agree. And I understand your desire to paint it. But we still have to believe in art as some kind of redemption, and act on that belief."

Pearson sat silent for a moment, "I've spent my whole life with a paint brush up my nose and what was it for?"

Burgh said vehemently, "What's the alternative? The problem for now is that your slashed works won't be understood. Maybe they'll be understood in the future, but for now, it's a no go."

"Understood? You mean it won't sell, and I should go on trying to kiss the corrupt asses of the Celia Loebs. They made this fucking world and my new work expresses it. Fuck them."

Pointing to the canvases, Pearson continued, "This is how I feel. Bloody hopeless. The world, my life, my art, bloody hopeless."

"Where can you go from here with this work?"

"With hopeless art? Nowhere. But, Pablo, I expected you to be more sympatico. Well, maybe I shouldn't have. You see with the eyes of those asshole critics and dealers you suck up to. Pollock always said you were a pathetic wimp. He was right."

Burgh stood, "I gotta go."

Pearson began to shout, "Wait up, you fucking creep. I'm not done telling you what I think of you."

"Cool it. Why the anger?"

"Who the fuck do you think you are, you hateful bastard?"

"All the hate seems to be coming from you."

"You smug son of a bitch. I loathe you."

He began to move toward Burgh, clenching his fists as he did. Burgh turned and walked toward the door. Looking back, he said, "You punched me out once, remember? Please don't try it again. Get a hold of yourself."

"Yeah, run you fucking fink! You get in my range again and you'll lose a couple of teeth."

Burgh picked up his mail. An announcement about a show of Pearson's work at the KA-BOOOM-KA-BAAAM Gallery, a venue he had not heard of. The show was titled "ART IS DOOOMED." The card came the day of the opening.

The gallery was a poorly lit, rundown storefront on the lower Bowery. When Burgh arrived, a group of bums were loitering outside the window. "Spare a quarter, sport," said one with a mass of matted hair. The people inside did not look much better than those outside. Pearson stood in the middle of a group of young men and a woman, each with a plastic glass of wine. He saw Burgh, walked over, and said, "Well, well, Pablo Burgh, welcome to the lower depths. What do you think your bitch Loeb would make of this?"

"Hi, Little Mike, good to see you."

"But not my work."

"Give me a chance to take another look."

Burgh walked off but he could hardly bear to look at the slashed canvases. As he edged close to a circle of what looked like artists, a large young man with a scruffy red beard and a black bandana over unkempt hair, wearing faded overalls and a plaid shirt, snarled at Peter, "You're Peter Burgh. Fucking establishment man. I don't know if you're welcome here."

"You're not going to call the cops, are you?"

A small, clean-shaven man in the group, somewhat more kempt, laughed, and said to Burgh, "Hey, I'm Sol Gutstone. This one's Bob Red Beard, BRB for short. These guys are Sheila, Tom, and Jake. Come on BRB, who do you think the fuzz will drag off to the pokey? Him or you?"

Burgh looked from Bob Red Beard to Gutstone to Sheila, a straggle-haired blonde in an ill-fitting blouse and skirt and heavy paratrooper boots, whose slouch and scruffiness did not quite hide her good looks. She stared at him, at first with hostility, then as if she wanted to discover something, perhaps some clue to his being or creativity, and finally, with slightly lowered eyelids, a signal that she was available.

BRB said, "I've got your number. You know Mister Burgh, you don't mind if I call you 'mister,' I think your work is capitalistic crap. Useless. It doesn't say a goddamn thing about the hell we're living through."

"Maybe more than you think. But I paint it like I feel it. Who said that, not my old buddy Bill Gropper, Stalin's gift to American art?"

"Ain't enough, Mister Burgh."

"If I stopped painting abstract pictures would that hasten the revolution?"

Gutstone interjected, "Doesn't it make you sick that the museums, the critics, and the stinking rich collectors swallow your pap?"

"Not really. It worries me sometimes, but I keep painting. I don't think much about it. And I didn't give it much thought when no one wanted to buy anything."

Bob Red Beard said scornfully, "Let's weep a tear for the poor old days, Mister Burgh. But now, the merchandise you manufacture is making big bucks. You want us to believe you haven't sold out? On top of being a shitty painter, you're a phony."

"Listen sonny, I'm trying to be friendly but I don't really give a flying fuck what you losers believe."

Pearson ambled over, "My comrades giving you a hard time, Pablo? Well, they're the real thing and they tell it like it is."

"Sure, sure, I know they're genuine revolutionaries. Their body odor tells me that. Little Mike, I came here to wish you the best, not to spar with these commie pussy-cats. I know you too well to fake some bullshit. I've always admired your work, you know that, but I can't accept the violence and chaos in these here. I'm still your friend, but I've got to go. Good luck on the show."

As Burgh turned to go, he heard Bob Red Beard say, "What'll you do, Mike, when the show is over—chuck this work on the garbage pile?"

"The thought has occurred to me. It would make sense. But I'll donate it to the Museum of Modern Art. It'll hang next to Burgh. They deserve each other." The remark elicited laughter.

Burgh turned, his face reddening, and in a choked voice, he rasped at Pearson, "Don't you dare destroy your work. Whatever it is, it's art. Your art may be a bitter critique on art but it isn't anti-art. You're no frigging Dadaist."

Before Pearson could respond, Burgh wheeled around and walked quickly to the door.

Gutstone followed him. Outside, he said, "Hey, hold up, Mr. Burgh, don't let those would-be rebels get to you. BRB's got a trust fund. You know, I'm a painter. Can we talk?"

"Gutstone? I'll keep it in mind."

"Yeah, I'll give you a call."

Burgh smiled and thought, a little careerism, not unexpected. As he left the gallery, he took a dollar bill out of his wallet and slipped it to a bum.

"Thanks big spender."

* * *

Burgh called Pearson a week later. The phone had been disconnected.

* * *

Loeb met Morton Nichols, one of her collectors, at a gallery opening. He said, "There a weirdo artist showing slashed canvases in a gallery on the Bowery. A Mitchell Pearlman. We're back to Dada."

"Do you mean Michael Pearson?"

"Yeah, that's him. Do you know him?"

"Yes, we've met. He's a friend of Burgh's. They go back to the thirties. Have you seen the show?"

"No way."

"Peter once tried to get me to exhibit Pearson, but it was not destined to happen. We were like dogs and cats. So he slashes his canvases? I'm kind of curious to see them, I don't know why."

"It's the Bowery. Take an armed bodyguard."

Loeb visited the gallery the following Saturday, the safest day she thought. The canvases did not shock her. She saw through Pearson's attempt at violence to an underlying artistry, the formal design of the cuts. He couldn't help himself. Loeb smiled to herself. So, he's really a housebroken rebel.

She had dressed down for her gallery visit. But the sitter was not fooled. She stood beside Loeb, introduced herself as Sheila.

She said, "Think it's funny?"

"Not sure. What do you think?"

"It says, 'Fuck Park Avenue Bitches.'"

"It could be called 'Up the Undeserving Poor.'"

Sheila looked puzzled. Then she said, "Wanna buy it?"

"I just might. It's kind of pretty the way he makes his gashes, but I wouldn't hang it in the parlor. It could go in the hall. How much is it?"

"For you, a bargain price. A thousand."

"I'm serious."

"Well, how about a hundred?"

"The canvas is kinda small for that kind of money."

"I can see that you can afford it."

"Possibly, but I run a business. That's why I'm in the money."

"You win. You can have it for fifty."

"Can I take it home with me?"

"Why not? Cash or check?"

"I've got forty in cash, thirty-five for you, five for a cab."

"I dunno. Okay, it's yours. What's your name?"

"You trying to queer me with the middle class? Can you imagine what my rich bitch friends would think if they knew I actually paid money for this? Just call me 'Art Lover.'"

CHAPTER 3: Johnson
(January 4, 1957)

Neil Johnson ushered the young woman out of the loft affectionately but firmly, although he could not remember her name. She said wistfully, "Can't I stay?"

"Sorry, but I can't paint when anybody is around."

"Okay," she pouted. "When will you phone?"

"As soon as I finish this goddamn canvas. Maybe a week, no more than two. I've got to get it out of my system. And then we'll live it up, you wait and see."

Johnson shut the door, sniffed the stale air of sex, frowned, and threw open a window to let in a blast of winter air, took a deep breath, and shivering, closed it. He knelt and smoothed a tarpaulin he had laid over a vintage Persian rug inherited from his Aunt Helen. Rising, he moved to the reproduction Sheraton table in the kitchen alcove, a gift from his mother, where he downed the dregs of his coffee. He put the soiled cups in the sink, plugged it with a stopper, ran hot water, and poured in soap flakes. He flicked a speck off the drainer, walked into the bedroom, straightened crumpled sheets and blanket, and went on into the bathroom. He studied his reflection in a full-length mirror behind the door. Six-foot-plus, lean, regular features, sandy hair that billowed out over his forehead. He addressed the mirror, "Hi there, God's gift to art and women." After showering and shaving, he pulled on paint-spattered dungarees and a clean plaid shirt.

Entering his studio space, Johnson glanced at a canvas in progress. *What a fucking A-plus piece of a painting. Eat your heart out, Mister Peter Burgh.* He kept looking at the canvas as he sat down on the Eames chair, which he had draped with bed sheets to keep the pigment off. The door- bell rang. *Joseph Sawyer?* He had almost forgotten. He opened the door and waved the critic in. While Johnson hung Sawyer's coat, the critic stepped into the studio and stared at the canvas. He breathed, "Beautiful."

"Is that a compliment?"

Sawyer responded with a hint of a southern accent that, despite his four years in New York, he had not fully sup- pressed, "It certainly isn't ugly. Morgan and Silverman and the rest of Bill de Kooning's paint slingers will posi- tively hate it."

Johnson said pleasantly. "That's good to hear. About time I climbed out of de Kooning's bag, praise be."

"But now you're bonding with Burgh."

Johnson knew exactly what Sawyer was saying, but he answered tentatively as if this had not occurred to him. "Burgh? Why Burgh? You see Peter in it?" Johnson squinted at the canvas. "Well, we both do use a dab-like brush mark. But mine's not like his." Then with a serious expression, "Don't you see the difference? Peter has a fit when you compare his work to nature and Impressionism. Goes bananas when he's labeled an Abstract Impressionist. But that's what I am. An abstract nature painter, and yes, I own up to it proudly—an Abstract Impressionist." He asserted, "I believe that avant-garde art today needs a revival of Monet and Renoir, yeah, and the beauty of their painting, most of all the beauty. Can you imagine what Peter would say if he heard me now? Beauty? Fuggedaboudit. Another thing, my color is different from Peter's—more high-keyed, more like Hofmann, *nicht wahr?* Everyone puts the old 'Cherman' down but he's becoming a trendsetter. Imagine, at his age, and now. My gut tells me they'll soon take another look at him. *Ja.*" Johnson waved at his canvas. "Besides, the gesture is all mine." He paused and said earnestly, "Don't you see it?"

Sawyer nodded, "Yes, I see what you mean. That comma-like curlicue, it's like your signature."

Johnson said with an irritated edge in his voice, "It's not a signature. I don't fabricate. I find it—and everything else—in the process of painting."

Sawyer registered the put-down in Johnson's tone. *So now I'll witness the charade of the hotshot painter lording it over the lowly critic.*

Shrugging, Johnson said, "It's funny that when pictures by us younger guys don't look like de Kooning, then people say they look like Burgh." He added thoughtfully, "Yeah, I'm with Peter. His stuff is way more cutting-edge than de Kooning's. I'm glad that he's finally making it. You know, he's sold a picture for four thou?"

Sawyer said, "You say you're into nature, but there's

hardly a landscape reference, and nothing of the figure."

Johnson raised an eyebrow. "Landscape? Figure? That's passé. Paassay. Too ordinary. Everyone's painting faceless faces, like Jerry Waterman and all his clones. God help us, if I see another fucked-up figure I think I'll puke. What I'm after is the expansiveness of nature and its spirit. *Das geist von die natur,* or is it *der natur?* Don't you see?"

"But beauty can be too beautiful. It gets pretty."

"Yep, you hit the nail on the head. Boy, that worries me. Still, lyricism today is so far out, it's cutting-edge. Crazy, huh? Imagine beauty becoming the next move? *Mein alter professor,* Josef Albers, said, '*Angst is tot.*' No longer cutting-edge. I heard that at a dinner party the other night. Hill said that ugliness is *kaput.* That's where the smart thinking is today. Hans *und* Hill, what a weird duo! It hurts me to say something nice about that fat-ass critic because he's hyping those no-talent stainers Martin and Karl, and he sells their brand of decoration to his smarmy collectors. Face it, thinned paint soaked into raw canvas ain't beautiful, its pissy pretty. Pissy, pissing pigment."

Johnson laughed at his put-down. Sawyer smiled wanly. Johnson went on, "As for me, I love the heft of paint, physical stuff in the grand tradition—no piddling paint for me. My lyricism will have balls. And I'm gonna knock those fucking stainers off the wall."

"I dunno. Martin and Karl are painting some quite interesting pictures at the moment." *Payback, Neil, for patronizing me.*

Johnson shrugged, furrowed his brow, and stared at Sawyer. "You think so? Believe me, they're here today, gone tomorrow, just wait and see." With a swagger in his voice, he went on, "I don't like to boast. Well, why shouldn't I if the boast is true? I can paint rings around Martin and Karl and Morgan and Silverman and those other de Kooning clones. No, no. I take that back. It's not for me to say."

Sawyer acknowledged Johnson's boast with a nod. *All hail, virtuoso heir of Abstract Expressionism. This sad sack critic bows low before you. But why are so many of you young geniuses blowhards? Insecurity? Let it pass. We critics can't win. Pan a guy and he's your enemy for life. Rave and the artist thinks he had it coming. And if you don't rave enough, if you've missed some allegedly brilliant move, no matter how niggling, you get a finger-shaking lecture.* "What's important to me, Neil, is that you can really paint. I mean that. You've consolidated the innovations of the old guys. And that's what I find necessary at this moment. Consolidation. You know, good painting."

Johnson stood quietly in thought for a moment and said, "Another thing that I do and Peter doesn't—bulky forms—solid like rocks or mountains but also fluid. It's really much more Renoir than Monet."

He turned to Sawyer abruptly and said. "Say, let's check out the Cedar. Get a bite there. I'm starving. Give me a minute to change."

Johnson went into the bedroom, shed his dungarees and shirt, pulled on tailored blue jeans, wiggled into a new tan turtle-neck sweater, picked up his suede leather jacket, and slung it over his shoulder, Italian style.

Sawyer stared at the canvas. *Too much Burgh, maybe too much contrivance, but painted better than that of his peers*. When Johnson emerged, Sawyer said, "I'd like to do an article on your new work. Maybe for *Art News*."

"Sounds good. You know that of all the art critics of your generation, I most admire you. Let's kick your essay around over lunch."

As they left the studio, Johnson turned and glanced at his painting. Hill came to mind. *He could be of use. He had nodded amiably when I said I'd invite him to the studio.* Sawyer was eyeing the furniture. *Very, very swank. How does Neil afford this kind of plush? Not from the sale of his paintings. Where does the loot come from? Family? Probably. Lucky bastard.*

The mailbox near the street door had been stuffed with mail, gallery announcements. Johnson shuffled through them, jammed all but one letter back into the box, and tore it open.

"It's from the Whitney. I'm in the Annual. No big deal. Peter Burgh told me he's also in it. They'll probably hang me next to him. Those curators like to invent relationships to show how smart they are, the assholes." Johnson knit his brow. *I'll paint a big one, really big. Peter won't know what hit him. I'll show the old fart who's really big-time. It's about time that the art world learned who's who.*

Seated in a booth at the Cedar, Johnson and Sawyer ordered hamburgers and beer. Sawyer said, "Tell me about yourself. Where'd you grow up?"

"Pulleez, my past is passé. You're not going to write about that crap?"

"No, but I'd like to know your background."

"If you must. Born in Columbus, Ohio. Couldn't love

it even after I left it. Dad, a workaholic lawyer, made big bucks but was hardly ever around, and when he was, he didn't give me the time of day. Mostly drank and played poker with his fat-ass buddies and followed mom around. She was a social butterfly and do-gooder. She didn't stay home much either. We managed. She was distant. I never could figure her out. String of nannies. I made all their lives a living hell. Mom and Dad gave me whatever I asked for—out of guilt for neglecting me, I suppose. Should I really tell you the low-down? Why not? I hated my dad for ignoring me. Still do. But he keeps sending me a healthy allowance. *Pour l'art.*"

Sawyer said with a smile, "That makes him an art patron." *Father's money, father complex.* "Is Burgh your good-father surrogate?"

"In a way, I guess. I began to draw at about three days old. Grade school, fuggedaboudit. High school, did yearbook illustrations, ran cross-country, got laid. The big Buick dad gave me helped. Great pussy wagon. College, art major, over dad's dead body, but Yale was Yale, ran cross-country, got laid, drank a lot, bout of psychoanalysis. BFA, Yale. MFA, Yale. Came to New York. The rest is history."

"What was Yale like?"

"Albers' color course was of some use. Put two colors together to suggest a third that isn't there. I still play around with this. Didn't get much from my fellow students. Pretty mediocre crew in my class. The visiting artists from New York were useful. Learned about avant-garde art from them." *And what was hot in the Big Apple. What galleries to show up at and who to suck up to. And to get to*

New York as fast as I could.

"Who were you influenced by?"

"The usual suspects. De Kooning first of all. And Kline. Then Guston. Also Burgh. They were the big guns. All of the young hotshots in New York and at Yale aped them. Still do. In my gut, I felt closest to Guston and Burgh. Peter influenced me, and more than that, gave me the permission to do my own thing, and he became my friend."

"Apart from what we spoke about—you remember, Impressionism, nature, beauty, and bulky forms—how else do you see your art as different from Burgh?"

"We have different attitudes, totally different. I mean in the way we look at art. Peter loves museums, and he knows one hell of a lot about what's in them. But his knowledge has hardly any effect on what he's painting. In my case, art is my subject. It's like this. Peter's painting looks like Renoir, but it's just in its look, not its content. That why he hates it when people call him an Abstract Impressionist. My art has Renoir in its bowels. I don't care for his big bimbos, but the bulk and light really gets to me. Renoir found his light in nature. So do I, but unlike Renoir and like Peter, I also discover it in the process of painting. Peter uses improvisation to expose his angst, or so he keeps telling me. Not me. I'm a lyricist—after pleasure. And I'm a professional artist. If I want a certain kind of effect, I make it. And make it better than those de Kooning groupies. Like you said, I'm into good painting."

"Yeah, now I see what you mean and it really interests me. A lot depends on the way you make your forms three-dimensional and non-Burgh-ish, even though Peter's shapes have been getting more solid lately. But not like yours. There's something else I want to ask you. What makes your work new?"

'I don't care about newness." Johnson saw Sawyer twitch at that remark but went on as if he hadn't noticed. "I go by feeling. If the feeling's accurate, then it'll look like it's mine—or me—and that's new enough for me. I'm not on anybody's bandwagon. Bandwagon art makes me sick and bandwagon artists, like that Beth Morgan and her no-talent cronies, even sicker. They'll kill avant-garde painting, maybe already have. And that includes some of my best friends—those who holler the loudest about their originality—but don't ask me for names. Those fuckers are bad, but the MFA grads swarming into New York from the hinterlands are worse. We're up to our armpits in fucking hicks wearing Dutch sailor hats."

Johnson suddenly looked pensive. "You know, Joseph, when you get down to the nitty-gritty, I don't know what the fuck I'm doing. I paint and paint—stabbing in the dark—the pain of it. It can get physical, like palpitations or sweating. At one point, the picture takes on a life of its own, and becomes its own thing. That's the moment I'm after. It's the sign of my identity, my being. It takes a real struggle to discover it. I know what I'm saying is a cliché in our circle, but it's true." Neil paused and then went on, "It's guys like you. Guys who look hard at art, I mean really look, and have the eye—and the brain—to get it. It's guys like you that I look at to tell me about my work. And I mean that."

Sawyer tried to look sympathetic. *That's the best piece of sucking-up I've heard in a long time. And you didn't manage to miss a cliché. Brilliant the way you switched from pleasure-seeker to sufferer, not to mention from arrogance to ass-kissing, even the ass of a worthless art critic. You sure can recite the action painting rap better than all your buddies do. Still, I admire your painting, and that's what counts.*

Trying to match Johnson's faux earnestness, Sawyer said, "Thank you Neil for the testimonial, but critics have to have something worth looking at in the first place, and that only you artists can provide."

* * *

Johnson was waiting for Burgh at the Cedar. As he sipped a beer at the bar, hands from behind suddenly cupped his eyes. It was his dealer, Celia Loeb. Johnson said, "Celia, old girl, what are you doing downtown? Slumming?"

"I'm here with your favorite collector, none other than Morton Nichols. Just checking out you peasants."

Johnson looked Loeb up and down appreciatively. *A touch too fat, but still stacked, hair in Marilyn style, but bleached a touch too blonde, lipstick, too red, eye-shadow, more than a touch too dark, and that blouse, too Bronx. Ugh.* The white gloves and little hat that looked so out of place at the Cedar caused Johnson to smile. *Good in bed though. A-minus.*

"Stop ogling me, you naughty boy."

"Can't help myself when confronted with a hot-looking babe." He lowered his voice, "But I like you better in the buff."

Loeb's face reddened and she turned to see if anyone had overheard Johnson.

He went on, "Nice suit. But I'll buy you a better-looking blouse."

"Thanks, but spend it on one of your floozies."

They looked out of the window. Burgh had stopped to chat with Franz Kline. Johnson said, "That Peter's amazing. I agree with you on him. What is he, forty-five, fifty? Hardly any gut. Terrific head of hair. How does the old geezer keep it looking kempt and tousled at the same time? Looks like he stepped out of a French art film. And that tan and those wrinkles, they make him look distinguished without looking old. If he penciled them on himself, he couldn't have improved on them. He could screw any broad in the art world, lucky bastard. If he put out a call, you'd be first in line. Come to think of it, you'd rather screw him than me."

Loeb nodded slightly and smiled enigmatically. "Bite your tongue, you bad boy. Be nice. And don't you dare bad-mouth Peter." *And yes, I'd rather screw him than you or anybody else.*

Johnson looked shocked. "Bad-mouth Peter? Never! He's like a father to me, the father I wish I had."

"I know, I know. I'm also here with Herbert Stein. He's trying to talk me into donating something or other to the Met. Maybe I can change his mind about your pictures."

"Don't waste your breath. The asshole hates my work. I think it's too hetero for him or I'm too hetero or both."

"Nasty, nasty. See you soon, big man. And give Peter a hug for me."

"Yeah, and give my undying love to Stein."

Johnson's eyes followed Loeb's legs appreciatively as she walked back to her booth.

* * *

Johnson studied the canvas he had stapled to the wall. Ninety by eighty, his biggest yet. He had loosely brushed the upper half with red mixed with orange touches and the lower half with a flurry of green and blue brush stokes. *Now what? No signs of de Kooning. Passé crap. There's Burgh, a bit too much of him. What if I put a big, blue geometric form smack in the red? But where? Jutting in and up from the lower right corner. A big oblong but not hard-edge. Show the brush marks. Not flat like that Kelly guy paints, but in sync with it. The smart money says he's a comer. Color? Make it blue, yeah, keyed up, like Big Hans but not as heavy. Nobody's painting anything like it. It will make those Hillites eat their hearts out. Problem is to get it all to work together and hold onto the volume of it all. Once it's up at the Whitney, it'll run away with the show.*

* * *

Burgh sat in Johnson's loft looking at his latest canvas. He pointed at it.

"Striking image and beautifully painted, but a touch too elegant and eclectic for my taste. There's Bill over there and below it there's me, and there's me again. Too much comes from other art."

"So, what's wrong with that?"

"I can't really say, but I guess I mean it's removed from your self. You certainly can paint, no question about that. But I'm not sure..."

Johnson said with a touch of irritation, "You mean the painting ought to come from somewhere deep, deep down in *mein seele* or *von das zeitgeist*? Maybe the music of the spheres? You know, Peter, the difference between you and me is that I'll try anything, riff like a jazz man, to keep myself open and fresh. I don't think you do."

"You're right, I don't. I no longer have the time to experiment. Besides, I want to zero in on a zone of compulsion, not get more open. You make it sound like you paint for kicks."

"I certainly do. I wouldn't want to bore myself."

"Of course." *But can't you see that creative thievery and shrewd pastiche are not enough? You're gifted alright, but will anything come of it? Am I being too harsh? You're still young. Maybe you will find...authenticity. You've got the talent alright.*

Johnson stared at his canvas. "Sure I've been influenced. Who hasn't? But this picture is me now."

"I understand. But it seems also to be about what's up-to-the-moment now."

Johnson hesitated and said, "I hope so. Okay, so I'm not into angst. Or sweat. I like some coolness, distance." *Isn't it about time you stopped peddling your existential bullshit?*

He pointed to a Burghesque passage. "Sure, I still take my cues from other art, like that bit from you. I'm the first to admit that. But I've tried to make what I borrowed mine, with an eye to the beauty of nature and, yes, Impressionism. And in this work, there's the intrusion of an alien geometry. Nature and geometry. Don't you think I've succeeded in integrating them?" *Succeeded isn't the right word. It's a real breakthrough. If you can't see that, tough shit. There's nothing in art like it today, and it's better painted than even what you can do. Is that beginning to worry you, old fart? Is that why you're putting me down? This baby is cutting-edge and has style—and it's gonna sell.*

Johnson's face clouded and he tried to control his annoyance, but Burgh sensed it and decided to say no more. *As Ad Reinhardt once quipped, "How do artists become prostituted? First they do it for love, then for others, and finally for money." That's mean-spirited. It doesn't apply to you, not yet.*

Johnson said with an edge of sharpness, "You know Peter, you're always pointing to the influences of other artists in my work, but you won't to any in yours. Come on now, what about Monet?"

"My work may occasionally look like his but there is no other connection."

"Then who are you influenced by? I mean artists, not ideas."

"This may be hard to believe. But the most important artist is a fictitious painter, name of Frenhofer."

"Who? Never heard of him."

"He's the hero, if you can call him that, of a novel by Balzac, *The Unknown Masterpiece.* For ten years, Frenhofer, poor bastard, works and reworks a painting that he wants to be the ultimate masterpiece, an image of pure feeling, pure passion. Finally he shows his picture to two painter friends, one of them is Poussin. They tell him that all they can make out is a confused mess of colors and lines. When his friends put down his painting, Frenhofer realizes that his long labors have yielded "Nothing! Nothing!" He kicks out his two friends, trashes his work, and commits suicide. How pitiful, but I empathize with the poor dupe."

"Sounds like an asshole to me. So you really relate to that nut?"

"Yes, to his ambition."

"What about his suicide?"

"In a way. You kids haven't experienced death like I have, as commonplace events. Lugging dead friends off a battlefield. Frenhofer's life had become intolerable. What was he to do? Suicide seemed the best option."

"You're talking crazy."

"I know. But...let's change the topic."

* * *

Johnson picked up the phone on the fifth ring.

'Hi, it's Joseph Sawyer. That article we talked about? *Art News* gave me the go ahead. Happened last night when I met Tom Hess at Beth Morgan's party. I had hoped to see you there."

Pause. "Oh yeah, I got tied up. Thought I could make it late, but it didn't work out." *Shit. Party? Beth Morgan? I wasn't invited. Shit.* "How was it? Who did I miss?"

"Oh, you know. The same old, same old crowd. No new gossip. But Dorothy Miller put in a rare appearance. She doesn't make the scene much these days. I'd like to meet to talk about your article."

"I'm free Monday. Come up for a drink. How about six?"

"You're on."

"Good, I've just finished a new canvas." *I know that I'm*

*low in the pecking order of the de Kooning clack, but I'm
not on the outs. What bug does Beth have up her ass?*

Johnson added, "Let's do dinner. I'm treating. How'll
that be?" *I could use a drink.*

"Dinner sounds good."

* * *

Through the window of the Cedar, Johnson saw Beth
Morgan and Milton Silverman at the far end of the bar.
He approached them and said nonchalantly, "Hi guys,
how's things?" Silverman looked away. Morgan stared at
him drunkenly and said coldly, "Can't complain."

Johnson stood at the bar next to them and ordered a
beer. Silverman turned back to him and said, "Yeah, we
were just talking about what a crummy painter Peter
Burgh is."

"Not in my book. The old guy's on the ball."

"It's crapola. Fancy looking *shit*. Some jerk I read in *Arts*
wrote that Burgh's as good a painter as de Kooning. Can
you believe that?"

"Why keep score? I like them both."

Morgan interjected, "Yeah, but you kiss Burgh's ass, and
that's why your work is getting limp, like your prick."

"Hey Beth, that's kind of rough." Johnson responded.

"Tough shit."

Johnson downed his beer in one gulp, dropped some
coins on the bar, and said, "Well, back to the old drawing
board. See y'all," and sauntered out. *So I'm banished from
l'ecole de Kooning. Thelonius Monk is playing at the Five*

Spot tonight and Beth and Milton are bound to be there. We'll go for round two.

Johnson made sure he got to the Five Spot late. He saw Morgan and Silverman with Frank O'Hara and Jimmy Schuyler sitting at a table near the bandstand. He ordered a scotch at the bar and, on his way over to their table, stopped to greet Celia Loeb, who was with some people he didn't know—collector types he guessed—and after introductions, he chatted about how lucky they all were to be at this jazz joint tonight. It was going to be incredible. He moved on to where Morgan, Silverman, O'Hara, and Schuyler were sitting, casually pulled over a chair and sat down. He said hello to O'Hara and Schuyler, who returned his greeting, but ignored Morgan and Silverman, who looked away.

Johnson said to O'Hara, "I really liked your article on Franz Kline, first-rate, and the poem was right on. I just wanted you to know."

"Gee, thanks."

"And I also liked what you wrote about Burgh. Really put down the assholes who think that de Kooning is the only great painter today. What do you know? There's Franz himself over at the bar. Haven't seen him in a chunk of time. Must say hello. Ciao."

Kline was standing with Paul Cobh, who published a little magazine that featured avant-garde painting and poetry. Kline greeted Johnson in his usual friendly manner and went on with his monologue. When he was through, he turned to the bar to order another drink. Cobh said to Johnson, "What's with you and Burgh? He's always putting down Bill and the boys. The creep's poison."

"You make it sound like some kind of war. Peter never bad-mouthed Bill to me. They're both my friends."

"About time you wised up."

Cobh turned away from Johnson, who stood there uncomfortably until Kline turned to him and said in a faux English accent, "Here's one you haven't heard. Queen Elizabeth herself told it to me. This limey sailor picks up a floozy at a bar, takes her to his hotel room and begins to grope her. He reaches under her dress and she pushes his hand away. 'What's up?' he says, flustered. She replies, 'Ere. Ere, erbert, titties first.'" Johnson laughed loudly, in case he was being watched by Morgan and company. Then, Monk took the stage. Suddenly, the only sound to be heard in the Five Spot was the jazz. Glasses stopped clinking, and even Kline stopped talking, such was the emotional force of Monk's playing. When he finished, prolonged applause. Kline looked down and said quietly, as if to himself, "That's what I want my painting to feel like." Johnson nodded in agreement.

* * *

Johnson and Sawyer met for dinner at the Cookery. Over drinks, Johnson said casually, "Say, what the fuck is bugging Morgan?"

"Aah, you know, she's always down on somebody, and this week it's you."

"Why?"

"Who knows? She thinks you're in Peter's bag and against Bill."

"I don't understand. Just because I admire Peter's work, does that mean I've betrayed Bill?"

"That's the party line."

"I don't get it. Have things really become so polarized?"

"So it seems. I think Beth's being egged on by Cobh."

"What a creep! She's trying to brown-nose him to get an article in his rag."

"Whatever it takes. But it looks like you're their butt."

"But you're as much into Peter as I am."

"Yeah, but I'm a critic and they can use me. Sure Tom Hess is in Bill's corner. He won't raise a finger to promote Peter if he can help it. But Tom needs someone on Peter's side at *Art News* to give the magazine scope, but someone not too important. And that's where I come in. That's the politics of it."

"I must admit that I feel hurt by Beth and Milton. I always thought that they were my friends."

"Morgan's vendetta is no big deal."

"Yeah, you're right." *It is a big deal. With de Kooning's gang against me, Tom might pull the article. And if O'Hara listens to those guys, I'll have no chance at MoMA. And then, there's that snake Cobh.*

Johnson shook his head and said sadly, "That Beth is a genius at back-stabbing. These groupies just can't stand an artist who insists on doing his own thing. Well, fuck them."

* * *

Three days later, Johnson walked into the Cedar and saw Morgan and Silverman in their usual places at the end of the bar. He had a drink and walked to the back as if to go the men's room. As he approached them, Morgan said, "Here comes the itty-bitty burger, shitty-bitty burger."

Milton laughed, "A pun, my word."

Johnson countered, "Quelle devastating wit. Now what did I just hear about you, Beth, that you don't copy Bill de Kooning, you illustrate him? Or was it about you, Milton?"

Silverman spun off his stool and turned angrily to Johnson, "I'll kick your goddamn ass."

Johnson feigned a falsetto voice. "Oh, pleath big sir, pleath don't strike itty-bitty me. You may be a cock-a-doo-dle-doo in Beth's sack, but I'm not bending over."

The bartender, sensing trouble walked over, "Now cool it guys."

Morgan's face reddened and she hissed, "Why don't you fuck off, you fucking loser."

Johnson flicked a middle finger in the air. "Score one for my side." And slowly walked away.

* * *

Johnson had recently painted a series of canvases with Hill in mind. He phoned the critic with some trepidation. *What if he's not friendly?* But Hill responded cordially and set a time to visit the studio. The night before the visit, Johnson felt agitated. *Why the tension? Just because Hill's coming? Big deal.* He had heard that the critic affected artists that way, but not him, not Neil Johnson, no way. But he couldn't shake the feeling of fear. In the morning, he selected eight of his canvases and stacked them against one wall. Then he removed a bottle of scotch, the good label, from a cupboard, some ice cubes, and set them out on the table with two glasses. A painting that Burgh had given him caught his eye and he removed it from the wall and put it in his painting rack.

Hill entered and said hello curtly, looked around, sizing up the apartment, and said, "Whatcha got to show me?"

"Like a scotch?"

Hill grunted.

"Ice?"

Another grunt. Johnson spooned a few cubes in a glass and poured four fingers for Hill and two for himself in another glass. He walked over to the stack of canvases, picked up the top one, and carried it to the painting wall. As he did, Hill turned away. Then he wheeled quickly, stared at the work, and grunted.

"First impressions count most. Let's see another."

The process was repeated until Hill had viewed all eight paintings.

Hill said, "Let's go through them again."

Of the first, he said, "Nah, it's not working."

"What do you mean?"

"Just what I said. It's not working." Hill waved it away impatiently. Nah with the second, and the third. Johnson was beginning to get irritated at Hill's rudeness, but he had heard that this was how the critic acted and he kept quiet.

At the fourth canvas, Hill blurted, "Yah, yah, that's it, put that one over there, face up."

"Why? Why that one, Mr. Hill? Is it because the paint is thinner?"

"Nah. That's the good one, the one with quality. That's all that counts, quality."

Hill dismissed the fifth, set aside the sixth, and waved off the seventh and eighth.

Johnson poured Hill another scotch and one for himself. He said, "Let me tell you what I had in mind."

Hill made believe he had not heard Johnson and, ignoring him, pointed to the two pictures he had singled out, "Put these together on that wall." He studied them and said, "Now, that's the way you should be going. Hold on to the volume but kick up the color. Painting thin, even staining, will help with that and keep the picture plane flat. See?"

Johnson nodded and said, "I see what you mean. Yeah." *Makes sense that you prefer the paintings that most resemble Martin's and Karl's but are also bulky, which makes mine different from theirs. You've fit me into your Color-Field clique. So that's what it will take to join your stainer's club. Fatten the forms but paint them thin and flat. Play it cool, Neil.*

Then Hill sat down and accepted a third scotch. Johnson did not join him in this. Hill's tone became friendlier.

"Did'ya see the de Kooning show? What did'ya think?"

"Disappointing. The only pictures that he's painted that are any good are the forties black ones." *That's the answer Hill wants. This is a test, and I'm going to pass it with flying colors.*

Hill grunted, "And Burgh?"

"Oh, I used to admire him and was even influenced by him, but I've just about got him out of my system. He can't compare with Pollock or Newman."

Hill nodded, downed his drink, and said, "Sorry that I've got to make this visit short, but I've got another appointment that I have to go to."

"Thanks for coming, Mr. Hill."

"Call me Marshall, and phone me in a couple of weeks. I'd like to see what you come up with."

"Will do, Marshall, and thank you for coming and for your thoughts." *You're a shrewd one, Neil Johnson. Painted just what Hill wanted to see and told him just what he wanted to hear.*

After Hill left, Johnson poured himself four fingers of scotch—with difficulty because his hands were shaking. *What will I do? Quit the schmearers and join the stainers and make some sales? Why not, but I'll also go on painting what I have been but will keep it out of sight. Who the fuck does that arrogant son of a bitch think he is? Berenson?*

CHAPTER 4: Herbert Stein & Morton Nichols
(February 5, 1957)

Herbert Stein's morning mood was invariably morose, even on a cloudless February day, even after he had a buttered bagel and coffee. That is, until he climbed the grand staircase in front of the Metropolitan Museum of Art. With every step, his spirits lifted. Standing outside was Fred Sparks, the aged guard. As Stein approached the door, Sparks opened it and, with an exaggerated low bow, ushered him in as he did most every day. It was their private ritual. "Upwards and onwards, illustrious curator of modern art." Stein put his nose up, pursed his lips, and with exaggerated loftiness, waved a limp hand in the air, and intoned, "For the greater glory of art."

Stein sat down at his desk, glanced appreciatively at a black abstraction of 1949 by Willem de Kooning, which hung on the opposite wall, a canvas he had acquired for the museum. He looked distastefully at his mail. He began to shuffle envelopes, barely glancing at gallery invitations. Flipping them into a nearby wastepaper basket, he noted with satisfaction that about half made their mark, a better percentage than most days. *Take note New York Knicks.*

The phone rang. "Hi Herb, Nichols here. I was thinking about you last night, actually when I was in bed with the wife. It's time I gave the museum something to thank you personally for all your tips on collecting, and don't think I won't tell your boss why I'm giving it. I've decided to donate my big Neil Johnson, you know, the green one. Let me know when you can have it picked up."

Stein paused and said tentatively, as if to himself, "The Johnson?" He paused again, then said softly, "How about your Pollock or de Kooning or one of your Rothkos? That'll really count."

"All in good time, all in good time. We'll start with the Johnson. Alright? That'll be a major addition to the Met's holdings."

"Not in my book. You remember, Mort, when you decided to buy the Johnson, I told you that I was not a fan of his painting. I'm still not. I don't think I can recommend this gift to the acquisitions committee. But it's not my decision. It's theirs, as you know."

"What's wrong with Johnson? Everybody says he's an up-and-comer Abstract Expressionist. He sure can paint. What you got against him?"

"Yes, he can paint. He painted de Koonings better than de Kooning did. And now he's outdoing Burgh. It's all second hand. When do you suppose Johnson will paint Johnson?"

"That's not fair. He's as good as Beth Morgan and she rips off de Kooning. You bought a big one of hers, paid lotsa cash."

"Not really, we bought the Morgan for pennies. And her work is fresh and personal in a way that Johnson's is not."

"Gimme a break. I'm giving you the Johnson for free, and it's a damn good picture. Better than most of what you collect."

"So it's good. But is it good enough for the Met?"

"Good, but not good enough. What the fuck is that supposed to mean? And you decide the difference, like some fucking god?"

"Look, Mort, like it or not, that's what I'm here for. But it's not only my personal opinion of Johnson. There's more to it than that. I'm beginning to have serious doubts about second generation Abstract Expressionism, and I'm not alone. Are we getting glutted with copy-cat smeary painting?"

"Smeary? Isn't that what we used to call 'painterly' in the good old days, like last week? And you propose to bury it already?"

Stein took a deep breath. Placating him, he said, "You know better than that, Mort. You know the difference between the exceptional and the mediocre. Your collection proves that."

"Yeah, and an artist by the name of Johnson is in my collection. Look, asshole, this is the last time I try to give the Met something."

Nichols slammed down the phone.

* * *

That afternoon Stein received a phone call from James Canning, the museum's director. "What's this I've heard about your objecting to a painting that Mr. Morton Nichols has offered us?"

"Nichols can submit the picture to the acquisitions committee. I just won't support it."

"Well, the committee follows your advice. Nichols can be a valuable asset to the museum. And Sheldon Green, one of our trustees, is very upset about your attitude. He's done legal work for Nichols. He's also made generous contributions to the museum. Green's a trustee I don't want to alienate."

"Look, Dr. Canning, I've been courting Nichols for three years, advising him on what to buy, and letting him store loads of his works in our racks. That's staff time and that's my time. And he's given the museum nothing, nada. Not even a drawing. I told him I didn't care for Johnson's work when he bought it. And now, that's the only picture he wants to give us. Not his de Kooning or Rothko. Why Johnson now? Is it because the art world is beginning to catch on that Johnson is second rate? I don't think the museum should acquire it, even if it is a donation."

"It's Green that concerns me. You may have to give in on this one."

Resigned, Stein said, "I understand."

* * *

Stein's conversation with Canning disturbed him and he kept chewing over it. *Have I already made too much of a fuss? I'll do what I'm told. But first, I'll do some conniving. I'll show that vulgar asshole.*

After work, Stein took a taxi downtown to the Cedar Tavern. He knew there would only be one or two NYU professors having an after-class drink, but no artists, not until after ten o'clock. Still, maybe a friend or acquaintance would show up, but none had. He sat at the bar and ordered a beer and some potato chips. Then surprisingly, Beth Morgan sauntered in, sat down beside him and greeted him fondly. She said brightly, "Why so glum chum?"

Stein smiled at her wanly and responded, "It's been one helluva lousy day."

"So buy me a beer and cry on my shoulder."

"Nichols offered the Met a Neil Johnson canvas and I wouldn't back it, and the shit hit the fan. What am I saying? I shouldn't blab to you. Please keep this to yourself."

"You did the right thing for the Met. So Nichols put the squeeze on you. Fuck him and fuck Johnson."

Stein knew that within two hours a large segment of the art world would get the word.

Milton Silverman came in and walked over. "Hi, Herbert. Hi, Beth. I'm heading over to that paint sale I told you about. Still want to join me?"

Morgan said, "Sure do. I'm just about out of cadmium red." She turned to Stein. "Stay cool, bubeleh, don't let that creep get you down."

Stein overheard Silverman say to Morgan as they were walking along the bar, "What creep?"

Morgan replied, "You wouldn't believe it."

Stein finished his beer and chips, paid his bill, put a dollar on the bar, and left. *Mission accomplished.*

* * *

At seven-thirty the next morning, Neil Johnson phoned Celia Loeb in a fury. "Did you hear? Nichols wants to donate a painting of mine to the Met, and Stein, that fucking fairy, is screwing up the deal. He's a friend of yours. You gotta do something."

"Calm down, Neil, calm down, I'll give Herbert a call and see what I can do."

At eight-thirty, Loeb phoned Stein. "Sorry to call you this early, but Neil Johnson's on a tear. He told me..."

"Yeah, I know."

"Look, Herbert, we're friends, and I never asked you for a favor. But just this once..."

"No can do, Celia, not this time. I know the Met owes you, but I don't care for Johnson's work, you know that, and neither do a lot of our friends. And I don't like being pushed around by a collector. He's a shrewd one, old Mort. Wants to get a great tax break and look like a big-hearted philanthropist. After years of kissing his ass and getting zilch for the Met, if he wants to give the museum a painting, give us his de Kooning or even his Burgh, but I'd rather have the de Kooning. I'm going to hang up before either of us says something we'll regret." *Poor Celia, but I've got a touch of my self-respect back.*

"Too bad, can't say I didn't try, but I'm not looking forward to telling this to Neil."

* * *

An enraged Nichols phoned Stein. He shouted, "What the fuck is this you're telling people that I'm trying to rip off the Met?"

"I said no such thing. I just mentioned to a friend that you wanted to donate a Johnson painting and that I wouldn't recommend it. Nothing more."

"Well, I've just withdrawn it and I'm quits with you."

Stein took a deep breath and said, "In that case, please remove your paintings from our storage."

"Don't you dare talk to me like that you fucking pansy! This is Morton Nichols you're talking to, not some nobody!"

"Look, I'm sorry if I offended you. But there's nothing more to say."

Stein hung up. *I'm getting to enjoy this. But be careful. Don't get carried away.*

* * *

That afternoon, Canning phoned Stein. "This Nichols matter is getting out of hand. Sheldon Green called and said that if we didn't accept the Johnson, he'd resign from the board."

"I've looked Nichols' gift horse in the mouth, and it's got a bad case of halitosis. I hate to speak up for it, but of course I will. Dr. Canning, I love my job and I'm told by people we both respect that I'm good at it. Sure I'll give in on the Johnson, but my reputation means a lot to my job—and to me of course. Maybe I could call in sick when the acquisitions committee meets."

Canning said quietly, "Let's not do anything hasty. The

acquisitions committee doesn't meet for three weeks. We'll all give it more time and thought."

* * *

Stein didn't feel like lunch and certainly not like working. He shuffled some loan forms that the Los Angeles Museum had sent him and looked at his watch. *Two o'clock. I've got to get out, get some air. Maybe have a drink and a chat with someone. Take a cab to the Cedar.*

It was Stein's luck that Milton Silverman was leaning on the bar nursing a beer. Stein walked over and sat beside him. "Hi Milt, painting giving you a hard time?"

"Been fighting this sucker for two weeks, and it keeps screwing me. It's cost me a hundred bucks worth of paint, a big C-note of Winsor & Newton. What a waste! I'm gonna go back to house paint. What brings you to this whorehouse on a workday afternoon?"

"Just practicing to become an alcoholic, like a lot of our friends."

"Yeah, I've heard you're a terrific drunk, one swig and you swing on chandeliers. Is that Nichols still bugging you? Is that why you're slumming?"

Stein answered, "Maybe I thought alcohol might help."

* * *

Stein stumbled drunk into his apartment just after eight o'clock. He phoned his answering service. Calls from Canning, Nichols, Sheldon Green, Tom Hess and Mark

Wall. The latter was an art critic for the *New York Times*. Stein knew he was in no condition to talk to anyone, certainly not to Green, Hess or Wall. The calls would have to wait until the next day. But he smiled to himself. *Some brouhaha.* Followed by a pang of fear. The phone rang. Stein waved it off with a flick of his hand. When it didn't stop ringing, he picked it up. It was Nichols shouting. Stein cut him off. "Look Mort, I'm in no condition to talk now. I've decided late in my life that I don't like being pushed around. Okay, so the 'H' in Herbert now stands for 'H' as in Hard-Ass. I'll do whatever is best for the Met."

"You're drunk. Don't hang up. Look, I'll sweeten the deal with the Johnson. You accept it, and I'll throw in a Rothko."

"Yeah! Now you're talking."

Nichols hesitated, and then added, "On extended loan."

Annoyed, Stein replied, "Why not just give us the Rothko and lend us the Johnson?"

"Come off it. It's a terrific offer."

"All it means is that, instead of storing your Rothko in our racks, we store it on our gallery walls with your name attached to it."

"You haven't heard the last of this you fucking queer."

Stein hung up.

* * *

Ten minutes later the phone rang and kept ringing. It was Canning. "Word has gotten to me that I'm putting pressure on you over the Nichols business."

Stein slurred, "I never said it."

"Have you been drinking?"

"Much more than I should have."

"You know you are well liked and respected at the museum and in the art world, and you've been doing an excellent job. But we will accept Nichols' donation."

"Nichols just offered me a Rothko—*on extended loan.* And he expected me to cry hallelujah. And when I wouldn't, he called me a queer."

"I've heard he was vulgar, but that he has a first-rate collection. We ought to think of him in the long run."

"Look Dr. Canning, this Nichols business is not worth the fuss. I'll support the Johnson.

* * *

As Stein entered his office at eleven o'clock, still a little woozy, his phone rang.

"Green here. Is this Herbert Stein?"

"Yes, sir."

"I hear that you've reconsidered your opinion of the Johnson offer."

"I have, Mr. Green. I was hasty in my take. The Johnson offered by Nichols is one of his best paintings and we should accept it. But there's something else. Nichols offered us a Rothko on extended loan. I really want that painting for the Met, but to own it. Why don't you suggest to Dr. Canning that he personally phone Nichols and thank him for offering us the Johnson and the Rothko, but that he give us the Rothko—not lend it. Perhaps, for his generosity, he might be put up for the board. Dr. Canning can be very persuasive.

What do you think?"

"I'm sure Jim will agree." Green paused, "You know, we have never really talked. Can we meet for lunch?"

"I'd like that."

"On Thursday at the 21 Club at twelve-thirty."

* * *

Over crab cakes, a martini for Green, and a glass of white wine for Stein, Green began the conversation. "I've agreed with most of your acquisitions of new work. When I don't, I think I understand why you bought or recommended them. Shrewd, very shrewd indeed."

"Thank you."

"I'd like to know more about that, but first I should tell you that I've checked you out. I hope you're not offended. Grandfather came from Russia in the early 1900s. Jewish, wasn't he? Built a successful shoe manufacturing company, Stein's Smart Shoes. I wear their loafers. Father took over the business, and made it even more successful. Bought real estate. Put you through Boston University. You majored in art history. I guess your father wanted you in the business but you went on to Harvard and acquired a Ph.D.— dissertation on Matisse. How'd you stay out of shoes?"

"I tried the business for a while, a very short while, but found it boring—that's an understatement. My father gave me a hard time, but I stuck by my decision, and he paid for graduate school. One of my brothers took over the company and is handling it quite nicely. In the end, my father now brags about me being a doctor of philosophy and working at the Met. And please call me Herbert."

"I'm curious about your acquisitions. How do you decide?"

"I'm pretty open-minded. I think I've got a good eye, or so Marshall Hill once told me. But I also have a good ear. I follow art world opinion closely, sophisticated art world opinion. It's not hard to pick the truly superior artists who drive avant-garde art in a new direction. As for the newcomers, I'm on the lookout for what's fresh and creates a buzz in the art world. I've managed to avoid most of the hyped, hot-off-the-griddle stuff that my gut tells me is second rate. Then I use my discretionary funds to quietly buy the best works by the best artists before they get scooped up by savvy collectors and the prices jump. I think my track record has been alright. And the guys on the acquisitions committee have generally backed me up. On top of that, I try to understand how the art world works, who is doing what for whom and to whom, and for what reason. I try to find out who's got a finger on the pulse today, people like Dorothy Miller at MoMA—you'll keep that between us. I hope my monologue wasn't too windy."

"No, please, go on, I find this very informative."

"Well, at the moment people whose taste I admire are beginning to question whether, on the whole, the second generation Abstract Expressionists are mediocre, not the likes of Mitchell or Frankenthaler, of course, but the hordes of newcomers. There are now way too many of them to be a vanguard. More likely, they make up a new academy." Stein took a sip of his wine. "There's one new guy not known in New York who interests me, Richard Diebenkorn, a Californian. He's a strong painter. Another young artist, Robert Rauschenberg, who pieces together city junk, has the art world riled up, pro and mostly con. He's been attacked as neo-Dada, but as I see it, his work is too formally adept to be anti-art. Whatever he's doing, it's really brand new. And I also have my eye on Ellsworth Kelly, whose painting—It's been labeled Hard-Edge—I saw in his studio. And the work of all three is still relatively inexpensive."

"Really? I don't know Diebenkorn. Don't care for Rauschenberg, but I'll take another look. I've seen a few Kellys in the back room of the Betty Parsons Gallery, and I've liked them. Still, it hasn't occurred to me to buy one."

"If you do, please promise it to the Met. or buy two, the price is right, and give us one. Pardon the pitch."

Green laughed. "I just might do."

Stein thought, my gut tells me that this man is intelligent, perceptive, worldly. I'm glad we finally met and talked.

* * *

The following day, Stein walked by the Burgh on the way to his office, but this time, he stopped. *It still looks too namby pamby, but it's got something. I'll give it more time.* He recalled that he'd hung it because the trustee who had donated it was a good friend of the museum. *I'll give it more time.*

* * *

The next morning, Stein brought a folding chair into the gallery and sat in front of Burgh's canvas. Canning came in on his daily tour, walked past Stein, turned, and looked back at him.

Stein looked up and greeted him, "Oh, good morning, Dr. Canning."

"What are you so deep in thought about?"

"It's Peter Burgh. I respect him but I've never given him more than respect. I know that he's influential. Now I'm beginning to wonder whether I underestimated him." Stein paused and said quietly, "Maybe I looked too fast. The more I stay with this picture, the stronger it gets."

Canning nodded. "I was about to send a memo to you. I spoke to Mr. Nichols, and he's giving us both the Johnson and the Rothko. Mr. Green tells me that it was your idea. Thank you."

"Thank you, sir. I'll give Nichols a call and mend my fences."

* * *

Stein was studying the prices of the latest Sotheby's auction when the phone rang. It was Canning. "Have you by chance seen the latest issue of *The Higher Standard*? Calvin Fischer is on a rampage again, using the Peter Burgh as his bludgeon. I recommend that you do nothing, but should you write a letter, clear it with me."

The magazine was near the top of a pile that had accumulated over weeks. Stein opened it and read:

It comes as no surprise that the fashion-mongering bureaucrats at the Museum of Modern Art and the Whitney have each acquired an abstraction by Peter Burgh. Recently, a collector has donated one to the Metropolitan Museum, and it was accepted. The museum, which has been the bastion of humanism, high art, and good taste, is now corrupted. I had hoped the Met's sole mission would be to preserve and advance the grand tradition of Western art, which for millennia, has prized standards of quality and has communicated universal messages about love and death, courage and sacrifice.

No such luck! With the acquisition of a canvas by Peter Burgh, the museum unabashedly promotes cynical art that dehumanizes art—and life—and what is worse, is nihilistic. For shame! Mr. Burgh's painting informs us that the universe is devoid of purpose. To promote this kind of art is to ally it with the evil forces of destruction and alienation that have made life in our century a nightmare. It nullifies values that have made our nation great. Why does the Metropolitan give this degenerate outlook credence?

One would have thought that in buying Pollock, de Kooning, and Kline, the museum hit rock bottom, but its curator, Dr. Herbert Stein, has shown that it was possible to stoop to still lower aesthetic depths. In acquiring the Burgh, Dr. Stein has done just that. Where will our trendy curator hang this new treasure? Next to the Metropolitan's Rembrandt or Velazquez? In order to demean these masterpieces? But perhaps this is precisely where the Burgh should hang. To juxtapose excellence with meretriciousness should teach the public about quality in art.

The American public has a right to know what role the Director and the acquisitions committee played in this travesty of acquisition. What in the name of humanist values were you and your cronies thinking, Dr. James Canning?

* * *

Stein did write a short letter to the editor of *The Higher Standard*, cleared it with Canning, and mailed it. It read:

> I'm sorry that Mr. Fischer objects to the Metropolitan Museum of Art's acquisition of a major Peter Burgh. He might also have mentioned that we had recently acquired a superb Milton Avery and our third Andrew Wyeth, which we have displayed prominently. It has been and will remain the policy of the museum to collect art of quality no matter what the style. Peter Burgh is a major Abstract Expressionist. The painting that we acquired, like it or not, is one of his major works.

Stein did not mention that he had been lukewarm to the purchase of the Wyeth, and, in the wording of his letter, he made sure that the adjective "superb" did not apply to it.

In a memo Stein sent to Canning, he wrote. "I would like to curate a Burgh show. What do you think?"

* * *

Nichols phoned Burgh and read him the Fischer article. Burgh said, "So, what else is new. These latter-day humanists sling the same tired hash and make believe that they've said something new. But the innuendos do get nastier, like that fashion-mongering slur and the Met's having fallen lower than rock bottom. And putting me on the side of evil— did Fischer mean in bed with Hitler and Stalin? These neo-humanist guys must really be desperate. Mort, old buddy, don't give it a second thought."

But Burgh was annoyed.

Stein's letter the following month eased some of Burgh's

irritation. He knew that the curator was no admirer of his work, but now he thought he would like to get to know him better.

CHAPTER 5: Morton Nichols
(September 20, 1957)

Burgh was so caught up in his painting that the phone rang four times before he registered it. It was Johnson. "Hi, Peter. Neil here. Are you going to the Whitney opening tonight? If so, can we go together?"

The doorbell rang. Burgh said to Johnson, "Shit, that's the door. Is it noon already? Who am I supposed to see? Nichols? Or is it that curator from the Met, Stein? Wants to talk to me about a picture the museum recently acquired. I don't think he much cares for my work. Now I remember, it's Nichols. Hold on while I throw him the key." Burgh stuck his brushes into the jar of turpentine. He opened the window to gusts of rain, looked down on Nichols, waved, flipped the keys to him, and shut the window.

Returning to the phone, Burgh said, "I should have told Nichols to see my dealer, but he would have been insulted. The asshole loves to deal directly with artists. Gives him the feeling of an insider and lets him bargain, the cheap bastard. But you know that. God, what a bore. But I can use the money. Aside from Hill's crappy article, the reviews from my last show were good, but the sales weren't."

As Burgh heard heavy footsteps on the stairs, he said, "Yes, let's do the Whitney. I'll call you later to arrange where to meet." Hearing Nichols at the door to his loft, he let him in. The collector, his fat face redder than usual, breathing hard, rasped, "Peter, Peter, great to see you. What gems do you have for me?"

"Hi, Mort. You look wet through and through. You should have put off your art experience today. The *Times* says it's the wettest it's been for months."

Burgh pointed to a chair facing his painting wall. "Sit here, and I'll show you my new stuff. Like a drink?"

"Too early in the day, but awright, maybe a little nip to dry me off."

Peter poured Mort a scotch and one for himself.

"How's Esther?"

"Awright, awright. I would have brought her here, but I'm looking for a gift to surprise her. And you know she grooves your work—and your body. Watch out!"

Nichols guffawed loudly. Burgh forced a smile. He pulled a painting from the rack and propped it against the painting wall.

Nichols said, "Have you been to the new club on Fifty-fifth Street off Second Avenue? That's the new in-spot, you know. Marshall Hill turned up a few nights ago. He said your painting once had a certain something but you lost it."

"That remark isn't going to get you a discount, Mort. I saw our primo critic at the Cedar not so long ago. Told him he was too blinkered to ever understand my work. Mort, listen to your wife. She's got a better eye than Hill has. And she looks harder than him or, for that matter, you."

Nichols waved the put-down away. Burgh was not sure that Nichols had even glanced at the painting in front of him but he replaced it with another.

Nichols continued talking, "Did'ya hear that Neil Johnson is screwing his dealer?"

"Oh?"

Burgh brought out another canvas. He asked, "So?"

"You know Peter, the picture's awright, but the passage on the upper right ain't working."

Burgh studied the canvas and nodded sagely. As he brought out another canvas, Nichols stood up, pointed, and said excitedly, "*Awright,* that's it! That's your newest masterpiece. That's for me. How much?"

"Five thousand."

"Aw, come on, Peter, that's what your dealer gets. How about three?"

"Now Mort, you picked my best picture. That's the one I want to keep for myself. I can't let it go that cheaply. Come to think of it, I'm not really sure it's for sale."

"Touché. Won't even bargain anymore. How about four thou? But that one's for me. But give me a break on the price. For the wife, I'll take the orangish one. Now you got to let that one go for three."

"I can never win with you."

"I'm in a good mood. Throw in the smaller one for two. That's nine thousand American greenbacks." Nichols wiggled a finger in the air at Burgh, "But I buy on one condition—that you never tell Hill I bought three. He thinks I listen only to him."

Peter replied sarcastically, "Not to worry. He wouldn't hear anything I had to say, even if I bothered to say anything to him."

Nichols went on, "Nine thousand smackeroos. My wife and I will starve. You'll have to buy us a crust of bread. But for now, I'll take you out to lunch."

"Thanks Mort." *Even for nine thousand, lunch is asking too much but what can I do?*

As they were leaving the loft, Nichols glanced at the racks and pointed to a canvas. "What's that? Let me see."

Burgh pulled it out.

Nichols waved his hands at it and said, "It's sensational. I want it."

"Not for sale."

"Oh, come on, how much?"

"Alright, but it will cost you."

"How much?"

"Five thousand."

"Look, Peter, I just spent nine thou. Make it thirty-five."

"When will I learn how to say no to you. I want to keep this one, but I'll take four."

"Done. I can't resist great art, particularly yours."

"Thanks." *Four works? Why that many? Why am I thinking that Nichols has something else up his sleeve? Is this my paranoia rearing its ugly head? Or...I wonder.*

Seated at a table at the Second Avenue Delicatessen, Burgh said, "How's business?"

"Don't ask. It's terrible, but even if it were good, I'd tell you it was terrible. But it's better than in the old days, in my Pop's time. I don't think I told you, but Pop quit high school to work in a schmatta store. Opened his own place before he was twenty. He was smart. And tough. Knew exactly how much to charge, enough to make a profit, enough to under-cut the other stores. Stole their business away, saved some money, upgraded his merchandise. Had a partner, Sam Black, but not for long. A lot of rumors about how Pops got rid of Sam, stuff about the Mob. But nothing ever proven. He never said anything to me. Then he began to manufac-ture suits. He taught me that you don't take any prisoners in the clothing business. But I'm not like him."

"Sure, sure, Mort, you're a sweetheart."

Nichols disregarded the sarcasm. "I truly am, truly. But if you fuck with me, watch your back. I'm good at business. I've made and lost a number of bundles. I would have really liked to be an art dealer, but I got no education and can't be hoity-toity like Celia Loeb. Or pretty like you, so I can't fuck for sales, not that I would mind, but who would take me up on it? So I buy art." He smiled. "*Pauvre moi.*"

After they ordered, Burgh said, "How did you happen to become a world-class art patron?"

"You wouldn't believe this. In my younger days, I wasn't a bad looker. I had the hots for this blonde model. She was a hard nut to crack. So very refined. So I would take her to the theatre and the museums. She turned out to be a lousy lay, but after I dumped her, I kept on going to museums, then galleries. Don't ask why. I dunno. One day, I dropped in at an auction. A Ryder came up for sale. You couldn't imagine how cheap it was. I thought, I want that baby and I can afford it. Later, I made a thousand percent profit on it." Nichols nodded smugly. "But it wasn't only the money. I really loved the art. I never learned good manners, but I know a good picture when I see one. You know that. But I also listen hard, like to you, Celia, Marshall, and Herbert Stein. I think I told you how Stein tried to fuck me up with the Met, but we're friends again. Ahh, enough of me. I just bought four Burghs, gen-u-ine Peter Burghs, for thirteen grand. That's how my life in the art world turned out. Not bad."

* * *

Leaving the delicatessen, Nichols flagged a cab. Burgh turned down the offer of a ride back to his studio. To get Nichols out of his system, he needed a walk, despite the rain. He sauntered west as far as Washington Square and then doubled back to the studio. He phoned Johnson. "That frigging Nichols, what a philistine. Philistine, that's what we called those creeps before your time. I keep thinking, how much do I really need the money? Is it worth dealing with the likes of Nichols? Then I think, hell, I put in my time living where dogs would die, as Franz Kline said. Not anymore. The Nichols' will keep me afloat with their filthy lucre. Is there clean money? So, I'll kiss the Nichols' asses and hate myself for it—and despise them as well."

"Come on, Peter, Mort's not so bad. Sure he's crass, but he really digs art, good art, our kind of art. And he buys it. That counts for something, doesn't it?"

"I guess so. He just bought four pictures for thirteen thousand. Give Jones his cut. Leaves me eight plus. Jackson and Bill get more, but price-wise I'm in Franz's class. That's the kind of thinking that I hate, even when I'm thinking it."

"Eight plus big ones sound good to me. Come on, Peter, you don't really expect me to feel sorry for you. Look at it this way, Nichols bought your work because it's great."

"How great? Andrew Wyeth makes a lot more dough. Does that make his art greater? What's success? Am I a success? Does Nichols make me one, or the powers at MoMA? Would Hill, if he wanted to? Who am I as great as? The 'P's,' maybe? Pollock? Picasso? Piero? And what if I wasn't selling like my buddy, Little Mike, always broke and crying in his beer? Would that make my stuff bad? Is Little Mike's work no good?"

Johnson interjected, "It's not worth breaking your balls over." *He's got eight plus fucking big ones and he's still crying. Eight plus fucking big ones.*

"You're right. Screw it. But it bothers me. Eight thousand. Why do I need that much? That would have lasted me for two, three years, maybe more, not so long ago. I remember we used to say that what made great art was character. And that art and business, never the twain shall meet. Yeah, back then we had dreams—to make great art—and we starved. But that was okay. At least we didn't have to kiss the asses of the money men, not that we even had the chance. The frigging creeps were our enemies. Now they're in bed with us, or think they are. And we're catching their money-grubbing fleas. The hell with 'em, except when I need the money, or think I do. Then I'll sell 'em my goods, oops, masterpieces. Even to Nichols."

"Yeah Peter, now you can moan and piss all the way to the bank."

"Yeah, shed a tear. You won't believe this, but our Mort

told me to fix what he called a "passage" in a painting. Maybe I will. After all, money talks. Hey, about meeting tonight. How about at the Cedar at six, have a genuine drink, and go on to the Whitney together and swill their cheap wine?"

* * *

A week later, Nichols sat on an Eames chair in the middle of Johnson's loft, facing the painting wall. He leaned back, the chair creaking under his weight, his flabby belly protruding, as he looked at a painting—the fifth Johnson had shown him. He announced pompously, "It's awright. Not bad, not bad at all."

Johnson responded in a half-macho, half-vulnerable tone. "Not bad! It's a damn sight better than not bad, Mort. If you knew what a struggle went into this sucker, you'd say more than 'not bad.' I mean, I stand here day after day sweating, not knowing what the fuck I'm doing, stabbing in the fucking dark, trying to dig deep, daring to go to the core of my being."

He paused, then said brightly, "Then, if I'm lucky, my vision takes over. When it does, I can't control it. It's like a fucking orgasm." Vulnerably, "You know, Mort, there aren't many people I can open myself to. You're one. That's because you can really see and you really care. My work is my life. It's costing me, God knows. It's costing me, but that's the price you have to pay."

Nichols commiserated, "Neil, I understand, believe me, I understand. And your commitment shows, right there on the canvas. I'd like to buy that one. How much?"

"A thousand dollars."

Nichols' eyes widened in feigned shock "That's kinda high." *High? It's highway robbery. What do you take me for? Some hick or do-good charity? Nobody suckers Morton Nichols.* Nichols pointed. "And those two?"

"Same price."

"I'd like to have all three, but I can't afford your price. Tell you what I'm gonna do. I'll take all three for one-five. Awright?"

Johnson stiffened. *You son of a bitch. You know my market is down.*

"Oh come on, Mort, sweeten the pot. The paintings will be worth triple tomorrow or even tonight."

"Nah, I wish I could, but that's my limit. Business has been slow, you know, damn slow."

"How about paying in installments then?"

"Nah, can't take the risk. With the schmatta sales what they are, who knows if I'll have a red cent tomorrow. Awright, I'll tell you what I'm gonna do. I'll give one canvas to the Cincinnati College of Art Museum, that's where the wife's family lives. Now that ought to make you, the museum, and Esther happy." *And they'll love me in the sticks. I'll take a tax write-off, sell one picture at auction if Neil's market picks up, and keep the third for myself.*

Johnson said, "Mort, if it was anyone but you, I'd tell him to go fuck himself. But it is you. And over my broken heart—and my even more broken wallet—you've got a deal." Johnson looked crestfallen. *You cheap shit. I ought to tell you off.*

"Awright, Neil. It's a good deal. Let me tell you something. When word gets out that Morton Nichols bought three of your pictures, other collectors will be breaking down your studio door. They're all following me. And let me tell you, they know Morton Nichols got an eye. Even Marshall Hill admits that."

Johnson nodded. *Maybe Nichols is right. The publicity might be worth a measly one-five.*

Nichols paused, "There's another thing I want to talk to you about. I probably shouldn't say this, I mean, mix into your business, but we're friends, and I'm one of your major collectors. Do you really think the Celia Loeb Gallery is where you ought to be?"

"Oh, selling is slow at the moment, but she's done okay for me in the past."

"Face it, she was doing okay then. But is okay okay enough now? Why isn't she moving more of your work? Tell me that."

"You've got something in mind, Mort. What?"

"There's this young dealer, Dick Wheatley. He's a real live wire, on his way to the top, right to the top. He'll even give Jones competition, wait and see. He's looking for artists."

Johnson looked quizzically at Nichols. *What's in it for you? Are you backing Wheatley?*

"Celia's on her way down and out for the count. A smart guy like you ought to see this. Lemme give you the lowdown on your dealer, and if you ever tell her I did, I'll deny it and never talk to you again."

"Mum's the word."

"She really doesn't have the class to deal with big-time

collectors and curators. Sure, she's able to sell to Bronx and Brooklyn climbers, but there's not much dough in that market and it's drying up for her. I don't want to bad-mouth Celia. I like her and buy art from her now and then—but even I find her crude. She can't help it. It's in her genes. What do ya know about her?"

"Nothing very much."

"Well, lemme fill you in. I knew her old man, a schmatta salesman, just like mine. She inherited whatever business smarts she's got from him. With his loot, she got a college degree from somewhere. Vassar, maybe, who knows? I dunno if she even studied art history. But she learned some manners there and how to dress right and talk proper, more or less. Then she stumbled into a job at the Jones Gallery and learned the business, a lot of it in the sack with the boss. Opened her own gallery with money her old man lent her—d'ya hear, *lent* her. I heard the cheap jerk made her pay it back with interest yet. That kind of cheap runs in her family. She knows whose advice to take. Mine, for one. For that, I'll give her some credit. The bottom line is, she ain't got class. Let's face it, she's a slut. Not like Dick Wheatley—he's a Wasp Yalie, like you, with connections. He'll be big. Mark my word."

"Yeah, Mort, I've met Wheatley and like him. But he's in Hill's bag and wouldn't give me the time of day."

"Don't be so sure."

When Nichols left, Johnson phoned Celia Loeb. "Nichols just bought three paintings for one-five, half of what they're worth. The skinflint knows I'm not selling at the moment. But it might be worth it to be heavily represented in his collection and he promises to give one to a museum. Would you give up your commission? I really need the five hundred that's owed to you. After screwing me, the bastard tried to talk me into leaving you and joining some new gallery, the Wheatley Gallery."

Loeb responded coolly. "Really? That's interesting. Wheatley, huh? Neil, I love you, but we have a business arrangement. There's the gallery's rent to pay."

"Come on, you can afford it. Give me a break."

"Okay, we'll split it. But don't make a habit of it."

"How about I buy *you* dinner, and we have ourselves a roll in the hay?"

"Pick me up at eight."

* * *

Loeb was bothered by Johnson's report on Wheatley. *So he's muscling in on my turf. But what's Mort up to? He has to profit somehow. Better watch my back.* She paced impatiently up and down her gallery, looked at her watch for the tenth time in ten minutes. The doorbell rang and she let Johnson in. "About time. It's eight-thirty. You're a half-hour late. We'll miss our reservation."

Johnson grabbed Loeb's hips, drew her close, and pecked her on the cheek. "So, time for a quickie."

He held her away, looked her over, and said, "Hey, hey, not bad. Not bad at all." *For a forty-year-old broad. Fucking for business and for fun.* "Sorry about being late. Had to see Peter."

"Yeah, yeah. There's no time to undress."

They walked down a spiral staircase which led to her apartment.

Loeb simulated passion, making all of the requisite moans and gasps. Johnson did his usual "professional" performance. He came, she didn't.

Johnson winked, "Not bad, not bad at all."

"Thanks for the testimonial." *C-plus, you arrogant asshole.*

Dinner was depressing. At one point Loeb said, "Would you leave me for Wheatley?"

Johnson looked startled. "It never occurred to me. Why would I?" *Unless it was worth my while.*

Loeb smiled. "That's nice of you to say." *Oh, you would.*

CHAPTER 6: Morton Nichols & Celia Loeb
(December 13, 1957)

Nichols phoned Celia Loeb. "Can I drop by this afternoon? I've got a proposition that I know will interest you."

"Sure. How about six-thirty, after the gallery closes?"

"Awright, I'll be there."

"Why am I thinking I'd better watch my back?"

"Bitchy, bitchy, but I love you, Celia, so you're forgiven."

* * *

Nichols looked Loeb up and down. "My, my, you look healthy—and prosperous. Business must be good."

"Can't complain. But if healthy means fat, bite your tongue."

"I'm about to make you richer than your dreams. Can we go down to your place?"

"Be my guest."

Nichols followed Loeb down the spiral staircase, stopped, and looked around at her apartment. He quickly registered the leather couch, the glass-topped coffee table with artfully placed magazines, and the Breuer chairs. His wife Esther had taught him enough about interior decoration to spot this decor as exemplary 1956 *House Beautiful*.

"Nice. Very, very stylish. Me and the little lady are thinking of buying a split-level house in Westchester County. Maybe you could do the interior decoration."

"If Esther will let me, which I don't think she will."

"Awright. Here's the deal, and I think you're really going to go for it."

"Shoot."

"I believe that Peter Burgh is a great painter—and an undervalued one—not only in reputation but in bucks. And I know you do too. I've been buying him on the sly—got a nice group of a dozen or so. I think he's as good as de Kooning and Guston. He's in for the long run. Even though the Met and MoMA own a few, big-shot collectors are still blind to him and when they finally catch on, his prices are gonna skyrocket out of sight. I'm gonna squirrel away his paintings until that day—and make a bundle. But I want more of his works, as many as I can afford. If word gets out that Nichols is buying as heavily as I mean to, I'll be a patsy for the sharks and what's worse, the copycats. That's where you come in. I want you to buy Burghs for me on the sly. I'll give you a five percent commission."

"So, you want to corner the market."

"Give the lady a kewpie doll. You're pretty damn smart for a broad as hot-looking as you. I propose to put up one hundred thousand dollars. That'll buy me about twenty-five Burghs. I need a dealer as middleman—*pardonnez-moi*, middlewoman—to do the buying. Comprenday?"

"Give me a moment to think about it." *Mort's scheme could work, and if it doesn't there's nothing to lose. Peter's paintings would still be worth more than he invested. But if I agree to work with him, I'll have to watch him like a hawk.*

"Something's bothering me. It doesn't seem ethical."

Nichols snorted, "Ethical? Oh come off it. It's business. It's Morton Nichols you're talking to. We're birds of a feather, remember? We love art and we love money. Will you do it or not?"

"If it's business you're talking about, then it's no deal."

"No deal? What d'ya want? Five grand is pretty mucho."

"I want in for more than that. I'll put up fifty thou and take my share plus three percent more of what we sell. I'll be doing all the work. A dozen plus more paintings on top of what you'll buy or stash away, and that adds up to oodles of Burghs."

"Awright, But three percent on top? That's pretty steep. Make it two percent."

"Settle for two and half?"

"Awright. You're a tough nut. It's a deal. You and me. Let's shake. Now, let me catch you up on where you fit. Our first problem is buying the Burghs. We'll have to deal with Sandy Jones without him knowing our plans. You tell him that a new Parisian gallery is planning to open next year with a Burgh show. It'll be called the Galerie Global. You are its contact gallery in New York, making all the arrangements. They want everything kept secret for now. So, your first job is to buy a dozen or more Burghs from the early 1950s from Sandy Jones, cash up front, and put them in the Parke-Bernet warehouse. We'll move them later to a more private storage and keep them there. No one's to know. One last thing. We'll need an agreement that says how we share in ownership and profits of our deal, except for the added percentage you get. I don't want my share in my name, but in my company's name, Penny, Inc., and I want it kept secret."

"Is it legal?"

"Of course."

"Then there's no problem." *I'll bet there is a problem, but how to investigate?*

What Nichols did not tell Loeb was that Penny, Inc. was an offshore shell company that couldn't be traced back to him, and that half of his stake was being put up by the Brooklyn Mob.

Nichols said, "Also, we've got to begin a campaign to promote Peter. Stir up interest in the art world. That'll mean investing a couple of thousand. We split that. Okay? Joseph Sawyer is writing an article on him for *Art News* and we'll get it published elsewhere as well. And Elaine de Kooning in her review of art in New York singled out Abstract Impressionism as the latest thing. She doesn't mention Peter but everyone knows who's who. The Club people have scheduled a panel with O'Hara and Guston. So, we're off and running."

Loeb said, "Sounds good. Let's have a drink over our deal. Scotch?"

"Why not? The good stuff and no ice."

Loeb walked over to the liquor cabinet, took out two glasses and a bottle of single malt scotch, and poured two fingers into each. She walked back and handed Nichols one. *My daddy and yours. Crooks of a feather. And equally crude, and you're your father's son.*

Loeb faked looking apprehensive and said hesitantly, "Listen closely Morton, don't you dare try to screw me, and, I might add, screw Peter. I won't stand for that. And stop ogling my tits."

'Great tits and mighty fine ass too. And talking about screwing, how about sealing our deal with a little cuddle?"

'Why not? A quickie. Do it like the beast you are, Mort. And we won't tell Esther."

"Oh-ho. You're a bad one. Do you think she'd mind? It's not her fucking night."

"Naughty, naughty, Mort."

Loeb raised her skirt, pulled down her panties, kicked them off, and fell onto the couch. Nichols struggled out of his pants and jockey shorts and climbed on top of her.

"Easy, easy, Ben, I'm not ready yet."

But Nichols rammed his hard penis inside her, grunting with each thrust. Loeb began to meet his thrusts down with her own heaves up, his grunts with her huhs.

"Yes, yes, Ben, fuck me like the beast you are!"

But Nichols was too intent on thrusting to have heard himself called Ben and to register that Ben was Loeb's father's name.

"Now, Ben, give it to me, now. Yeah. Huh, huh. Now, now, huh, huh, huuuuh."

Nichols' grunts stopped. With a deep sigh, he said, "That's one for the books. You were mind-blowing, and I could use some other kind of blowing."

"Mort, what you just got is too good for a vulgar asshole like you."

"Am I hearing any complaints?"

"Mort, you are a prime asshole. But you sure can fuck."

"Thanks for the compliment. How about an encore sometime?"

"Don't press your luck. Well maybe, if you get Esther's permission."

"I think I'll bring her along. She could pick up some pointers. I've gotta go."

Loeb watched Nichols leave, sat down on the couch, picked up a *Vogue*, and thought of Peter Burgh. *He didn't fuck like a beast. He was heavenly. Would I ever make it in bed with him again? So I'm in the sack with Neil, that pompous asshole who hates Peter and makes believe he loves him, and Mort, that money grubbing prick out to make a buck on Peter. So what does that make me? I need a drink.*

Loeb poured herself another scotch.

* * *

Loeb approached the desk at the Metropolitan Museum and asked to talk to Herbert Stein.

"Who is he?"

"You must be kidding. You mean you don't know your own curator of modern art, and you work here?"

"Don't get testy. I'm just a volunteer. Yes, here's the number." Pointing, "You can call him on that phone."

"Hello, Herbert, I'm at the desk downstairs."

"Be right down."

Settled at a table at the Stanhope, Loeb smiled coyly at Stein. "Have you seen the new *Vogue*? Pretty picture of you with Jayne Mansfield. Brought it for you to brag about."

She turned to the page and held it up.

"Oh, my God. I didn't know I looked so pretty. Put it away."

"Cheating on me with Jayne. Just for that I'll read the text. 'Hip young curator. And tall, dark, and handsome too.' Want more?"

"Food first."

As Loeb scanned the menu, Stein looked at her. *Even in that Chanel suit and Vassar accent, you still can't hide the Bronx. But you're money smart, smart enough to pick my brain—for a measly five grand donation—designated for the curator of contemporary art to travel and a tax break for you. Every now and then you donate a picture you can't sell, a good one that you let me choose, for another tax break. And when I return from a trip, you buy me dinner and get the word of what looks good out there. Then there was the night when I took you home after a Whitney opening, both of us loaded, and I ended up in your bed. Good lay.*

Loeb said, "I think I'll have the salad special. I'm dieting. What about you?"

"The cold salmon plate."

"Now, tell me all about San Francisco."

"Not much to report. The scene's pretty dull. A lot of smeary figuration. The best things in that style that I saw were paintings by a Richard Diebenkorn. He's the real thing and a comer. I looked him up. He's cultivated and a real gent. He'll go far."

"Has he got a New York gallery?"

"Not yet."

Over dessert and coffee, Stein said, "You remember, Celia, our night of love? It was sensational. How about a repeat performance?"

Celia responded brightly, "I'd love it. How about tonight? It just so happens I'm free."

Stein was the opposite of Nichols. Finding erogenous zones and slowly caressing them. He had Loeb moaning with pleasure, but no climax.

While resting and smoking a cigarette, Loeb said, "I'm curious. There's a Burgh I like, from 1954. Price seems right. What do you think of his work?"

"Do you mean, how do I assess his market?"

"That too, what's the projection? Peter is still out of the big money. Will he ever really make it?"

"About now, or soon, I would say."

"Neil Johnson thinks he might have already peaked."

"The smart players know better. And that goes for Johnson too. I really don't like to talk art and money. But, sexy sex puts me in a good mood, so here goes. The sale of the Pollock to the Met—incidentally, the director did that, not me—was the icebreaker. Thirty grand ain't hay. Now, word filters back from Europe that collectors there are beginning to buy. In my book, Celia, old girl, if Europe buys, within a year, we'll buy. How does Burgh fit in? Bet on him. He's a sleeper. Number one is Pollock, now in the tens of thousands. Number two, de Kooning, at what, eight, nine? Rothko, say seven. Next on my list, Kline or Guston, maybe five, six. Then Burgh. What's his price—four, five? My prediction? Buy Burgh at these prices and before you know it, you'll sell at fourteen, and that's for openers."

"I'm glad to hear you say that. Peter's high on my list. I am really moved by his painting, and I must confess, guiltily, that I am moved by Peter too, but don't you dare repeat that."

"No way." *And no need. Everybody knows.* "Having been to bed with you twice, it occurs to me that I don't know much about you. And we've been friends for a long time. Tell me more about yourself."

"Want me to let my hair down, pubic first, now head, huh?"

Stein laughed, "Yes, the naked truth."

"We'll begin with Vassar. There I was the New York Jew. Wandering in the wrong places. Bet you had that problem too."

"Yeah, but there were quite a few of us at Harvard. It wasn't so bad. Besides, I played varsity tennis. Jewish jocks had it easier, particularly if they could drink and hide their grades. "

"None of those skinny blonde Wasps at Vassar said anything bad to my face, but I knew what they were saying behind my back. How I hated them, but I copied them. Learned their talk and manners better than they did. I took courses in art history to show how sophisticated I was, not like my papa. But I did get to love the art. In a kind of revolt against Wasp uptightness in my senior year, I became a bohemian of sorts. I dressed in black and hung reproductions of abstract paintings on my walls. When I graduated, what to do? Marry some schlub in the clothing trade? Never. So I asked, 'What does a girl who's a refined bohemian, and who likes art and money—the part of papa I couldn't rid myself of—do?' Didn't have to think hard or long to come up with the answer. Become an art dealer. Jones liked my ass, gave me a job, taught me the trade— and fancy fucking, the old lecher." *But no orgasm. Good at faking one, just like now. Still it was pleasant enough, even if the earth didn't move. You can't have it all.* "Then I opened my own gallery."

Stein responded, "For the greater glory of sex and art."

* * *

Nichols continued his promotion of Burgh by phoning Wheatley. "I'm no philanthropist but every now and then I like doing something for the art world without using my name. You know I've got enemies and they'll use even something good against me. This year I want to help art criticism and was thinking of giving five hundred dollars to a young critic. Make up some catchy name about it. Like the Annual Anonymous Grant for an Art Critical Essay on a Living Artist."

"Why not call it the Wheatley Gallery Grant for Art Criticism?"

"I'm so impressed with Burgh's work, why don't we pick him as the subject of the first article."

"Sounds good to me."

"And we'll give the gallery a lot of publicity."

* * *

After Sawyer completed his article on Burgh for *Art News*, the Whitney announced it was mounting a show of Burgh's work. That generated an additional buzz about him in the art world. Nichols said to Loeb. "Time to start cashing in. Raise Burgh's prices to eight thousand dollars."

Two collectors tried to buy Burgh's paintings from Jones and were told that his gallery was sold out, but that Loeb had acquired a number. When one of the collectors approached her and was told the new price, he said, "That's nuts." She replied, "That's the market today, and I predict it'll go up." She phoned Nichols and asked, "Can I sell at six? Eight seems to be too high."

"No way, not yet. No bargains."

CHAPTER 7: Peter Burgh
(January 30, 1958)

Peter Burgh received a call from Harvey Ravin, the art critic, who asked, "How about me doing a studio visit to see what the old master Abstract Expressionist is up to? Are you still making stabs in the dark?"

"What else? Maybe you could light my way?"

"How about I bring a flashlight next Monday at five?"

"I'll have drinks ready. I recall that you're a single malt scotch man. I'm lucky you don't come over too often or I'd go bankrupt."

"I promise to take only a few sips."

Ravin was an old-time ex-Marxist intellectual who had been schooled on soap-boxes in the 1930s and had debated with the best of them. Since he and Burgh had met at the Artists Union back then, they had both enjoyed sparring verbally. At a lecture at the Club, Ravin had chided painters for over-intellectualizing their art. Cerebration got in the way of intuition and feeling. The way forward was through spontaneous improvisation.

During the question and answer period, Burgh had told

Ravin that an article he had written on Abstract Expressionism was brilliant, except that it parroted the same old Duchamp crap about artists being dumb. Burgh said that he and his fellow painters hadn't disposed of their minds. They could think as well as feel. He added, "And besides, Ravin old comrade, You may be a world-class intellectual but you've got a tin eye." He later apologized for the tin eye crack and told Ravin that he had been drunk when he criticized him and that now sober, he wanted to make amends. It took the critic several weeks to forgive Burgh, but he finally said, "We go back too far for me to hold a grudge, so far back that you should have learned something about modern culture in the interim, but no such luck." Burgh responded with a smile, "Really, Harvey, I couldn't help being a dim-wit. I'm just a visual type, as you know, ain't too good with ideas." Ravin began to laugh and shook his hand. Despite their long acquaintance, however, Burgh was surprised that Ravin wanted to see his work. After all, the critic was in de Kooning's camp and hadn't phoned in years.

Ravin had a bum foot and Burgh could hear him clump his way up the stairs. Burgh greeted him with a glass of scotch. "I'll bet the reason you're here is because you heard that Hill hates my work and that led you to love it."

"It's because I've been neglecting you too long. But it's true that I'm predisposed to like anything that phony hates. His formalism is pure unadulterated bullshit."

"He has nice things to say about you too."

Ravin was big man who looked larger than he was and seemed to fill any space he was in. Burgh had put a half-dozen canvases around his studio and Ravin walked about casually looking at them. He said enthusiastically, "They're great. Hill's missed the boat again. I hear you gave him the finger at the Cedar."

"Yes, he deserved it." *Thank you, Harvey.* "You versus Hill makes me nostalgic for the 1930s, when we crossed swords over Stalinism and Trotskyism, art for the masses and avant-garde abstraction. We're still at war but with new camps—de Kooning versus Pollock, Color-Field Painting versus Action Painting. The polemics haven't subsided, or the hatreds."

"Oh yes. You have something there. Maybe the only way to end the art war is to shoot Hill or hang him."

"Ship him off to a gulag, like they did in the workers' paradise."

"Too good for the son of a bitch."

Burgh poured them another drink and said, "Tell me something, Harvey. I know you see Bill de Kooning, but I haven't talked to him for a long time. His followers have a humongous hate on me. But what does Bill himself think about my recent work? I'm curious."

Ravin responded seriously, "Bill is disposed to anyone who, like him, goes back to the thirties and has stuck it out making art, even though he didn't like the work then—or now. He also enjoys the kudos of his followers. But he lets them babble without saying much himself. Plays it close to the vest. As for your work, we both looked at your painting in the Whitney Annual, what was it called, *Journey*, I think? And Bill said, 'That's terrific.' Which is about as enthusiastic as he gets. Beth Morgan was with us. She said nothing but looked as if someone had pissed in her beer. I get the feeling that Bill doesn't know where he stands with you personally. Why don't you make the first move? Give him a call and invite him to lunch or a drink."

"I think I just might. It's been a long time since we've talked."

"Oh, and another thing, you're getting to be his main competition. Show him a little deference. Even with all of his accolades, he's still insecure because he still thinks of himself as a Dutch immigrant. Incidentally, one reason I'm here is that young artists I meet are talking more and more about you. And I want to get on the bandwagon first or early. And, yes, fart in Hill's face."

* * *

Burgh phoned de Kooning, told him how moved he was by his recent show, and invited him to lunch at the Cookery. As they were ushered to their table, they passed Marcel Duchamp eating an omelet.

Duchamp waved a limp hand at them. Burgh waved back and smiled. "The devil incarnate himself. Nose up like a French snot. He's history—I hope."

"I'm not so sure. Young guys are talking him up, like this Rauschenberg fellow. Nice kid, good manners. He turns junk into art. They call his stuff Neo-Dada, but it ain't. He asked me for a drawing and told me he would erase it. I gave him one, a good one. Would you?"

"No way. It's like Cage erasing music, like his composition of silence, four minutes and thirty-three seconds of nothing to hear. Cage's other stuff is just noise. Our friend Duchamp sitting over there is his guru. What I don't understand is why Cage likes my work."

"It doesn't surprise me. Even Cage can't help responding to mastery, much as he tries not to. He says he doesn't want to be a great artist, but I don't believe him."

"He wants to turn everyday life into art. I strongly disagree."

De Kooning nodded, "Or art into everyday life. Reinhardt says, art is art and it comes from art. I'm with him. Gorky's ghost in art heaven keeps haunting me. He never got Picasso out of his head. Neither have I. Yet, I try to make my painting out of my life."

"For me, it's Piero, but the kids say Monet."

They finished their second drink and ordered another. De Kooning said, "You know, my followers bad-mouth you. They think I'm running for mayor of the art world or something and they gotta beat the competition—you. As if, if I win, they win. So it's about them." He shrugged. "You also got guys in your corner, but they aren't as loud-mouthed as mine."

"But my fans are afraid to attack you. And we both got Hill on our backs."

De Kooning sneered, "He's a fat fart in the wind. Back in the good old days, the geometric guys tried to rope me in. They were a lost cause, but I was with them, not their brave new world crap, but their modernism."

"I was with the commissars. They hated anything new and even demanded that I purge the bits of Surrealism in my work. I wouldn't, but they didn't kick me out of the Communist Party because they could use me for my reputation as a painter. So it was a standoff. We dreamed of a future utopia, and they murdered millions in that cause. What did it all add up to? A lot of lousy art."

After a third drink, de Kooning said, "I wish my followers would stop bad-mouthing you. Please don't hold it against me."

"Never! I'm moved that you respect my work. I wasn't sure that you did."

"Respect's not the right word. I respond to the angst in your painting. The kids don't see it. They don't understand it. They think they suffer for their art. It's not the same as painting it."

They parted with a handshake. Neither artist wanted to let go.

Burgh said, "Let's do an encore soon."

* * *

Burgh had been ignoring phone calls for days. But once, when the ringing didn't stop, he picked up the receiver, and was about to put it down when he heard the voice of Stanley Jones, his dealer. "C'mon Peter, answer the goddamn thing."

"What for?"

"Oh, you're in one of your jolly moods. I've been trying to get you for two days."

"Aw, this fucker of a picture has been taking up all of my time and my life. I'm in a deep funk."

"Sorry to hear that. But we've got business. Two big collector couples want to see your latest work. I mean big.

Sheldon Green, the trustee at the Metropolitan Museum and his wife, Mildred—they're friends of the Nichols'. And Robert Wright, CEO of Northeast Railroad, and his wife Jane. They'd like a studio visit. Are you up to it?"

Burgh answered despondently, "Why not? Can't paint anything I care to look at and got nothing better to do. It ought to be worth a prime place on a fat-cat's wall."

"Peter, Peter, puhleeze, that's just the kind of talk I don't want them to hear. Will you behave yourself? I'm sure they'll buy."

"Yeah, sure. I'll be nice and not say a single word, promise."

"We'll be there for drinks tomorrow at six. Serve the good stuff—and clean the place up."

Jones arrived with the Greens and the Wrights. Burgh greeted them cordially and offered drinks.

Robert Wright said, "Neil Johnson told us to look you up. Said you were the most undervalued Abstract Expressionist, both in reputation and price."

Green added, "And Nichols put in a good word too."

Burgh began to show them his paintings, one by one, placing them along the studio walls.

At the fifth, Mildred Green said, "That a nice one. I like the color. What do you think, Shel?"

"How much?"

Jones answered, "Six."

Wright raised an eyebrow, "Isn't that rather steep? I happen to know that Burgh's prices are around four."

Jones said, "The market has taken off recently."

"Is that so? What is it about them that made you up the prices?"

"The market has finally caught up with Burgh. I've been advising you for some time to buy his work. And we hear from Europe—even France—that New York has replaced Paris as the center of world art. When the Europeans buy, the Americans buy, and up goes the market."

Wright said, "Well, at least these are paintings, not drippings."

Burgh looked askance and was about to speak but Jones cut him off. "Bring out another canvas, Peter."

Jane Wright laughed and said in the direction of Burgh, "My husband likes being provocative. It's a game with him."

Burgh nodded, "I understand, except that I believe Pollock was a great painter."

Green interjected, "Greater than you?"

"Price will tell."

"You can bet your bottom dollar on that."

Jane Wright provocatively said, "What do you think, Mr. Burgh? Are your new prices too high?"

"I really can't say. I don't pay much attention to the market. That's Stan's department."

Wright rolled his eyes.

Mildred Green had moved a few steps away from the others and had been staring at one of the paintings. "Tell me Mr. Burgh, what are you trying to express?"

Burgh smiled at her. "I'm not exactly sure. I guess I want a painting that is as intensely felt as I can make it."

Mildred Green nodded and smiled back.

Green registered his wife's smile and interjected with an edge of hostility, "Why should I care about how you feel? Why should anyone care?"

Burgh answered quietly. "People do respond. They feel the emotion. They also respond to the painting's authenticity."

"Whatever that means."

"There's a philosophy I find meaningful called Existentialism."

"I've read about it. Some Frenchman invented it, Sartre's his name, I think."

"Yes, he's one."

Mildred Green interjected, "What's it about?"

Burgh replied, "It starts with the premise that life is absurd, because it ends in death. In the face of this, each of us has to make himself or herself into what we want to be, but our desires must be shaped by what we want mankind to be."

Green interjected, "So you want your painting to speak for us all?"

"No, it speaks for me and my desires. You have to decide whether it speaks for you or to you."

"That's a pretty tall order for a piece of cloth smeared with some pigment. My desires are less cerebral and of a lower order, much lower."

Burgh busied himself with placing a picture on a sidewall. He quickly turned it away.

Green called out, "What are you hiding there?"

Burgh replied, "I think it's finished, but I'm not exactly sure."

"Let's take a look."

Burgh turned the canvas around.

Mildred Green said to her husband, "I like that one,

really like it. Can we buy it?"

Burgh said quickly, "It's not for sale," but his visitors ignored him.

Jane Wright said, "At six thou? Really Mildred?"

"If I have to, I'll use my allowance."

Green snickered, "Didn't you know, the wife's a do-gooder. Helps starving artists. But she's right. I like the looks of that one. What do you think, Robert? You've been awfully quiet."

"You know, Shel, I've checked out Burgh. Johnson's advice was good. For price, I always go with the market."

Wright looked at Burgh and added, "And I overheard Herbert Stein say nice things about you. But I won't accept that Pollock is a great artist. Is he better than Dubuffet?"

"They're both good. I like Pollock more."

Jane Wright said, "Well, me too. I made Robert buy me a Pollock, a big one. Got it for nine-five."

Wright said, "I still prefer Dubuffet. Matter of fact, I recently bought one of his at eighteen. It was a bargain. Is a Burgh worth a third of that? You may not understand the market, Mr. Burgh, but I do."

Jane Wright said, "You do remember, honey, that Hill thinks Pollock is the greatest."

"Yeah, but he doesn't care for Burgh. I trust Jones more. Still, six is too high. But if you like that one, Jane, I'll buy it for you."

"Thanks, but I'd like a better price."

Jones looked to Burgh. Burgh nodded.

"We'll take five."

"Oh honey, let's buy it."

Green said sarcastically, "We're in luck. Mr. Burgh deigned to sell a masterpiece at a bargain price. The little lady can't live without it. Sold!"

* * *

A few hours after they left, Jones phoned Burgh. "Thanks for almost behaving yourself. Your 'price will tell' worried me for a moment."

"Do you think the asshole got my drift or is he as dense as I think he is?"

"He got it loud and clear. He's vulgar but not stupid. And this may surprise you, but he's an art junkie."

"An art lovebird. Sure he is. Now Stan. Please don't inflict any more of your asshole collectors on me."

"They're generally pleasant, not arrogant like they were on this trip. Something about you turned them off."

"They sensed that I was the enemy, the class enemy. Besides, Mrs. Green made goo-goo eyes at me that Mr. Green didn't like."

"Are they really your enemies? Are you their enemy? Look, these people buy art, your art. They just shelled out more than five thousand dollars and you suffered for less than an hour. And you even got to bite the hand that feeds you."

"I hate to admit it, but you've got a point. I'm certainly not about to shout 'Up the Revolution' or turn my studio into a barricade on behalf of some cause, like I did a long time ago. That's over."

Jones laughed, "Telling Wright you wanted to keep the one he wanted was brilliant marketing."

"Actually, I didn't want to sell it."

"Of course not, but anytime you want to quit painting and become a dealer, you're hired."

"Thanks for zilch."

* * *

Roger Prince, the TV talk show host, phoned Burgh and asked if he would appear on "Newsmakers Today."

Burgh said, "No, I'd rather not."

"Why not? You know you're news. We reach tens of thousands of people. Don't you want them to know about your art?"

"I'm leery of the boob tube. I don't like the way it dumbs down our cultural and intellectual life."

"You haven't answered my question."

"Tens of thousands, huh?"

"Actually, many more. Sure, most of them will be yahoos, but a bunch of them won't. They're the ones you want to talk to. Besides, how can we upgrade television, if people like you avoid us?"

Burgh protested, "But what I have to say will be swamped in small talk and soap commercials."

"We gotta try, don't we? I'll do my best."

"Okay, I'll give it a shot, but please keep it on a high level."

* * *

"This is Roger Prince on 'Newsmakers Today.' We have with us Mr. Peter Burgh, an Abstract Expressionist artist who has been making a big splash in the art world, not the kind of splash Jackson Pollock made—they called him Jack the Dripper, didn't they, Mr. Burgh—but a splash nonetheless. This is what one of Mr. Burgh's pictures looks like. It looks like Monet to me—but I understand you don't like the connection. Why not and why don't you paint things that people would recognize?"

"Monet's painting is about nature, light in nature, outer light, and mine is not. I try to paint what you might call my inner light, a personal light."

"But why? Why is it abstract?"

"I paint the way I do because I can only paint what I feel, honestly feel, while I'm painting. And what I *feel* can't be represented by recognizable things."

"Looking at the picture on the screen, Peter, doesn't it look like you're just messing around? People simply won't understand it. Don't you want them to?"

"Of course I do. I recognize that most people will find it hard to relate to the work because it doesn't represent anything and they think that art should. But many people do respond. That's why you invited me here. Perhaps, in order to fully appreciate my painting, people will have to learn something about the half-century tradition of abstract art. Still, it's enough to look at the painting and try to feel it. I can only hope that people will give it a try."

"What I'm asking is, why don't you try to paint something the American public will understand without getting a Master of Fine Arts degree, like Andrew Wyeth does."

"Because I'm not Andy Wyeth."

"Well, what do you think about his pictures?"

"I find his work well made but sentimental and, therefore, shallow."

"Are you saying Wyeth is a bad artist?"

"Not bad. What he does, he does very well. But in my eyes, and in my eyes only, his work is thin. You're free to admire him, of course."

"Oh I do, I do. I don't want to put your work down, but to be honest, I'd rather we had Wyeth's pictures on the screen instead of yours."

"Then why didn't you invite Wyeth here? Why me?"

"Because, you're making a big, big splash in the art world, and I and my viewers would like to know why."

"It may be because my work moves people."

"Or, like Emma Jenner writes in the *Herald Tribune*, you're putting something over on the public."

"Why would I want to do that?"

"You tell me. Jenner says it's for money. People actually do buy your stuff."

"Some do, but do you think they're dumb or duped? All you're really telling me is that Jenner is very interested in money and attributing her own petty money-grubbing desire to artists. Sure, a few collectors, a few museums buy my work. Enough for me to get by. If I wanted to get rich, I'd paint like Wyeth or go into the stock market."

"Come now, Peter, I'm told that smears like yours and the other Abstract Expressionists sell like hot cakes for tens of thousands of dollars."

"Mine don't and I doubt that theirs do, either."

"I've got an article here by Calvin Stockman, the editor of the *Higher Standard*, who says that you paint the way you do because you hate people."

"That's nonsense. I'd like to ask you a question Mr. Prince. I assume that you've invited me on your program because I've achieved some reputation as an artist. Why don't you quote critics who understand my work, like Professor Meyer Schapiro of Columbia University or a major art critic like Harvey Ravin?"

"I like to give a rounded view."

Burgh looked straight at the camera and said, with a mixture of anger and passion, "That's *your* view, Mr. Roger Prince, and it's hardly rounded. I'll give you my view. American abstract painting is the foremost in the world today because of the efforts of Pollock and a dozen of his associates. And does the American public hail these great artists? No, these artists are labeled money-hungry frauds, accused of trying to put something over on people. And someone like you, Mr. Prince, who's in a position to inform the public, doesn't. Do you? You put us down and claim you're giving a rounded view. For shame. But it doesn't really matter. The art is magnificent, and because it is, it will, in time, convert growing numbers of people. As for myself, let me say that I paint the way I do because I have to. It's that simple. I'd like to say something more to your viewers out there. Look at the painting, and try to put aside your ideas about what art ought to be, your prejudices. I mean, try to feel the work. If you do, you'll understand."

"Well, our time is up, Peter Burgh. Thank you for coming on 'Newsmakers Today' and sharing your art and thoughts with us. Let's have a round of applause for Peter Burgh,

Abstract Expressionist painter. And now we'll meet a panel of women whose children strangle themselves for sexual pleasure, moderated by America's favorite psychoanalyst, our own Dr. William Downing. But first, we'll take a minute to learn why Fine Sheen Shampoo will end your bad hair days…"

Burgh crossed University Place to the Chuck Wagon and ordered a grilled cheese sandwich and coffee. There was no one he knew there. He began to review his performance on "Newsmakers Today." He had held his own but did he appear pretentious? Or was that unavoidable? It's silly to defend art. It doesn't need it. Only boors think it does. *I should have stayed in my studio.*

* * *

Burgh phoned Stein. "I know it's been weeks since your letter to the *Higher Standard*, but I want to thank you. Just the right tone."

"Thank *you*. I was about to phone you, Mr. Burgh. We've met on and off but never really talked. I'd like to. I also would like to do a show of your work at the Met."

"At the Met? With the big guys? Sounds great. Let's meet for a drink. Are you free this evening? And please call me Peter. Even my enemies do."

"Unfortunately, I have a date with an old art history professor of mine, Ashton Tite."

"You could bring him along, if you like."

"Could I? I know he would love to meet you. He even mentioned he'd like to do an article on you. He's an authority on Baroque painting, but wants to move into contemporary art. What time shall we meet and where?"

"How about the Cedar at six. A break from painting."

"Suits me fine."

Burgh was sitting at a table at the back of the Cedar sipping a scotch when Stein came in, spotted him, and walked over. After greeting each other, Stein sat down next to him and ordered a beer. Burgh looked toward the door and said, "There's your professor. That's him, isn't it?"

"How'd you know?"

"Easy. Leather patches on the sleeves of a sports jacket. That's a dead giveaway."

"He's not forty yet and he looks fifty. As a professor of mine, he was not much older than I was. He was a real hotshot, destined for scholarly glory. And more than a bit full of himself."

Tite looked around, saw Stein, and walked over to the table. He said heartily, "Herbert, my boy, it's grand to see you. And I am glad indeed to see that my former prize student is doing so well in the Big Apple."

"Professor Tite, welcome. This is Peter Burgh."

"I'm honored to meet you, sir."

He sat down across from Burgh and enthused, "I'm a great, great admirer of your painting and I mean to do an article on you. That is, after I finish one on Willem de Kooning."

Burgh looked at him quizzically. "I understand that your field is Baroque art. Why do you want to write about today's painting?"

"You see, I want to branch out. My book on Guido Reni has gotten good reviews and is selling reasonably well for a scholarly monograph. Before starting a new study on Baroque space, I thought it might be interesting to wade into the present, from Baroque play with space to Modernist flatness, as it were, or maybe from three dimensions to two. Say, both would be good titles for essays." Tite paused, "But, that's not the real reason. I'm bored with academic art history, all of that iconography. I've been in therapy for six years, and I've been fascinated by psychoanalysis. I thought I might formulate a new methodology for art history based on Freud, and living artists I can interview."

"Like psychoanalyze them?" Burgh interjected.

The waiter walked over. The professor ordered a cognac. He looked around. "So this is the famous Cedar Street Tavern. It looks rather drab. I would have expected artists to choose a livelier, more stimulating environment."

Burgh said, "But that would attract a livelier and more stimulating crowd, just the kind of people artists don't want around when they want to talk to each other."

"Ah, yes, yes, of course."

Burgh asked, "How will you use Freud's theory in your article on Bill, that is, if you wouldn't mind saying."

"Mind? Not at all. I'd like your opinion of my approach. Now consider de Kooning's 'Women'. I've come to think that the key to them is his mother fixation. Of course, I'm simplifying." Tite continued, "Let me explain. De Kooning's image of woman is fierce and dominating. She's an oppressive and threatening presence. She's his 'big mama.' I imagine de Kooning as a child looking up at her feeling anxiety at his insignificance, yes, and anger at his impotence. I read that his mother ran a sailor's bar in Amsterdam. She must have been a very tough woman. And now his anger has surfaced in his art. As for Freud..."

Burgh interrupted, "You don't find the 'Women' funny as well as scary, the mythic New York bimbo? Do you deal with the way Bill's women relate to billboard images, or to Picasso's and Leger's females, as well as, formally, in the way they're painted?"

"Other writers have dealt with the 'Women' from socio-logical, art historical, or formalist standpoints. But the psychoanalytic approach is unexplored, you see. And I hope to talk at length to de Kooning."

Burgh asked, "In the article on me, will you deal with my mother?"

"Yes, your painting is most unlike de Kooning's. He's aggressive, you're passive. He's awestruck by mother but is driven to confront her furiously. My thesis is that you did your best to be unobtrusive. I would like to interview you about such matters."

"Like analyze me? Would an interview, or a number of them, provide sufficient information? A friend of mine has been seeing a shrink for half his life and still doesn't know his ass from a hole in the ground."

"Freud and his followers have given us a valuable method to analyze the unconscious, if one is perceptive, that is."

"You say I was unobtrusive—what an odd word. I have no memory of ever being reticent around my mother. I was a pretty self-assured kid."

"Your conscious memory, you mean. Maybe unobtrusive is not the best word. I'm looking for what you've repressed, what's hidden in your unconscious. And what your defense mechanisms inhibit you from revealing."

Burgh suddenly saw the image of Frankie on Guadalcanal. "Yes, the unconscious…" He paused and looked away. "Gotta watch out for defense mechanisms. Come to think of it, I'm always forgetting my mother's birthday. But I phone her every month." Peter shrugged, "or maybe every other month."

"Well, you've just made my point."

"I don't know. I would agree that my paintings are about my life, psychic self-portraits of sorts. But they are also about the world and how social events impact our lives. How does that matter?"

Tite didn't answer. He was watching a large, unkempt man, obviously drunk, who was stumbling toward the table, right at him, and who sprawled next to Stein on the bench. Burgh introduced Little Mike Pearson to Professor Tite. "This man's a marvelous painter, named after Michelangelo. I've known him for more than thirty years. You ought to interview him about me for your article."

Pearson learned over the table to the professor and, slobbering, said loudly, "An article on Peter? Ashk me anyting. Peter'sh my besh fren. Peter'sh my only fren." Tite tried to lean away from Pearson, but the big man moved even closer, overturning his glass of cognac. Flustered, Tite pushed his way past Pearson out of the booth. He stood up, composed himself, straightened his pants and jacket, and said expansively to Burgh, "Well, I must be off. It was nice meeting you—and illuminating. I'll send you an offprint of my essay on de Kooning. And phone you soon."

Burgh nodded.

"Well, goodbye Herbert. Keep up the good work. How much do I owe?"

Burgh said, "No, no, please. You're on my turf. It's my nickel."

Tite thanked him and hurriedly left. Stein said to Burgh. "I don't think my professor will ever forget his introduction into our art world."

"Did he know that I was kidding him?"

"I doubt it. A sense of humor is not his strong point. You are a wicked man."

"I guess. I couldn't resist spoofing what turned me off academe—and psychoanalysis. I don't mind following Bill de Kooning in Professor Tite's pantheon, but not Guido Reni."

Stein looked at Burgh quizzically, "Why do I think you invented that bit about forgetting your mother's birthday? I read somewhere that your mother's dead"

Burgh laughed.

"What'll you say when Tite includes your mother's resurrection in his article?"

"It was a Freudian slip. Or I was misunderstood. Or that I invented it. Isn't that what artists are supposed to do? Be imaginative? I can look solemn and say that in my mind she's still alive or that I plumb forgot. In the end, I can fall back on the idea that us artists are crazy bastards. One even cut off his ear. I guess you'll have to sort it out in your article on me."

"Whosh ah bashtard? Whosh calling whosh ah bashtard? Shay, buy me a drink, Peter, old comrade."

Burgh called out to the bartender, "John, put all of this

on my tab. Hey, hey, Little Mike, time to go bye-bye. I'll buy you a burger and some black coffee at Rikers." Stein got out of the booth and Burgh hoisted Pearson to his feet, grabbed him by the arm, and steered him toward the door. Turning to Stein, Burgh said, "We'll talk another time soon. Give ma—I mean, me—a call. I hope our future meetings are as amusing."

CHAPTER 8: Diane Knight
(February 21, 1958)

Burgh met Diane Knight at an opening at the Hansa Gallery. She said she was a painter and an admirer of his work and asked if she could see his most recent canvases. They went to his studio. Their animated conversation about art took a personal turn. As Burgh mounted Knight he softened. *Please God, not again, not now.* Eileen came to mind. *Relax, dammit, relax.* Knight sensed his difficulty and began to caress him gently, whispering, "Easy, easy does it, lover man, shshsh. Easy does it." Burgh looked down on her thick blonde hair and firm, full breasts. Caught up in her aura of sexual excitement, he felt himself harden again and regain control. The more he thrust, the more sure he was of himself. Knight's excited response helped.

As they lay together relaxing, she said, "Happy day! I just had sex with the great Peter Burgh and it was terrific."

He replied, "More terrific than terrific." He marveled that he ended up in bed with this handsome woman. He smiled at her and said, "I can't help thinking of French movies."

"How so?"

"Middle aged man seduces young beauty."

"What would you title it?"

"Triste Amour."

"Why *triste*?"

"Middle aged man had trouble getting it up."

"His mamselle knew a trick or two."

"For which he is eternally grateful. I'll never go limp again, not with you."

"You triggered a super orgasm that was not at all *triste*. And see how I've messed up the sheets."

"While they dry, let's celebrate. Go to the Jumble Shop for a feast."

"Celebrate our anniversary. How long has it been? Two and a half hours?" She pointed to the sink. "But first I'm going to wash some dishes and pans and clean this mess up, ugh and ugh."

"No, please don't."

"Where's the soap and a clean towel?"

Naked, she got up and turned toward the kitchen. Watching her perfectly rounded buttocks and patch of blonde hair aroused Burgh so that, before she got out of reach, he grasped her arm and drew her back into bed. Knight laughed, "Well, if you won't wait, the dishes will have to."

Later, at the restaurant, Burgh said, "I'll have a scotch for openers. What about you?"

Knight replied, "I'm not much of a drinker. A small beer, maybe, or a glass of white wine. But okay, it's a party and I'll make whoopee. I'll have what you're having. But you mustn't let me get drunk. I hate being hung over." She paused. "I didn't get a chance to ask you. What were you doing at the Hansa Gallery opening? It's Hofmann's turf, and I've heard that you don't think much of him."

"The guy showing there, Billy Abbott, may be a 'Hofmannerist' but he stretches canvases for me and we've become friends. And there you were." *A hot-looking blonde, a little broad in the beam, but not bad.* "What really grabbed me about you was your milk-white skin. Then I remembered that Harvey Ravin once said that Aristotle or somebody, said that whenever he read 'milk-white skin' or 'wine-red sea' in a book, he slammed it shut. I eyed you and you eyed me, and here we are. I can't imagine what a glorious young chick like you saw in a sagging old cock like me."

"No accounting for taste."

"You can say that again. I must admit that when I invited you to the studio, I thought you'd turn me down."

"I just wanted to see your latest paintings. I'm a fan, you know. But I liked what it led to."

"Ditto." *A perk for being a big-time artist.*

After his second scotch, Burgh said, "I can't help noticing your southern accent. Where are you from and how'd you get to Hofmann? I don't even know your last name. Tell me about yourself."

"Name's Knight. Southern accent? I thought I had already become a 'Damn Yankee.' You want my life story? Why not? I was born on a Marine Corps base in North Carolina, Cherry Point, and was raised as a Marine brat. My dad was a sergeant. He was killed when I was eleven, run over by a tank on maneuvers. I still miss him."

Burgh looked downcast.

Knight laughed. "Oh, Peter, you're not thinking that you're a father figure to me?"

"No, no. You suddenly reminded me of a Marine comrade who was killed in the Pacific."

"Oh, you were in the Corps during the war? I want to hear about that."

"Another time. Go on with your story."

"Three years later, my mother remarried another Marine noncom, and we were stationed in Charleston. My stepfather was a cold fish. We were civil and kept our distance. I was one of those child prodigy drawers, and everyone we knew oohed and aahed over my pictures. I kept at it in high school and then at the University of Virginia where I went on a scholarship, but I had to work part-time waiting tables. Took a BFA in painting in 1953. I fell for a halfback—a 'Big Man on Campus'—who was also ROTC. He bought me a humongous diamond ring on the installment plan—it'll take him most of his life to pay it off—and we got married. Big mistake. Clyde became a junior executive in a farm machinery company, and in his spare time watched sports on television, messed with his car, did some carpentry, drank with his buddies, and bored the pants off me. He didn't like the idea of my continuing to paint and became downright hostile when I decided to go back to the University to earn a Masters. Then Erle Loran came to teach for a semester, you know him?"

Burgh nodded.

"I had seen reproductions of his work and just had to take his course, but it was in the evening, once a week. My husband blew his top. I said to him, 'Look, you take a night out every week, sometimes two and even three, to be with the guys.' He said, 'Yeah, but I'm a guy.' But I enrolled anyway. One night, I came home from class, he was there, watching boxing on the tube. I remember every detail of that night. I noticed the light was on in the cellar where I painted. The mean bastard had slashed all of my canvases, cut them up into pieces. He said smugly, 'It was them or me. I decided it's me.' He then said that he had done the world a favor, saved it from all the abstract crap I was shitting out. And he laughed. I was too shocked to even cry or rant and rave. I just said, 'Okay, that settles it.' But not the way the SOB thought. You know, even after I began to sour on my husband, I still enjoyed the sex. But that night he wanted some, to really show me who's on top. I tried to beg off, telling him that I was too upset, hoping he'd understand. But he'd have none of it, and if married sex can be rape, that was it. I had squirreled away some money, and the next day while Clyde was at work, I salvaged a portfolio of drawings that had been stowed out of sight under the bed, packed a bag of my stuff. Then I got somewhat crazy. I wrote with lipstick on the living room wall, '*You* said art or me. I choose art. So, bye-de-bye.' Clyde had been keeping a folder of snapshots, mostly of him, as a football star and me as his trophy wife. The last thing I did was to cut out a few pictures of me, baked the rest of me in the oven, and put the ashes on our bed. I thought that even a jerk like Clyde would get the symbolism. Funny, but when I was about to go out the door, I went back and took a scrapbook that I had been keeping since I was a girl, filling it with clippings, photos, any mementos of events in my life. Then

I took the bus to New York, changed my name so my ass-hole husband couldn't trace me, pawned my humongous ring, used the money to rent a teeny apartment, and got a part-time job waiting tables on Thirteenth Street. Loran had liked my work and had raved about how great a teacher Hofmann was. So, I showed Hofmann my drawings and he accepted me into his school. That's where I am. Then I seduced you. And that's the story of my life to date."

"The bastard slashed your paintings? I can't think of anything more rotten. I would have spattered his brains over your destroyed work."

"The thought crossed my mind, but there was a kind of silver lining. The next morning, when I went into the cellar and saw the cut-up paintings, I remember crawling on the floor, crying, trying to put some of the pieces back together, like jigsaw puzzles. Looking at how the parts were painted, they didn't look so wonderful. I remember thinking, I've got to do better. At that moment, I knew, really knew, that I would become an artist. Nothing would stop me, nothing. Funny, instead of being depressed, I felt elated."

* * *

For the past two months, Knight had been seeing Burgh once or twice a week at his loft, generally for lunch and an occasional love-making session in the afternoon, because by evening he would get nervous and want to paint. When she felt comfortable, she invited him to her apartment. She led him into a living room which doubled as a bed-room and said, "That green bedspread was given to me by my real dad a year or so before he died. I bought the green pillows to match. He also gave me that ragdoll around my seventh birthday. Made her clothes myself. They're mostly green, but with yellow trim. So I figured that green was my color. You'll see a lot of it in my work. I sometimes wonder why. Maybe something to do with the beautiful park across the street from an apartment I lived in with my real dad. I loved playing in the grass. I really don't know."

Knight led Burgh past a closet-sized kitchen into a small room she used as her studio. She had hung a few of her paintings on one wall and, on the other, some dozen photographs and illustrations cut out of magazines. She began to show her paintings—small, thinly painted green fields with images of apples and plums composed of intricate patterns drawn with charcoal and colored chalks.

Pointing to one, she said nervously, "See, a lot of green."

He sat silently for a long time and then said, "Your canvases really surprise me. I didn't expect what you painted, not from a Hofmann student. That's so different from what he teaches."

"Is that bad?"

"No, that's to your credit."

"My drawing has always been central to my work. I don't think Hofmann cares for what I'm doing, but he has made some suggestions and I'm following his advice, and they're getting better. I never want to push and pull paint, like he teaches, and he accepts that, although he's cut back on giving me crits. He did say to keep on with what I was doing. I stay with him to listen to his ideas and to be with his students. They've become my friends and keep me on my toes. But do you like my pictures?"

"Yes, but you should be leery of the opinion of someone like me, who paints big abstract pictures with a sloppy big brush. Your brush is so tiny that it's hard for me to feel the paint. But I can say without question that you are talented and on to something of your own. Like Hans said, keep at it."

"I know you don't paint like me. But could you tell me how to make them better?"

"I wouldn't know how to advise you."

Knight said, "What I mean is, look at the apples. How can I improve them? Or the drawing?"

"I would ask, how could you make it more felt, more you?"

"Yes, I understand that. But I mean on the technical level. How, can I make the painting of those apples better?" Knight's lips curled down. *Why was Peter holding back?*

Burgh sensed her disappointment and said, "I did have to crit student work when I was teaching, but it felt phony to me, so as soon as I could quit, I did. One thing I can say— I understand the form your painting is taking, getting the open green field to work with the complicated drawing, but what does it have to do with apples and plums? What do the subjects say? What do apples mean to you? What do you feel about them? Do you love them? Or what?"

"Well, Hofmann set up a still-life. I needed a subject and that was as good as any."

"But do you really need it? Isn't your expression essentially what the field color and the drawing are doing? Isn't the fruit distracting? Why not cut them out?"

"Hofmann says we must begin with nature. I need a subject."

"You want to know what I really think? Okay. You're damn good, and I mean it. But, as I see it, the aim in art is not to be good, but to be inspired. That sounds pretentious, I know, but that's all that counts."

She sighed, "I'll need time to be inspired in the way you mean it. My problem now is to make better pictures. For the moment that's all I can handle. But I hope to find my style."

He looked at the wall across from where the canvases were hung. He said, "What's this? There's photos of me and of my paintings. And there's Hofmann, Kline, and Guston and other stuff, like pictures of a girl, is she you? There's Central Park and Washington Square, an opening at a gallery, looks like Parsons, and Metropolitan Museum postcards and Marines on maneuvers."

"Yeah, some are mementos I brought with me to New York, a Happy Valentine's Day card from a grade-school admirer, a *Life* magazine illustration of the kind of tank my father used to drive. Here's the receipt from my bus ticket to New York, and there, the menu of the Genuine Southern BBQ a high-school crush took me to. Other pictures I took here and cut them out of old catalogs and *Art News*. I buy them for dimes at local second hand stores. So I'm doing a New York scrapbook of how my life is changing. Sort of the new version of the one I kept since my childhood. I think I mentioned that to you."

"Yes, I remember."

She shrugged, "It amuses me. Nothing special."

"They look like you composed them on the wall carefully."

"I didn't give it much thought."

He pointed, "Is that John Cage?"

"Yeah."

"Why him?"

"Well, I went to a concert of his last month. This may sound corny to you, but the New York art world—I mean the museums, the galleries, the lectures, and poetry readings—it's a brand new world, and I love exploring it and recording it on my wall scrapbook."

"I was at that concert. What did you think of Cage's music, if you could call it that?"

"I can't say whether I liked it, but I was intrigued. I couldn't understand why people walked out, and one guy cursed it out loud."

"I often feel like walking out of his concerts, but I can't. We avant-gardists have to stick together. Besides, he's a friend." He paused. "You know, I really like the design of these photos, the way the cut-outs on the lower left balance the two on the right and the one in the middle creates a kind of bridge between them. You've got a terrific sense of composition."

Knight shrugged, but didn't reply. But she looked hard at the wall collage.

* * *

Over lunch, Knight asked, "Why don't you like Hofmann's paintings?"

"I don't dislike all of them. Some are very well painted.

But I've never been able to accept Hofmann's outlook. It's just too healthy for me."

"Why is that bad? What about his idea that art ought to express the highest artistic truths?"

"That's the German in him. Building Dachau with their heads in the clouds. That's nasty. He beat it out of the Third Reich and is married to a Jewish woman. But we live in a pretty shitty world. We don't bask in the wondrous light of eternity. At least I don't."

"But Hofmann says we have to struggle beyond the crap to something higher, something spiritual in people and universal in art. He says that all great art, no matter when or where, has that something and that's what makes it timeless."

"And can he tell you what that is?"

"There are laws."

"I'm not sure about the laws. It may only be formal problem solving. That's not necessarily bad, but it's limited. Much of Hofmann's own work strikes me as Teutonic gymnastics, as Guston once said."

Diane then said, "You know I think you're a great painter, better than Hofmann, but your painting could be more humanistic. Why does it have to be so off-color, so down?"

"Because that's how life feels to me. Hofmann says that underneath the crap, man's innate humanity will win out. I say that what you feel now is real, and art that doesn't reveal that reality is shallow."

"No, I'm with Hofmann. We have to reach above it all. You know that canvas, mostly all green with the yellow edge I showed you? I thought it was finished. But then I saw how to make it better, which means higher."

"Formally better is not necessarily higher, whatever that means. It might only be a kind of glorified craft, craft without vision, without feeling or meaning. Art needs more."

"I'll settle for craft, for now, and the Hofmann school is useful. I'm honest enough with myself to know that I need his teaching, that is, until I really know what I *need* to paint. And to be honest, I just don't know—not yet."

"Fair enough. When a student said to Duchamp that he didn't know what the fuck he was doing, the old *fakir* said, 'Keep up the good work.'" Knight did not smile.

* * *

Knight would not accept Burgh's thinking about the purpose of art and its formal analysis and she found their conversations increasingly frustrating. His angst also depressed her more and more. But he did introduce her to the inner circles of the art world and for this she was grateful. One Friday night, he took her to a panel at the Abstract Expressionists club, or, as the artists called it, the Club.

Burgh had explained, "The Club was founded in 1949 by us older Abstract Expressionists. It meets every Friday night at ten for lectures and panels, after which there is drinking and dancing. Bill de Kooning is the top painter, which means that I'm a second fiddle along with Pollock and Rothko. But I often go because I like the art talk and drinking and have nothing better to do. You should know, Diane, that women tend to be patronized, except for a few tough ones, like Elaine de Kooning and Joan Mitchell, so you have to overlook slights or be labeled a bitch."

The first evening that he took her to the Club, the door-man, Landes Lewitin, greeted him and looked over to Knight, "She'll cost you fifty cents."

Burgh replied, "She's worth a damn sight more. You know *cher maître*, you're referring to one of the finest younger painters."

"Then why are you taking her here? To learn how to become a loser, like schmeer-meister de Kooning—or you for that matter?"

"No, I was hoping the great Landes Lewitin could teach her a thing or two."

"Nothing she couldn't learn at the Metropolitan Museum."

"She thanks you for your profound advice."

As they walked into the darkened room full of lines of chairs, Knight said, "Do you always joke like that?"

"I'm not sure we're joking."

They sat down. She looked around and spotted many of the artists she greatly admired, recognizing them from photographs in *Art News*—de Kooning, Kline, Guston, Mitchell, and Hartigan.

The topic of the panel was, "Has the Situation Changed?" The participants were Harold Rosenberg, Thomas Hess, Ad Reinhardt, and Elaine de Kooning.

Sawyer introduced the panel. "As you know, this is the Nth session on this perennial topic, which is one thing in our world that doesn't change. Another thing is the non-payment of dues. Will the freeloaders who owe please cough up some dough and give it to the warm-hearted Landes Lewitin, who has graciously—very graciously, I might add—offered to collect it? Our moderator tonight is Tom Hess."

Elaine de Kooning said, "I'll begin. Ten years ago, we could use improvisation and really not know what the picture would end up as. We now know. We no longer have to make a fetish of spontaneity."

Voice from the floor, "You sound like a German professor."

"And you sound like a New Jersey hick."

Hess, "Elaine has a point. Spontaneity led to bad painting. The mission today is to consolidate the innovations, that is, to paint better pictures. And that takes brains and control. How can we have it both ways?"

Rosenberg, "Won't what I termed 'Action Painting' become academic if it's controlled? Won't it turn into a new academy?"

Voice from the floor, "It already has."

Hess, "Will you kibitzers out there please wait for the questions and answers?"

"Only if you all tell it like it really is, minus the bullshit."

Reinhardt spoke up, "You all know what this 'schmear kunst' signifies. This idea of stabbing in the dark is nonsense. A guy painting for forty years ought to know what he's doing. As for art, it should be art and nothing else. Pure! Eliminate all that crap you've been peddling about 'life as art,' expressing your piddling selves. Art should be pure."

"You mean all black like you do it?"

"At its very least it's not spilling my guts."

Rosenberg, "Ad, the world is in the pits. Action painting won't change it or make it better, but at least it'll reveal what life is like today."

Having presented the basic ideas, the debate continued for another two hours.

After the panel, the chairs were cleared. Knight and Burgh stood near a wall nursing whiskeys in paper cups.

She said, "I enjoyed the panel, but is that the real reason the likes of de Kooning and Guston are here?"

"Only a part of it. I think artists, even them, come here to escape the loneliness of their studios. They come for mutual support and proof that what they are painting is not off the wall, no pun intended."

Sawyer walked by holding a basket. Burgh threw in a five-dollar bill.

The critic smiled, "That'll keep the troops happy for about thirteen minutes."

Knight looked quizzical and Burgh explained, "The whiskey bottle's empty so they pass the basket for another. Those that have money pitch in, those that don't, don't. Puts everyone on an equal footing. Oh, they're about to start the dancing. Would you like to stay?"

"I'll take a rain check. I want to paint tomorrow."

* * *

Knight kept attending Club sessions, even though she had to fend off macho types who thought they could show the lady painters how to fuck and teach them how to paint. Lewitin remembered who she was and collected her fifty cents with one of his rare half-smiles. He soon put her up for membership, a rare act for one who blackballed as many applicants as he could.

* * *

Once, as Burgh and Knight were lying stretched out in bed, he turned to her and said, "What bothers me is your total lack of interest in politics."

"Please, Peter, we've just had great sex, and with that rare February sun streaming in. Why not just relax, enjoy the double glow?"

"No, I want to get serious for a moment." *She's right. Shut up.* "You know I was weaned on politics and painted politics in the 1930s. I no longer do, but politics still obsesses me and I wonder if my abstractions are still political. Given my work, I guess I should be interested in psychoanalysis, but I'm not. I'll still take Marx over Freud. What really bothers me is that America doesn't give a shit about art. Our fellow citizens have become cogs in vast bureaucracies, money-grubbing conformists, living ugly lives in ugly houses in ugly cities. In their spare time, they're chained to their television sets, sucking up pap manufactured by hucksters. And they hate any serious art worth anything. That's only the half of it. You don't seem to care about that."

"Oh, Peter. There's nothing I can do about it. Besides, people seem to be happy. We're at peace. Eisenhower had something to do with that."

He snorted, "We're on our way to fascism. Even Eisenhower knows that."

"Okay, so I don't care much about politics. You're trying to put me down, and it hurts. Why?" She turned away.

He said contritely, "You're right. Why am I bugging you? I'm sorry. Sometimes I don't know what gets into me. But next to my painting, politics has been my most important concern. At one time, it even topped art." He reached out and hugged her. *Why am I such an asshole?*

* * *

Later in the week, over drinks and between sets at the Five Spot, Knight asked Burgh, "Why is painting such a misery to you? Why all the suffering? Why?"

"Let me turn to question back to you. You've told me that you think I'm a terrific artist. Why? What do you see in my work?"

She said slowly, "It's hard for me to say. I love painting, your painting. The way you put paint down, it's magical. I think it's beautiful, and I know how you hate that word."

"But what does my work mean to you?"

"It's expressive, and, please, don't ask me about what. I don't know. But I feel it, really feel it. Why isn't that enough?"

Burgh sat quietly. Then he said, "I wonder if my painting would be expressive if it wasn't agony to make it and if the feeling didn't show somehow. Maybe not. But might what you see as beautiful be a case of mistaken identity? You ask, 'Why the misery?' It's so hard to be honest. I mean, you start with a bare canvas, nothingness, and go by feeling. There are so many possibilities. Why paint this and not that? It's pure agony trying to figure that out. Is every one of my moves genuine, what Camus would call 'authentic?' It drives me crazy. You've had a front-row seat. You can ask, why is it important? Because if I'm utterly honest with myself, I'll end up with a picture that's somehow me, warts and all, no matter how beat down—the real me. We live surrounded by lies. Political lies, corporate lies, media lies. At least what I make is real, or so I hope. And it seems to me that, in today's world, it's important to make that kind of statement—or, as we used to say in the thirties, a 'socially significant message.'"

She answered, "I would like my painting to be enjoyable, beautiful. Delight people. Make them happy."

"There are people who think my work is beautiful, whatever that means, but I certainly don't start out to make a beautiful painting. Look, I can't paint a picture if I don't feel it. It's not a very happy time, is it? And I like to think that my painting is of the now."

"I think I understand." *But it's not my now.*

* * *

Knight stapled a piece of canvas to the wall. She studied a line-up of tubes, picked four, squeezed out mounds of green, red, yellow, and white onto a glass pane she used as a palette, humming as she did. She took her rag doll and propped it on one edge of the palette. Turning its head toward the canvas, she said to it, "You tell me, Dolly, what to paint. Ain't talking? Then let me talk to you, like we did when I was a little girl. You were my best confidante then. Still are. Now, Dolly, what to paint? That?" Diane pointed to a vase of flowers that Peter had given her. Blue pot, red roses, yellow table. *Make the background green.*

"Very nice." Knight looked at the canvas, then turned to her doll. "Peter would ask, 'Why that subject?' Hans would say, 'It doesn't matter. Nature is only a way of getting into the painting, *nikker*?' He's always saying '*nikker.*' I wonder what it means?" She thought for a moment, then said, "Peter would say, nature gets in the way of painting." *Paint abstract?* She shook her head.

Knight picked up a charcoal stick, then put it down. She would see if she could push and pull, like Hofmann taught. She squeezed some blue from a tube. She whispered, "So, here goes. First, pull the image of the still-life apart and spread it over the canvas, to treat the canvas as a whole, give it pictorial structure and activate the picture plane. *Nikker?*" She quickly brushed an image in blue on the surface, adding red and yellow. Then she whispered, "The blue of the pot is falling out. Whiten it. Push it in. Yes. Cut back the red. Better. Red's still jumping out. Pull it back. Yellow it. Good. Kick up the green around it. Spread the green more. No, that's what I'm trying to get away from." Then Knight took up the charcoal and stopped. "This takes me back to square one. Okay Mr. Hofmann, I'll lay off green and charcoal and see what happens."

After an hour, Knight stepped back and said to her doll, "It's a mess, but it's getting interesting. Very interesting."

* * *

Knight kept adding photographs and magazine illustrations of art world figures and scenes and New York sites to her wall collage. One evening, on impulse, she picked up a small photograph of herself and her birth father in a heavy frame and, without thinking, attached it to the wall. *A three-dimensional collage. That's interesting.*

Most every evening, she would cut out new images and add them to her wall scrapbook. When the wall became too crowded, she had the idea of rearranging the parts, according to loose categories: family, childhood, the Marine Corps, the South, New York, and the art world. It soon occurred to her that she was creating some kind of visual autobiography. Was it serious? She didn't know but she enjoyed the activity and it didn't interfere with her painting, so she kept doing it.

Knight became friendly with the janitor, an elderly African-American man who had emigrated to New York from Alabama decades ago and who, in his southern accent, kidded her about hers. She invited him to see her paintings. He examined them closely and then looked at her three-dimensional collage. He said, "I don't understand abstract art but this wall is really interesting, particularly the part about the South. My people were sharecroppers and I know that world. You've captured how it feels."

"Thank you, Mr. Scott."

"Please, call me Jeremy."

"It's kind of cluttered." She nodded. He added, "If it's of any use to you, there's a big empty closet in the cellar that you could use to store some stuff. You could even put a lock on the door."

"I could really use the space. I'll pay you rent."

"No, no, I've got all I need, but I'd appreciate it if you would lend me one of these paste-ups. Brighten up my apartment."

"I'd be delighted to put one together for you. You're my first collector, even if what you acquire isn't art."

"Why not?"

"I hadn't meant it to be."

"Well, I'm still going to enjoy it." He hesitated and added, "What would make it art?"

"I guess my intention would."

"What about my appreciation?"

Knight said with a smile, "I'll have to get back to you about that." But his question stayed with her.

* * *

As Knight added photos, magazine illustrations, and objects to her wall, she continued painting. Her subjects remained figurative but she now used Hofmann's push and pull technique to achieve an evenly intense painted surface. The resulting canvases pleased her, but she knew they were derivative and could not decide how to make them hers. When she invited Burgh to see them, he said, as he had before, "I like the complexity. But where are you in the picture?" *It's foolish of me to raise these questions again. How fatuous can I get? All they do is depress her. That's why she rarely invites me to her studio.*

Burgh introduced Knight to Johnson at an opening of Philip Guston's show. Burgh noted her smile as she shook his hand. *She's interested. Why not? He's young, pretty, and up-and-coming.*

Later that evening, over a drink at the Cedar, Knight said, "Tell me about this Neil. I've seen his work. Do you think he's a good painter?"

Burgh hesitated. "Good enough, I guess. He's got a good touch. Lots of talent. He's a friend, and he admires my work enough to copy it, so what can I say?"

"You don't sound as if you approve."

"Sorry, I didn't mean to sound negative. Copying me does count. And like a good Yalie, he can talk intelligently about art—and about other things. But he's a bit glib. He's on the make and will use me. How? I don't know yet. Please don't repeat that."

"Tell me more about his painting. Be honest."

"Well, Neil's beginning to face the problem that all young artists who've had a quick success face—selling and getting a lot of attention. When Bill de Kooning heard that Neil had a show just out of art school, he said, 'Showing so soon? Is he so lacking in ambition?' His work is still too derivative, but the art world says that's okay for a talented young painter. Yep, youth counts, counts a lot. However, at some point critics, curators, and collectors will want more. Neil seems to be at this point. The question is, will he recognize this and be able to dig deeper into himself? Or will he find some trendy image that'll sell to people looking for hip and glorified decoration? Will he sell out? We'll just have to wait and see." Burgh took a big swig of scotch. *Is that my envy of Neil's youth talking?*

Knight said, "I won't ever get into the happy state of

having to feel unhappy about selling out, will I?"

"It'll happen, wait and see. It'll happen."

* * *

A few days later, Knight invited Johnson to see her work. He sat in a chair as she slowly showed him a dozen paintings. When she wasn't looking at him, he was looking at her ass.

"Well, what do you think?"

Having shifted his attention to her breasts, he barely heard her. "Huh?"

"I mean, tell me what you think."

"I like what you're doing. But the color is too dark, too expressionist. You've got to make the image more lyrical, like Guston or Burgh. That's where the cutting-edge is today. You've got to tap into that. Use quieter colors like in that picture there. The red in the center would work better if it were yellow. That would be beautiful. Also that brush-work in the lower right. It's dead. Liven it up. You've got the hand to carry it off."

Johnson stood up to point at it. He and Knight stood shoulder to shoulder in front of the canvas.

She said, "Yes, I see what you mean."

"You know, Diane, from the first time I saw you I wanted to make love to you." He turned, pulled her to him, and kissed her.

She drew back. "Easy, I'm Peter's girl."

"I'm not going to steal you away from him. I just want to make love. That's all."

When he next kissed her, she put her arms around his neck. Most of the men she had known would then have begun to grope. Not Johnson. Stepping back, he began to slowly unbutton her blouse and helped her slip out of it, unbuttoned his shirt, unfastened her bra without fumbling, took off his undershirt. Then he drew her to him and kissed her gently on the lips and breast. She found herself marveling at his expertise. It was exciting but also somewhat off-putting. He seemed to be following a sex manual. *Fucking by the numbers. Now my skirt and panties. Then his pants and underpants.*

Johnson made all the right moves. All that was missing was emotion. Nonetheless, Diane found the sex enjoyable—and amusing.

That was the start of their affair.

When Johnson left, Knight looked hard at the canvas and, recalling Johnson's advice to improve it, decided not to change anything.

* * *

Dressed in Burgh's bathrobe, Knight sat in his loft, leafing through *The Stranger* by Camus that Burgh had handed her, but not really paying attention. They had just finished having sex and he had gone to the toilet.

He emerged in his underclothes and looked at Knight as she gloomily scanned the pages of the book. *We're falling apart. She's not getting what she wants from me. Advice? Encouragement? Have I begun to bore her? Or her me, with her vision of beautiful Art with a capital 'A'? Irrita-*

tion occurs in every relationship. Break it off? Never. She's no Eileen, that's for sure, but she's as good as I'll ever get. Thing's aren't going well. What should I do?

Knight walked over to the window and looked out over the garbage-strewn paved yard with a spot of bare ground on which a stunted tree struggled to survive, the last of its leaves bobbing in a brisk winter wind. *Why do I feel so low? My painting is going nowhere. Neither is my affair with Peter. Have I had enough of him?* She turned to Burgh and said, "I think I'll check out my studio." Knight dug in her purse and took out a rumpled piece of paper. "Listen to this, Peter. Bertold Brecht wrote it in a poem, 'To Those Born Later,'—that's me. 'What kind of times are they, when/ A talk about trees is almost a crime/ Because it implies silence about so many horrors?' That pathetic tree in your yard inspired me to copy it."

Burgh nodded in appreciation. "Brecht, huh? Yes, maybe it's up to you to paint a tree, even that pathetic tree out there, and make it mean something."

"I'd like to, but not that wretched tree."

She turned back to the window. "I don't know why I feel so lousy, like that tree. Oh, well, I'm off."

She dressed and walked toward the door. *Yes, off Peter. It's over.*

He called out, "See you. Around eight, okay?"

She looked back and said, "That's fine. Let's meet at the Cedar."

Burgh turned to his painting.

* * *

Knight's depression was immediately apparent to Johnson. He sat her down on the couch, put his arms around her, and said, "Tell me what's wrong. Talk it out. I'm listening."

She began to sob, softly, "It's my work and it's Peter. Neither is going well. Peter—one minute he's on cloud nine, the next minute, he's in hell. Crazy mood swings. Sometimes he scares me. But like he told me, his father was a depressive who blew his brains out. Craziness could run in the family, but how would I know? And one night, when I slept over, he had a weird nightmare about somebody named Frankie. I asked him who Frankie was, and he changed the subject. I'd watch him sit for hours staring at a picture. Then, in a fit, he'd scrape out a wonderful image he'd been working on for days. Then, he keeps saying that he'd never be able to realize his dream. Once he told me about some artist in a Balzac novel who couldn't achieve his vision and committed suicide, suggesting that this was his fate."

Johnson interjected, "Yes, he told me about him too."

She continued, "Peter's a great artist, I know that, but do I want to be with a manic-depressive who drinks too much? He talks on and on about the existential condition of the artist and how awful America is. One more bout of angst and I'll go bananas."

* * *

Burgh sat in Knight's studio, looking at her latest painting tacked to the wall. He turned to her and began to speak urgently. "I know you want a formal critique. I just can't do that. I can't even analyze my own work. What criteria would I use? What can I say? I'm dragged down by tradition that I don't believe in any more, not after what's happened in this god-awful century. What can art be today? Can there be art at all? And if there is to be art, what is it to be? As I see it, we've got to expose ourselves—without fear. No limits. Risk everything. Try to create an image that speaks to this post-Holocaust world. Have I done it? I don't know. I hope so. There are formal considerations. I put down a form. It's got to be flat and have depth. It's got to sit still but also appear to move. It's got to be expressive as a pigment but also reveal me—an image of me. All those different claims. I paint until they disappear. I paint part to part to whole for dreary weeks, sometimes for months, overlaying painting on painting. You've seen me do this. Scraping them out. Then, it happens, in an instant of vision—not planned, but not spontaneous either. All of a sudden, the parts pull together. Each keeps its own identity while charging the others. The light I'm looking for appears. Until that moment, my work is a lifeless doodle. Just decoration. Wow, what a mouthful!"

Moved by Burgh's rhetoric, Knight remained silent. Then she said glumly, as she had many times before, "Yes, I think I understand." *I've heard it all before. Live the forms. Feel the forms. Lose yourself in them. God, I wish I could. But I don't want to hear it again.*

Sensing her dejection, he took her hand in his and said, feelingly, "One day, Diane, one day, it will happen. A picture will suddenly come together for you, like magic. And you'll say, 'that's exactly how I feel,' and if you're really lucky, you'll say, 'I never knew I felt like that.' Auden said that, and he was right. At that moment, you'll become an artist." *How pretentious! She doesn't want to hear this. I've failed her again. But she's failed me too. No matter how she appreciates my work, she doesn't understand it, really understand what I intended. Eileen came to hate me as a person but she believed in my ideas as well as my painting. Is this the end between Diane and me?*

She said, "I truly, truly hope my day comes. But for now I think I'll go back to my work." *My, with a capital 'M'!*

"Fine, I'm off. Catch up with you later."

When Burgh left, Knight phoned Johnson and said that she was on her way over.

* * *

Johnson appreciatively contemplated Knight sprawled on the couch.

"You've outdone yourself."

"Thanks, but I wish I could paint as good as I screw."

"It'll happen." *Fat chance. Fuggedaboutit.*

"Neil, I've finally decided to leave Peter. And keeping us secret is a drag. Can't we come out of the closet?"

"Diane, I would love to. You know that, but Peter's a close friend, more like a father, and if I steal his girl it would really hurt him. I just can't. You know how fragile he is."

"He's a big boy."

"Look, you leave Peter. We'll keep it to ourselves for a month or so and then come out as an item."

* * *

Over dinner at the Cedar, Knight said softly to Burgh, "We've had a good run, you and I, but we've been growing apart. You're as aware of this as I am. I think it's time to end it. Before we both begin to make each other really miserable."

He looked down, "I would like to go on."

"Can't, Peter, it's over. I've got to level with you. I don't think you can imagine how rotten I feel. My life is the pits. So is my art. I don't blame you, but I've got to change things and that begins with us."

He nodded. "I understand. But if you'd stay with me, I'd try to change. I really mean that." He added forlornly, "Think it over."

Back in his studio, Burgh poured himself a four-inch scotch, gulped it down, and, in the haze, thought not of Knight but of Eileen.

* * *

Knight admired Johnson's knowledge of art. He had also introduced her to artists of his own generation, much of whose conversation stimulated her, and she was grateful.

Over coffee after a Ginsberg poetry reading, she said to Johnson, "I'm surprised that Peter has no use for the likes of Ginsberg. You know how cultured he is. He got me to read Camus and Sartre and the modern French poets. And he could talk beautifully about them. I learned a lot. Sure, he likes O'Hara and Ashbery. They're art critics as well as poets. But when it comes to Ginsberg and—bite my tongue—Kerouac, he sees red. He really likes the French.

He paints American, but his head is too often in France."

"I'm not all that sure he paints American. Yeah, Peter's French thing affects his painting. Makes it old-hat."

"Oh, I don't know about that."

Johnson blurted harshly, "I do. Take my word for it."

Taken aback by his vehemence, she began to rebut but answered softly, "If you say so." She suddenly thought of other remarks of Johnson's that had troubled her, like, "That picture almost has balls." He had said it with a slight patronizing sneer, that she'd caught and hadn't liked. *Big macho prick. Tell it to Georgia O'Keeffe. Or how about Beth Morgan? Does she paint as ballsy as you or ballsier? Let it pass.*

* * *

Mixing in the crowd at an opening of Mark Rothko's painting at the Janis Gallery, Knight lost sight of Johnson. For a moment, she saw him talking to a brunette. He then shook Rothko's hand, looked around until he spotted her, and walked over. "Sorry, Diane. Damn. Change of plans. I just met Paul Seaman, you know, that curator from Los Angeles. He wants to put me in a show and talk about it over drinks. It'll be a late night. Let's meet up for lunch tomorrow."

"Sure."

She left shortly after him, just in time to see him get into a cab with a woman. It looked like the brunette she had just seen him with, the one he had just met. *The two-timing bastard.*

Back in the studio, her anger growing, Knight picked up a brush and ruffled the bristles in her hand. Putting Johnson out of her mind, she stared at a painting in progress stapled to the wall and sat down on a chair, picking her doll up off the seat as she did. "Now what?" She said to it, "Big Master Hans is specific about the formal aspects of painting. But Peter says it's not enough. Big Cocksman Neil, the bastard, is also specific but his bag is what's the latest thing and what's not—and fucking bimbos, pardon my language. He says he's avant-garde, but he's really only trendy. Do I really care about fashion? Did you just say 'That's a bore?' I agree. Like a good little student, I've followed the dictation of Big Master Hans but not Big Cocksman Neil's cutting-edge crap. There, I've used bad language again, bad me. Now what? Peter says to follow myself. If you ignore his existential doodoo, what's he saying? Go with what feels right. Sounds so simple, but every time I try it, I back away. It *feels* right, but it doesn't look good. No, it isn't that. Whatever it is, it scares me. Why? Facing what I really feel? Well, I'll have to risk it. That's what Peter would say. Risk it! You know what, Dolly? It's time to give it another go and stick with it. Force myself to stick with it, no matter how it looks. I think I'm ready to dump Big Master Hans's laws and Neil's cutting-edge (and maybe Neil, the bastard, himself). What do you think? Now you sit there and watch me, okay? What part of this painting do I really mean—not like what it looks like—but mean, really? The green, of course. But that red in the lower right. Did I paint it because it looked nice but didn't mean it? The blue in the center. All wrong."

Knight picked up her palette knife. "I'll push the red into that spot. No, make it green. Big Master Hans says my green is too 'decorateef.' *Nikker?* But doesn't he also say, give it your all. And my all is in that little blob of green. Put green in your pipe, Big Master Hans. Now, Dolly, you take a nap. I'm on a roll. Make it a long nap."

* * *

The more Knight worked, the more she focused on what gripped her in her own painting, the harder and longer she worked. She soon began to paint early in the morning, with half dreamed thoughts of a picture in progress, even before coffee, and then, in every free moment, often until she was so tired that the brush seemed too heavy to hold. She didn't know if what she was painting was any good, but it didn't matter. She just wanted to lose herself, like Peter said.

Knight found what appealed to her most in her painting was its lyric quality. She really was a green person. Now and then she thought she would be happy with an allover green, green all by itself, no other color, the greenest green. She even painted a picture whose entire surface was green but hid it in the closet. She tried another all-green one but reached for yellow and a warm red. Her work occasionally reminded her of other painters' work—Peter's feathery brushwork and Hofmann's high-keyed color, whose *joie de vivre* she increasingly admired. She accepted what she borrowed if it felt right. For now, she thought, for now. And yet, she also recognized that her work was becoming distinctively hers.

Knight was not aware, not yet, that lyricism or hedonism was coming into fashion, as Johnson had predicted.

Johnson watched Knight's growing passion for painting with jealousy and discomfort. He kept repeating one criticism in different variations. "Okay, so it's your own thing. But push and pull is yesterday's style. It doesn't deal with today's avant-garde ideas about stressing the whole field of a picture. It's outdated." But Johnson's ideas no longer interested her, although she hid her indifference. She was able to paint—paint with intensity—and that was all she wanted to do. He sensed her disregard of his criticisms and became increasingly frustrated and angry. *Maybe it was time to break it off, but not yet. It's going to be on my terms, not that broad's.*

* * *

Knight was working so intensely that her chest would tighten and her hands shake. Then she would stop, get a beer from the fridge, turn on some Mozart, lie down on her couch, and look at her wall scrapbook. She would add a photo or move a form. That relaxed her.

CHAPTER 9: Joseph Sawyer
(January 8, 1958)

Before returning to the Metropolitan Museum, Stein visited the Sandy Jones Gallery to see a group show of Abstract Expressionist paintings. He stopped in front of the de Kooning but kept turning to the Burgh. Back and forth.

A voice from behind him. "What do you think?"

It was Joseph Sawyer. Stein turned. "Hi. I wish I knew. The de Kooning's great, assertive but ambiguous—and masterly. He makes ambiguity so clear. But the Burgh? It looks so tentative but then it's not. It does have its own kind of power. Power? It's more like seduction. It draws you in and holds you, so subtly. But how does he stack up to de Kooning, or isn't it fair to ask?"

Sawyer answered, "He's right up there with him. You know, you and I have never really talked. Can we arrange to meet sometime?"

"Sure. Are you free now?"

"I am."

"Then let's go to the Stanhope. I'll let you buy me a

drink. Critic treats curator. Sounds unethical, but what's a little whoring among friends? Nah, I'll buy you the drink. Flush curator rescues critic from starvation and invites alcoholism."

They ordered beers. Sawyer looked at Stein expectantly. "Tell me, Herbert, what do you think of me?"

Stein looked at him quizzically. "I admire your writing, but I've told you that."

"No, I mean about me, as a man. See, I really think you're amazing, one of the best things in the art world. And I think you're one of the most handsome as well."

"What are you getting at?"

"Do you like me? Am I interesting to talk to?" Sawyer hesitated and added, "What I'm saying is that I'm very attracted to you. Are you at all attracted to me?"

"Are you coming onto me?"

Sawyer paused and, with an edge of urgency, said, "Okay, cards on the table. Yes. Word has it you're gay."

"Really, who says so?"

"The gang. They all say you and Jerry Waterman are having a thing."

"He's not queer."

"Oh, a little."

Stein laughed. "It wouldn't surprise me. I think he may go every which way, dogs, cats, plants, you name it. But I admire him for his paintings, and he's become a good friend. You've been talking to Beth Morgan, haven't you? You know better than to believe anything she says."

Sawyer asked, embarrassed, "Would you please forget this conversation? If word got out....If my macho friends...

I'd be finished."

"What conversation?"

"Thanks. In propositioning you, I was looking for friendship more than sex. There's not enough communal feeling in our world, even at the Club or the Cedar. Artists hug one another face to face and as soon as their backs are turned, out come the knives. Knowing that, I'm shocked that I opened myself up to you. No, not really. In my gut, I knew you were a good guy."

"Friendship? That's fine. To change the subject, I'm curious about you. No hiding where you were born. Somewhere in the South. Accent shows that. How'd you ever get up 'Nawth'?"

Sawyer looked down and said quietly, almost under his breath, "To escape the desperation of my early life. I was born in Athens, Georgia. Grew up a sissy boy. Got beaten up a lot in school and had no friends. Found a refuge in books. There were some on art in the library and I spent hours daydreaming over the pictures. One of my high school teachers seduced me, and I discovered what I was. So did everyone else when we were caught in the boy's toilet after school when no one was supposed to be around. He beat it out of town. Dad beat the shit out of me and mom looked the other way. Dad was only a plumber, but a Sawyer, descended from the Virginia Sawyers. One was a confederate captain in the 'War Between the States,' what y'all call the Civil War, and we were distantly related to the Virginia Lees. Don't you Jews have a word for it, 'yeekees'?"

"It's *yichus*."

"I stand corrected. Dad was misery personified. An

honest-to-god relative of Robert E. reduced to digging shit out of redneck toilets. His southern heritage was the only noteworthy thing in his life, and I had defiled it. Ran away from home as soon as I graduated from high school. Escaped to Atlanta. Found a gay bar. You don't want to hear about the next year. But a rich dude fell in love with me. Paid my way through college. I studied art history. Graduated with honors. Rich dude and I moved to New York. He found a pretty boy five years younger than me and pitched me out. I supported myself as a waiter in a gay bar. I had met this curator who works at the Modern. No names, but you know who. He introduced me around the art world and encouraged me to write about it. I found out that I could. He got the word to *Art News*. Hess read some of my stuff and gave me my break."

"Ever think of writing a novel about your life?"

"I keep notes. But the time isn't ripe yet for a gay saga, if any time will ever be."

"Grapevine has it that you're writing an article for *Art News* on Johnson."

"True. He tells me that you have no use for his paintings. Why?"

"I don't believe in them. I question their authenticity. I'm not sure that any of the younger Action painters, except a few like Mitchell and Frankenthaler, can keep doing meaningful variations on the painting of the older Abstract Expressionists. And it seems to me that the more interesting young guys are turning away from the oldsters. I've met the composer, John Cage, who's got a new take on what art should be. He's rejected the sense of tragedy that his elders were after. He says that art ought to offer an optimistic vision of life. He's collaborating with a new choreographer, Merce Cunningham, who uses ordinary movements, like walking and falling, in his dance. And then there's Bob Rauschenberg who uses junk that signifies city life. His inspiration is both Cage and Cage's guru, Marcel Duchamp."

Sawyer interjected, "Isn't this anti-art?"

"Or a new kind of art. I mean, Rauschenberg is very interesting, far more interesting than Johnson."

"Thanks for telling me this. I'll give him another look."

* * *

Sawyer rang Burgh. "What are you painting? Can I take a look?"

"Just finished a new picture. Hardly worth the trek."

"If you're free, I can be on my way."

Looking at the new painting, Sawyer was overcome by an involuntary rush of emotion that he only felt before works of art he considered great. He composed himself and turned to Burgh, unable to think of what to say. But Burgh had sensed the intensity of his response and said, "Not bad, eh?"

"That's one monumental understatement."

Sawyer paused and said, "My reason for being here isn't only to see your work, but because I'm writing an article on you for *Art News* and hopefully will be going on to do a book."

"You? I thought you were in Bill de Kooning's corner."

"I'm in your corner too, and in nobody's corner."

"Did Hess say he would publish? I'm the 'Abstract Impressionist,' remember, Bill's competition?"

"He already gave me the go-ahead."

"When he runs your article, want to bet that Bill gets the cover of his rag? Has Hess come a long way—or have I?"

"You have. A lot of young painters are looking up to you. Hess has picked up on it and needs to cover your 'Abstract Impressionism.' Don't throw that chair at me."

"You want to do a book, you say?"

"Harry Abrams is interested."

"A book? Isn't that a bit premature? I'm not dead yet."

"I'm serious."

"Maybe the book would be a death sentence."

"Do I look like a pall bearer? Can I go ahead?"

"Why not, but only if you don't bother me—or make me read it."

"But you'll go see the movie. We'll title it, 'Move Over Monet.'"

"Only if I get a freebie. How about 'Move Over Bill and Franz'?"

"While I've got you, I'd like to ask you a question, and I'd bet that you've been asked it before. I know the answer—mine, that is—but I'd like to have your take. You say that you paint what you feel. Why should anyone care?"

"I could answer that by saying, why should I care about what anyone thinks, but I won't. I do care. Look, I once painted Social Realist paintings because I cared about the plight of the working class. I also did a Crucifixion or two way back then, not because I believed in it but because I wanted to try what the old guys did. I did alright by them…

well better than Mark Chagall. And I could've kept on turning out figurative works and selling them, but at one point I couldn't paint them with conviction. Same goes for the still lifes and landscapes I was turning out. So what was left for me to paint? The real me, what the Existentialists like Sartre and Camus call the 'authentic I.' Sartre says we've got to reveal ourselves, and painting is my way of doing it. Sartre and Camus also say, we're all going to die; life is, in the end, absurd. Why do I keep painting? There's some crazy kind of kicks in having a picture come off as authentic. Does this make any sense or is it just bullshit?"

Burgh stopped talking. Sawyer seemed to be thinking it over. After a silent moment, Burgh said, "There's more. Let me read you something." He went over to a pile of *Art News* magazines on the floor in the corner, picked up the one on top, and flipped the pages. "Schapiro, Meyer Schapiro, where's it at? Ah, here it is. Meyer writes that the new American painting is, and I paraphrase, deeply rooted in the self, and is opposed to a culture that's increasingly organized." Scanning another page, Burgh read, 'No other art today exhibits...the presence of the individual and the concreteness of his procedure.' Yeah, that's it. Meyer says it a lot better than I can. I believe that there's a social dimension in my ego-tripping, but it sounds pretentious to spell it out and maybe silly. Can't help regressing to my 1930s mentality."

While Burgh was rummaging through the stack of magazines, Sawyer was looking at a geometric abstraction hanging over the bed against the back wall. When Burgh finished reading, he pointed to the canvas and said, "One of your early ones, Peter? Thirties, huh?"

"Date's right, but not the artist. It was painted by an old buddy of mine. Mike Pearson. Do you like it?"

"From here it looks like a really strong picture."

"It is. But while you're looking at it, let me fill you in on the Mike Pearson saga. We call him Little Mike. When he was first introduced as Mike to Rothko in the thirties, Mark looked up at his six-feet-four and said, 'Not the late big Mike of Renaissance fame?' Mike lifted Rothko a foot off the floor and whispered in his ear, 'Naw, I'm just little Mike,' and the name stuck. We first met on the Federal Art Project back then. He had been a longshoreman in some port in the South, Savannah, I think, a genuine proletarian. Little Mike had a promising first show of Social Realist stuff at the ACA Gallery. Nothing sold, but it was the Depression and nothing did then anyways. We all predicted that he would go far. He was a communist. The Party kicked him out over the Moscow Trials in '37. He gave up 'art for the masses' and switched to geometric abstraction when it was still trendy. But he really believed that it had a message of good will to the world, the art of a future socialist utopia." He paused, pouring a drink, "Damn, he could paint."

"He went to war. Won medals in Italy. When he was discharged, he went back to geometric abstraction. But by then, it was pushed out of fashion by Surrealism. Still, Little Mike stuck with it. People stopped looking at his work. So he tried to 'action' it up, make it personal. It still looked good and us artist buddies admired his skill and, at first, so did a handful of critics, dealers, and collectors, but it didn't get mileage for long. The underlying geometry did him in. Five years now without a show. Even the few nice receptionists at galleries won't look at his slides anymore. And his temper tantrums don't help. On top of that, his life fell apart. As an ex-communist, Little Mike was called up by Senator McCarthy before his committee. When asked to name names he refused, took the Fifth, adding that he had left the Party long ago. Besides he wouldn't rat out his former comrades. He didn't go to jail—his war medals helped—but he lost his teaching job at Temple. Began to drink heavily. Booze and anger and poverty drove away his wife and most of his friends. Disaster after disaster. I watched out for him as best as I could, saw that he had enough to eat, held his hand, and talked things out with him. But even at his darkest, Mike kept on painting—terrific pictures that became looser and looser. He survives by doing carpentry and an occasional part-time teaching gig bestowed on the sly by some pal from way back for old-time's sake. For all I know, I'm the only friend he still has."

Burgh stopped talking and saw Pearson in his mind's eye. "God, he was handsome back then. Big muscled brute, broad shoulders but slim waist, and curly blonde hair. And smart. He could really talk."

Sawyer said, "You sound as if you really loved the man."

"Still do."

"He must have had it tough. Communists are considered the devil, even worse than homosexuals. I feel sorry for him."

Burgh again was lost in thought and didn't seem to hear Sawyer. Then he went on. "Every time I think of Little Mike, I think of me. What I'm about to say is something you can't write in your book. My doubts. What if I had stuck with Realism? 1946, 1947, I was Realism's golden boy. Like Little Mike, I changed styles, but why did I succeed and not him? I guess it was because I came up with something newer. Don't get me wrong, I believe in my painting and it's persuaded enough of the big guns in the art world. Little Mike believes in his work, but mere loosening up of geometry hasn't convinced the powers that be. But why do I keep thinking that there, but for the grace of the Big Guy above, go I?"

* * *

When Sawyer left Burgh, he walked over to Washington Square, thinking about his reaction to Burgh's painting. What was it that moved him so? Apart from its involuntary emotional impact, what else? Its originality? Or because it felt of our time? Was it because the painting had quality, whatever that was? He had asked these questions before, and he would ask them again and again.

* * *

Sawyer phoned Sandy Jones and told him about his proposed book. "Can I drop into the gallery and take a look at the material you've collected on Burgh? I'd also like to see the works you have."

"Certainly, we have a slew of photos, but no Burghs in stock. Those we had were sold recently."

"Oh, who bought them?"

"A new dealer in Paris, Galerie Global. Wants to do a Burgh show. Celia Loeb is acting as its go-between here."

"That means that a lot of Burgh's works have gone abroad. That really cuts down the number we have here in America. That's not good, is it?"

"I'm a businessman, not the protector of our national heritage. And I believe that Burgh has squirreled away a bunch of his canvases. The dealer over there paid money in advance, in full, and promised to send me the names and addresses of the collectors they sell the Burghs to. I'm still waiting."

"Can't we nudge him? Would you give me the titles of the works he bought, and any photos you've got?"

"Sure, drop by tomorrow morning, anytime."

* * *

Sawyer tried to find the phone number and address of the Galerie Global, but couldn't. He phoned Celia Loeb and asked for her help. She said that Jones shouldn't have told him about Galerie Global, since the Parisian dealer wanted to keep his moves secret for the time being. He had also sworn her to silence and she would say no more. Sawyer found her attitude strange.

The mystery was heightened a few weeks later when the Cincinnati Art Gallery asked him to curate a show of works from the collection of Nichols, whose wife was an alumna of the school. Sawyer and Nichols met at the Santini Brothers warehouse to select works. Out of the corner of his eye, Sawyer spotted the side of a Burgh sticking out from the rack. He pulled it out and propped it against the back wall, noticing a Celia Loeb Gallery sticker on the stretcher.

"What about this one? It's a beaut."

"Nah, not that one. I've got other plans for it. Put it back."

Sawyer persisted. "Too bad. Let's see how sharp my visual memory is. The title? Something about some novelist. Am I'm getting warm? Camus? That's it Camus! *Homage to A.C.* Date, middle fifties. Give the man a kewpie doll."

"Get on with it. I haven't got all fucking day."

* * *

A week later, while studying the photographic file of Burgh's paintings, Sawyer found the picture he had seen in Nichols' warehouse. He looked up *Homage to A.C.* in the inventory of works Jones had sold to the Parisian gallery. *Strange. How did it end up in Nichols' storage and why? Wasn't it supposed to go to France? Loeb and Nichols? It doesn't make any sense. Something smells funny in all of this.*

* * *

That evening, Sawyer sat on a canvas sling chair with a slash in the fabric that had been crudely stitched together, a piece of junk picked up off the street, and looked across the room at the bookcase he had assembled with planks set on bricks, which was stacked with books and magazines. The only other furnishings in the room were a small television set and the end table on which it was propped. He looked sullenly around his 'parlor,' as they would say in the Southland—his sumptuous parlor—seven paces from wall to wall. Sawyer turned to a grimy window looking out at the brick wall of the building across the alley. Through a door to the next room, he glanced at a minuscule kitchen, dominated by a bathtub whose ceramic top served as a table, a tiny, noisy refrigerator, a hotplate on a shelf, and a folding chair, all of it illuminated by a bare light bulb.

He could also see into the far room, even tinier than the living room. It contained a single bed on one side and on the other, a secondhand door propped on two secondhand filing cabinets, which served as his desk and on which sat an antiquated typewriter, a dime-store lamp, and piles of catalogs and books. Wedged under the desk was a three-legged stool. Toilet? In the hall, fortunately with a lock on the door. *My private Versailles. I'll give Nichols a call.*

* * *

The next morning, Sawyer phoned Nichols. "I don't know what to make of this, but there's something funny about Burgh's work. A lot seems to be bought by some gallery in France. I'll need to see them for my article and the book on Burgh that I'm planning. I thought you might know some-thing about it."

"I can't say I do. How 'bout telling me all about it over lunch. Say, the Four Seasons tomorrow at one."

"I'll be there." *Four Seasons? Kinda rich for a no-account critic. Nichols isn't known for his philanthropy.*

* * *

Sawyer dressed for the occasion and still looked like the have-not he was. After being seated, Nichols said, "Well, my friend, what's on your mind?"

"It's puzzling. You know that Burgh I saw in your warehouse with the Celia Loeb label on it? It was supposedly sold with a lot of other Burghs to a gallery in Paris. And yet, there it is in your warehouse. On top of that, I can't find the French dealer and Loeb won't tell me anything. It strikes me as peculiar."

"Why? I bought that Burgh from Celia. But her business is none of your beeswax."

"Well, I think it is. There's a story here. A secret deal involving a dozen Burghs sold abroad."

"What's that got to do with me?"

"I've been wondering what you and Loeb are up to." Sawyer took a deep breath and blurted, "Are you hoarding Burghs?"

"That's crazy. What makes you think that?"

"Lucky guess."

"Don't get smart with me Joe. If you know what's good for you, you'll drop this and keep your mouth shut tight. Fuggedaboutit."

"Now, now, Mort, old buddy, I think you've cornered a good chunk of the Burgh market. If what you have in mind is legal, I want in. Or I might go on asking questions about a French dealer with a piss pot full of Burghs who doesn't seem to exist."

"Oho, so the little art scribbler has a business head. And blackmail on his mind. I could tell you to take a flying fuck at the moon, but I won't. Awright, what d'ya want?"

Sawyer felt guilty suddenly, then thought of his apartment. "I'm dirt poor, but I've put some money away, money I decided never to touch, even if I was hungry. Almost three thousand. I've been saving for the proverbial rainy day—war, famine, pestilence."

"Don't be funny."

"Three thousand is worth about one Burgh. On top of that, you could also use my writing. If I write that article or better still the book, Burgh's prices go up. Of course, I would like a pittance for my efforts. And I'm sure there are other useful chores I could do. I get around in the art world like you collectors don't. You'll think of something."

"Awright, I'll talk to Celia. If you're in, you get the same cut we do, minus two and a half percent that Celia gets for doing most of the work—that is, the percentage of any rise in Burgh's prices on your three thou. But there's no agreement until I talk to Celia."

"Sure, sure, you do that, partner."

"If you have a brain in your head, you'll say nothing, not one fucking word of this to anyone or you can kiss your investment bye-bye."

"I hear you loud and clear."

* * *

The postcard mailed to the two hundred members of the Club read, "April 4, 1958. At 10 P.M. sharp. Critics at War: Hill vs. Sawyer. Color-Field vs. Abstract Impressionism. Harry Holtzman, moderator. Deadbeats, it's time to pay your $10 dues."

Herbert Stein arrived at nine forty-five. He had gotten himself invited by Kline. He paid his fifty cents at the door to Landes Lewitin, who looked at him suspiciously even though he had seen him dozens of times. Stein found a seat on the side. The room was dimly lit and shrouded in a cloud of cigarette smoke. Peering about, he could make out that most of the some hundred chairs, packed together, were taken. Burgh sat down beside him. Stein greeted him and said, "Does *House Beautiful* know about this dump? Should do a feature."

"Its shabbiness fits our collective mood. It even keeps art lovers like you out most of the time."

"Too shleppy even for the slummers, huh?"

Nodding in the direction of Hill, Burgh said, "Some art lovers still sneak in, like the likes of him."

At a quarter after ten, Hill, Sawyer, and Holtzman, who had been standing to one side, approached the table and sat down. Holtzman began by saying, "Lewitin said that this panel ought to be called the 'Battle of the Midgets.'" The audience broke into raucous laughter. "You all know these guys, the old heavy and the young contender in a fight to the finish. Let the mayhem start."

Hill's presence filled the hall. He looked around slowly, glowered, and said, "If I'm a midget, what are you guys, giants?"

Grumbling in the audience.

Hill stared at Sawyer, then challenged him. "The most important quality a critic can have is an 'eye.' That is one quality you seem to be lacking, Mr. Sawyer. How else could you possibly support Peter Burgh's painting? That pasty color and timid brushwork. Not that de Kooning is much better."

Louder grumbling.

Sawyer responded, "Burgh's pictures are very moving and they speak to our time. So do Bill's."

"Speak to our time, whatever that means. What I look for is quality, first and foremost, then what art needs to remain vital. Burgh and de Kooning are retards, Cubist retards, but have managed to convince a lot of people, pretty much all of you in this room, that they are forward looking. They are working in an outdated Cubist style that has had all its problems solved. Their work is not what painting needs at this moment. And when it comes to quality, Jackson's still the one."

"Sure he is, Mr. Hill, Pollock is *one* of the ones. But does art need the formalist agenda you're promoting and its groupies, like Martin and Karl, who follow it?"

"Yes, Mr. Sawyer, because their work has quality and is new—which, as I said, your eye doesn't seem able to recognize—and their painting opens up to the future."

"It's decoration. There are more important things in painting to express than decoration. You say the future, huh? You've convinced a lot of gullible people that you are some kind of prophet who can predict the future of art. And at the same time, you make it sound like it's already art history. Having it both ways is a real *tour de force*, turning wishful thinking into history. But it ain't necessarily so, Mr. Hill, not yet. And puhleeze don't patronize me with your superior taste—your great 'eye.' You can't tell me what quality is. And I don't believe that any critic who doesn't see the excellence of Bill de Kooning's work or Peter Burgh's knows shit about quality."

"My taste was right in the past when you were still a piddler, and it's right now."

"Well, Martin ain't no Pollock, and neither is Karl. None of the guys you champion are in the class of Mitchell or Hartigan or Rivers or Rauschenberg or Johns. Sure, you look hard, you do, but too often you end up seeing what you want to see, not what our best artists are painting."

"Like crappy Action Painting? It's dead and gone and Rosenberg's propaganda can't revive it. Do you really believe the Action guys when they tell you that they don't know what they're doing, that they're stabbing in the dark? And why do all those stabs in the dark look alike? Tell me, how many years does an artist have to work before he figures out what he's doing? Some of those mediocrities you're promoting have been painting for forty years. And how long does a style have to be around before it gets academic? As I've been saying for some time, there's a mainstream in art that is always threatened by academicism, and which needs repeated avant-gardes to keep it alive. The artists I admire, they're in the avant-garde. They confront what painting needs at this moment to be alive. They laugh at all your *sturm und drang* crapola about angst, the tragic artist in the grips of the *zeitgeist* or God. What bullshit!"

"Tell me, Mr. Hill, do you promote artists because they paint what art needs or because it appeals to your appetite for decoration? Am I wrong to define formalist painting as art that you happen to like and that you like it because it's pretty? What really bugs me about your criticism is that you're still flogging that old deterministic Marxist baggage with regard to art instead of the class struggle like you did in the past. Like the Marxist ploy of predicting the next move in Art History with a capital 'A' and 'H'. In the end, art dictated by your formalist agenda takes precedence over your vaunted eye and makes History with a capital 'H'. Ideology wins out over all."

"Let's get one thing straight, Mr. Sawyer. I don't champion art. I describe what art has objectively come to be and what it needs to remain alive. And what Burgh's painting tells me is that anyone who likes it has a tin eye. Whatever else you have to say doesn't matter at all."

"We'll just have to wait and see."

"Yeah, don't hold your breath."

Holtzman interjected, "We've waited long enough for the yokels out there to have their say."

A voice in the back called out, "What's going on here, a sales pitch for Martin and Karl? Does the Club take a commission?"

Malcomb Reming jumped to his feet. Shaking a finger at Hill, he shouted, "Who invited this creep here? Why are we listening to his baloney?"

Hill answered, "Listen up you. Two years ago, on this floor, I said that Action Painting had become timid and used up. Since then, it's gotten even more academic—and just plain bad, if that's possible."

Milton Linz got up and snarled, "You're not a critic. You're a fucking gravedigger. You're trying to bury us. We're painting great pictures, and you are too fucking blind to see it."

"Who is this 'we?' Yeah, I want to bury mediocrities like you."

"You're playing God, deciding who gets into heaven and who doesn't. If no-talents like Martin and Karl are up with the angels, I'd rather be in hell."

Karl spoke up. "The hell of lousy painting. You're there already."

Linz shouted back, "Better bad than pretty."

Another voice from the audience, "Why are we so hostile? Why can't we talk in a civilized way?"

"Because art is at stake, asshole."

Holtzman stood and said, "Time's up. Reming, Linz, and Karl have been very naughty and don't get good conduct medals tonight. The rest of you do. Time for booze and paying your dues to Monsieur Lewitin. Tightwads take notice."

CHAPTER 10: Neil Johnson
(October 17, 1958)

There was a spectator crush at Johnson's opening at the Celia Loeb Gallery. He stood a third of the way into the gallery greeting the guests. He was cordial and modest, if occasionally smarmy, to his elders, peers, collectors, and art world powers. To anyone who didn't count, he was the lofty prophet with a "big message to the world." But his mind was on who was there and, equally as important, who was missing. *Burgh and Guston? They'd be late. But where the fuck is Kline? Probably boozing at the Cedar. Who the hell is here from the Modern? Ah, Frank O'Hara just walked in. I wouldn't have expected Barr. But Dorothy Miller? No one from the Whitney? No, there's Goodrich. Here comes Kline, about time. Nichols with Bob Scull, the big-time collector. Interesting. The taxi mogul never gave me the time of day. No Hess. No Rosenberg. None of de Kooning's gang. Fuck'em. Hill, wow Hill! Who would have thought? Miller at last.*

He breathed a sigh of relief.

Loeb had her own agenda. She expected Nichols to show,

but not Hill or Scull. She was as surprised as Johnson was, and she would make the most of it. She took him aside and whispered. "Do you know Hill or Scull?"

"Yeah."

"Well enough to invite to them to dinner?"

"Hill, yes. Scull, not really. I've been to a party of his once."

"That's good enough."

Hill begged off, with a show of courtesy that did not escape Loeb. *He's signaling something. I wonder what?*

Sauntering over nonchalantly to Scull, she said, "Why Mr. Scull, welcome. Welcome. You remember me, I'm Celia Loeb. We met at the Picasso opening at the Modern."

"Oh, yeah."

"Neil, as you may know, is a great admirer of your collection, and has asked me to invite you to the dinner after the opening. Are you free?"

"I'll see. May I use your phone?"

The dinner was at the fashionable 55th Street Café. Loeb seated herself next to Scull. "Well, what do you think of Neil's new painting?"

"It's good stuff. I like it."

"Any particular canvas more than the others?"

"Yeah, the big red one on the back wall."

"That's the best one, and Morton Nichols has his eye on it. Look, I'd like to see that work in a collection as distinguished as yours. If you want it, I'll give you a ten percent markdown."

Scull knit his brows and said nothing.

Loeb turned to Frank O'Hara sitting two places down from

her. "Say, Frank, are you going to the Merce Cunningham dance concert next Tuesday?"

"That's one show I won't miss. You know Rauschenberg did a set."

Loeb gushed, "That alone is worth the price of admission."

Scull leaned over and whispered in her ear, "Make it twenty percent."

"That doesn't leave me much."

"How about if I took the blue one as well—also at twenty off?"

"That's more like it. I think Mr. Scull, like the man said, 'This is the beginning of a beautiful friendship.' But what'll I tell Nichols?"

"You'll think of something."

* * *

The *Art News* was in Burgh's morning mail. He opened it and scanned the table of contents. *An interview with Neil. Read it later. There's my name.* "Sure, Peter Burgh's my long-time friend. I was influenced by him early on, although there was really a good deal of give and take even then. And I'm grateful to him. But I've paid him back. His latest work owes a lot to me, you know, those heavy shapes, they're out of my painting." Burgh was shocked. *Owe Johnson what? That treacherous asshole. He was doing okay. He didn't have to climb on my reputation. Did he have no shame? What to do? Nothing! To hell with it—and with Johnson.*

At that moment, the phone rang. It was Joseph Sawyer.

"Did you see *Art News*?"

"Yeah, just now."

"That upstart shit. What are you going to do?"

"What can I do?"

"I'm writing a letter to the editor, saying that I saw the pictures you were supposed to have cribbed from Neil, months before he began to paint them. And he saw them too."

"Thanks."

"Yeah, and I just took the notes of the article I was writing on him and pitched them into the waste-paper basket."

Johnson called Burgh as if nothing had happened. Before he could say anything, Burgh said, "I'm pissed off about your interview in *Art News*."

"That's what I'm calling about. I never said I influenced you, Peter. Believe me. I never said it. The interviewer twisted it."

"Yeah. Write a letter to *Art News*, explaining that. Let's you and I cool it for a while. Goodbye Neil."

Johnson said urgently. "Peter, don't hang up on me. We're friends. Don't turn on me."

He heard the click of Burgh's phone. *The bastard cut me off. Just like my fucking father. God, I hate the sons of bitches.*

Sawyer's letter read, "I understand that artists are competitive. And that's to the good if it spurs them to paint better. But there are limits. Fiddling with the truth is one. Neil Johnson and I both saw Peter Burgh's paintings that Johnson claims he influenced five months before Johnson got around to aping them. His claim is, in a word, a self-serving ploy. He should be ashamed of himself."

* * *

Johnson read Sawyer's letter and knew his careerist ruse had backfired. When he showed up at the Cedar that night, he was in for a ribbing, even by his "friends."

"Hey Neil, what's this I hear about you influencing Picasso?"

"Naw, naw, it was Cézanne. Neil here taught him how to use orange."

"Or paint one."

"Or eat one."

Johnson would protest, "I was misquoted." Or, "The bastard got me drunk, led me on, and misquoted me. You know I would never say anything like that about Peter. Been like a father to me." Neil knew that the attention span of the art world was short, and even if he had blundered, it would soon be forgotten. Or would it?

Sawyer's letter was noticed. It became cocktail party conversation for a week. Art critics and collectors with a stake in Johnson's career spoke up in his defense. Burgh began to get phone calls from critics and curators, a number of whom had barely acknowledged him for years. Even de Kooning's people, Thomas Hess and Harold Rosenberg, took his side. When he entered the Cedar, young artists sidled over to be in his aura, shake his hand, so that they could later drop "Me and Peter" in their conversation. He waved off these homages, but was gratified by them. Even Johnson's dwindling supporters changed their tune. "It doesn't matter who did what first. They are both great." But no one was paying attention.

Johnson's sales had already slackened. The brouhaha over his comments about Burgh caused collectors to reassess his work and conclude that it had less substance than they had originally thought. The paintings of new artists replaced his on collectors' walls. Invitations to insider dinners fell off. Then, one of Johnson's works appeared at auction. This was the last straw for him. He phoned Nichols, "Why'd you put it up for sale?"

"Cash flow problems. I'll get a new one when business improves."

"Oh, come off it. Why didn't you sell a Burgh, goddamn it? You've got a bunch. It's that creep Sawyer's doing, that goddamn letter and bad-mouthing me all over town. I'll bet that Peter's behind this. Am I getting too big for him? Is that why he's breaking my balls? Has he taken you in?"

"Neil, you're talking crazy."

"Sure, sure. Cover up for him. I know the bastard's out to screw me."

Soon other of Johnson's works went on the block, including a second canvas owned by Nichols.

When Johnson asked his collectors why, one responded, "We're changing our direction." Another said, "We want to buy younger artists, like Johns."

"Johns? You must be kidding. He's a flash in the pan. You're making a big mistake."

Johnson found himself increasingly obsessing about his plight, particularly at night, and he couldn't sleep. *Am I becoming paranoid? What am I going to do? Lay low for a couple of weeks or months until my interview has become yesterday's news? Peter's pulling the strings. I did influence him, goddamn it, and the fucker knows it. He's getting back at me for spilling the beans. Still, I'd better try to sort things out with him.*

Johnson phoned. "Hey Peter, I've really got to make it up to you. That bastard from *Art News* made it all up. I never said what he wrote. You've got to believe that."

"Sure Neil, sure, but I'm in the middle of a painting now. Can't talk. Why don't you write that letter to *Art News* and clear up the misunderstanding. We'll talk then."

"Right, I'll take care of it." *Letter to* Art News? *Fat chance.*

Johnson's market did not improve, and his comment about influencing Burgh lingered in the art world's memory. As the weeks turned into months, his hatred of Burgh grew. It was fueled every time he saw a work by Burgh, or read a review of his work, or even a mention of his name in general articles, all of which appeared with greater frequency.

* * *

Sawyer was sitting at the bar of the Cedar when Stein walked in.

"Morning Joseph."

"Morning, Herbert. Kinda early for you, isn't it?"

"Arranged to meet Guston at his studio at twelve, and I'm early. Thought I'd kill some time over a coffee. What brings you here at high noon?"

"Writing a review of Neil Johnson's show for *Art International*, or trying to, without much success. I told Jim Fitzsimmons to assign it to another critic, but he said he wanted me. I'd like to be fair and forget what a jerk Neil is, but it's not easy. Sure, he's a good painter. But like Wallace Stevens said, 'goodness in art is as boring as goodness in people.' So, I'm asking, if Neil's art is a pastiche—art out of art—is that enough? Peter Burgh says that it can't have much to say. Maybe he's right. I think I'll make this the topic of my review. I'll start by declaring that Neil's art doesn't merit a review as serious as the one I'm about to give. You see, Herbert, how hard it is to be fair?"

"My advice is, forget what a creep Neil is. Answer the question you just asked."

"Yeah, you're right. But it's easy for you to say, cloistered at the Met. The knives can't cut you up there."

"Oh, but they can. It's just that the knife throwers wear better suits. That's about the only difference."

"Okay. Back to the drawing board to tell it like it is, or try to."

* * *

Sawyer typed, "For openers, Neil Johnson is a gifted painter. His work owes a lot to Peter Burgh's facture, Barnett Newman's Color-Field, and Ellsworth Kelly's Hard-Edge. Is that necessarily bad? Not really, if he's paid back in interest what he borrowed. Has he? He has patched his borrowings together in an individual way. His surfaces are planar fields of impasto strokes that manage to be weighty and are penetrated by rectangular forms. Johnson's marriage of the painterly and the geometric is visually stimulating and fresh. But there is little more to command interest. Still Johnson is young and this critic recommends a wait and see attitude."

Sawyer pulled the page out of his typewriter, read it, and crumpled it up. *Can't tell if it's too bitchy or not bitchy enough. Fitzsimmons will have to find another critic.* He was suddenly overcome by exhaustion. He looked distastefully around at his shabby apartment. *What a comedown for a descendant of General Robert E. Lee. What have I lost if I junk this review? Three dollars. Big deal. Is my love of art enough to justify working my balls off for pennies? For what? Some artist's career? What about my rent? So now, I'm a big investor in Peter Burgh. Every last cent of the pittance dear old dad left me, the hateful son of a bitch. Going to make some big bucks, at last. Conspiracy to corner the market. Sneaky but not criminal and not unethical. Is this why I feel guilty? A critic playing money games with art. It won't hurt Peter so why should I care. I wish I wasn't so tired.*

Sawyer retrieved the crumpled review, reread it, and decided to retype it and send it off.

CHAPTER 11: Diane Knight
(June 12, 1959)

At an opening of the Summer Group Show at the Tanager Gallery, the leading artists' cooperative on Tenth Street, Knight stood next to a middle-aged woman who introduced herself as Perle Fine, a member of the gallery. In their conversation, Knight mentioned that she was a painter. Fine asked to see her work. They arranged to meet the next day.

* * *

Fine studied Knight's paintings from across the small studio, then moving closer to them, examined the surface closely. Knight was touched by her attentiveness. After a while, Fine said, "I like what I see. I think you're ready to show your work. Then you'll get to see your paintings from the art world's point of view, hear the opinions of other artists. I'll see what I can do."

Fine asked several members of the Tanager to visit Knight's studio, and Angelo Ippolito, Charles Cajori, and Sally Hazelet came by. Like Fine, they looked long and hard.

They didn't say much but invited Knight to be in a group show in the fall. She was delighted. She couldn't imagine a better entry into the art world.

* * *

At the opening, Johnson said, "The picture looks better in the gallery than in the studio. But it still shows you're nowhere near there yet. Not by a long shot."

Knight was stunned. *When is an artist ever "there?" But "nowhere near" and "not by a longshot" are nasty—and hostile. Why?*

She said quietly, "Give me time."

* * *

Knight happened to be minding the gallery when Burgh came in. "Hello, Diane, I missed the opening of your show. Wish you had let me know."

"I would have Peter, but I wasn't sure how you felt about me."

"Water under the bridge."

"Thanks for coming."

He studied the painting.

She asked, "What do you think?"

"The truth?"

"Please."

"It's not original, but it's yours. And it's felt. And it has presence. Diane, I think you've come into your own. You've arrived. Stick with it. Push it."

"You mean that?"

"Ever hear me say anything about art I didn't mean? Not to you. That was our big problem, remember?"

"Yes, I remember. Thanks, and I can't tell you how much your response means to me."

* * *

When Knight got to know the Tanager members, she joined in their activities and perpetual conversations about art. Then, Ippolito phoned her. "We've just had a meeting of the Tanager members, and we've decided to invite you to join us. Think it over and let us know."

"No need to think it over. My answer is yes. I'd be honored to join." *Finally, artists' recognition in the world I want to be in. The Tanagerites live art. Not like Johnson and his buddies who no longer talk much about painting but babble on about galleries, sales, career. What a bore! How should I celebrate? Invite Perle, Lois, and Sally Hazelet to lunch at the Cedar. Ladies Day. How are my funds? Better make it a buffet at my place.*

* * *

The artist standing unsteadily at the Cedar's bar was drunk. As Johnson walked by, he slobbered, "It's Neil, I do believe, Neil, my old, old buddy. Hi, Neil."

"It's Steve Burns, by God. Haven't seen you in forever. You look awful. What's new?"

"Been out of town for a year doing a teaching gig at the University of Minnesota. Just got back. Been catching up on my drinking—and on what passes for art in New York. Been reading too. Saw that interview of yours in *Art News*. About you influencing Peter Burgh. That was good for a laugh."

"That's yesterday's news. Everyone knows I was drunk and misquoted. You've been in the boonies too long."

"Come off it Neil. Don't bullshit me. I know you, you meant it."

"I also said that you are an asshole. It shoulda got printed but wasn't."

Johnson looked at Burns and asked, "Did Peter get to you? Did that lying son of a bitch bad-mouth me?"

Burns looked flustered. "What in hell are you talking about? Peter did what? That's weird, Neil, real weird."

Burns' remark called to mind all the ridicule Johnson had suffered for months. Was still suffering. *If this loser could gloat and lord it over me, where did it leave me? When will the abuse stop?*

Moving to the far end of the bar, Johnson ordered a double scotch. Then another, and another. After the fourth, he decided he wanted to see Knight and headed out shakily to her studio.

He let himself in and even before he closed the door to her apartment, he began to shout. "Those bastards Burgh and Sawyer are still out to get me, and that damn *Art News* article won't die. They even got word to the boondocks, to that asshole Steve Burns, you don't know him."

He paused to give her a chance to agree with him. She looked at him sympathetically but said nothing.

"Ain't talking, huh? So, now you're on Peter's side, you

bitch. He's breaking my balls, and I'll bet you're grooving it."

"Come on Neil, I'm with you. You know that."

Johnson was too drunk to remember that when he had told her he had influenced Burgh she told him quietly that their work was too different for that to be of any importance. He shouted then that she was too fucking blind and stupid to see what he meant and she said no more. Now, he looked at her with hatred, went to the closet, took out a bottle of bourbon, and poured a large glass. She said, "I think you're over your limit, lover."

"Don't tell me what the fuck to do, lover."

Nodding at her canvas tacked to the wall, he snarled, "You call that painting, lover? It's crap, lover. Lady nose-picking crap, lover. Who gives a fuck about your itty-bitty sensitivities? Can you paint? You want the truth? You and all your other fucking lady painters, like that Morgan cunt, you haven't got the balls to be painters. You'd do the art world a favor by learning how to fuck and leave it at that, lover, or going off and having babies, *lover*."

He swung around and sloshed his drink onto her collage. "It looks better now. This piece of shit is better than what you call your painting, but it would make even Duchamp puke. At least that phony had the sense to quit."

"Neil, you're sloshed."

"Don't tell me what the fuck I am...lover."

She looked down not knowing what to do.

"Don't look away from me you no-talent bitch."

He subsided for a while, then said, "What I need is a fuck."

"No, not tonight, Neil."

"Yes tonight, you dumb cunt."

Johnson lunged at Knight, hurling a canvas off the wall as he did. She backed away but in the tiny room there was nowhere to run. He grabbed her. She pounded him with her fists screaming, "Don't. Neil, stop it. This is crazy." But it didn't seem to affect him. He dragged her to the bed, threw her down, ripped off her skirt and panties. She continued to try to fight him off. "Don't do this, Neil, please." He punched her in the mouth. Diane began to cry. She felt the blood ooze and, when he hit her again in the eye, she went limp. Neil fumbled with his fly, unzipped it, and tugged out his penis. It was soft. He passed out and fell into a drunken sleep. She looked at him with disgust and thought of her ex-husband. *That bastard battered my work and raped me. And you tried, you son of a bitch. Both of you had the same idea. Stop me from making art. Well, my dear hubby didn't succeed and neither will you, asshole. Neither will you.*

Knight put a cold compress on her mouth and eye, took a knife from the kitchen cabinet, tucked it under the pillow of her chair, curled up, and dozed on and off.

She was brewing coffee when Johnson awoke. Holding his head he looked woozily at Knight who continued to press a cold towel alternately to her swollen lip and black eye. He said, "God, what have I done? I'm sorry, really sorry."

"Let's cool it for a couple of days. Neil, please leave now."

"You know I didn't mean to hit you."

"We need a little time to sort things out."

He said angrily, his macho tone returning, "Come on, you're not going to make me pay for one drunken gaffe. I was sloshed. It was no big deal."

She looked at him impassively. "You hurt me. Now go."

"At least you can make me some coffee."

She turned away.

"Okay, I'll go. I'm sorry, but it was no big deal."

As soon as Johnson left, Diane put new sheets on the bed and had a locksmith change the locks.

He phoned in the afternoon. She said coldly, "I've known macho bastards before, and I've been raped, but my ex-husband never punched me like you did."

"Alright, alright, I acted like a bastard. I apologize."

"Now, you listen closely, you son of a bitch. I've talked to a lawyer, a local policeman who's a friend, and to Perle Fine. If you so much as look funny at me, I'll charge you with assault and attempted rape. And one last thing, your hatred of Peter had made you crazy. You better face up to that and get some help."

She hung up before he could reply.

* * *

The battering changed Knight's attitude, not to men, but to art. She dismissed Johnson as a creep but now hated what he stood for in art. *To hell with cutting-edge, the next move in art, and a career. Now, I'm going to paint exactly what I feel, really feel, as directly as I can, no matter what comes of it. No fudging, no compromise. Not a very original idea. Wasn't that what Peter was talking about all the time? But without his angst. I'll follow my feeling in everything—size of canvas, form, brushwork, light, everything. And so what if my paintings call someone else's to mind. They'll still be mine, and that's what counts. I don't have to answer to anyone. Forget*

Hans, forget Art News, *forget career. And if I don't make it in the art world, so be it. Win or lose, head held high.*

Knight felt her hands; they were clenched so tight that her fingernails cut into her palms. Looking around her apartment, she was suddenly annoyed. Aside from her collage, it was just the kind of place a lady painter would live in. She neatly folded the green bedspread and stored it in the back of a closet shelf. On top of the bedspread, she carefully placed her green throwaway pillow and her doll with the green clothes. She went out and bought a solid grey blanket and white sheets and pillowcases. The room remained much as before but its attitude had changed.

* * *

At the Cedar a few nights later, a young man in paint-smeared jeans asked what she did. She said she painted. He smirked, "Yeah, sure. Let me buy you a drink."

"Thanks, but I've got one."

"You should be nice to me."

"Why? 'Cause you're the Good Lord's gift to lady painters?"

"So I've been told. Wanna have a go?"

"I've got an alternative suggestion, big boy."

"Like what?"

"Like they say in the United States Marine Corps, 'Why don't you take a flying fuck at the moon?'"

The other drinkers within earshot laughed uneasily.

"You some kind of bitch?"

"Just in your case, big prick, so fuck off."

She turned away and smiled to herself.

Knight would later look back on the simple change of decor as symbolic of a radical change in her life. In distancing herself from Hofmann's dictums, Burgh's angst, and Johnson's trendiness, she felt liberated. Every now and then, a feeling of pleasure, more like joy, would surge up from some inner depth—while painting, listening to music, working on her wall scrapbook, walking the streets, anywhere, anytime. This feeling pervaded her painting. Hans Hofmann got one thing right. Life could be beautiful. Paint it!

* * *

Knight had painted ten pictures. There had been a cancellation of a show at the Tanager. The members offered her the slot.

* * *

Knight's first show at the Tanager was a downtown success, for a newcomer. Burgh came to the opening, of course, said little, but beamed. The arrival of Hofmann was a surprise. He hugged her and said, "*Nicht* exactly push *und* pull but you are going your own vay. *Das ist gut, nikker*? Keep it up." Diane reddened and said, "Thank you Mr. Hofmann for coming and for your kind words." Nothing sold, but little did on Tenth Street. The downtown artists liked her work. De Kooning, Kline, and Guston signed the book, and all three made encouraging comments when they met her.

The reviews in *Art News* and *Art Digest*, though brief, were favorable. As Ippolito said to her, "Super entry, kid."

* * *

Herbert Stein visited Knight's studio and praised her paintings. He also looked hard at her wall scrapbook. She said, "You seem to be taking the paste-ups seriously. I'm surprised. They're just old photos, some stuff from my this-and-that life torn out of magazines, and what have you—mementos that strike my fancy."

"They're really interesting. Makes me think of Rauschenberg, but they're different. He's about the city, you're about yourself."

"But are they serious?"

"As serious as Rauschenberg's combines. But if you are going to show them, be prepared for a lot of flak. Rauschenberg paved the way for you, but his work is still called Neo-Dada, the new anti-art, and so will yours. I'd advise you to forget that and keep on making them."

"I enjoy making them and I'll keep at it." She said it matter-of-factly. *I like this man and would like to see more of him.*

* * *

Two weeks later, Stein phoned Knight. He said, "I have tickets for a concert by John Cage. Would you like to join me?" Cage's concert consisted of dozens of radios tuned to different stations. Stein was respectful but cool. Knight was fascinated.

Over sandwiches, he said, "This radio medley was not as far out as Cage's piece titled *Silence*, which was just that, four minutes plus some seconds of silence. Not my cup of tea."

"But is it music?"

"It couldn't be anything else, like your bulletin board is art. Cage's piece wasn't all silence. There was sound, of course—people noisily making for the doors, shuffling, coughing, chairs creaking, insects buzzing. Cage meant that to be his music. But as I said, 'Not my cup of tea.'"

Stein looked at Knight quizzically. "You seem very interested."

"Everyday sounds as music. Yes, I am interested."

"He's giving a talk at the Club in a couple of weeks. You can meet him there."

* * *

Stein advised Celia Loeb to look at Knight's work. She bristled, "Give Peter's ex-bitch a show? Not in my gallery." But then Knight was a Burgh reject, just as she was. Still, she would never take on that slut. Nonetheless, she made the trek downtown. She was surprised to find that Knight's painting stirred her. She couldn't think of why, but sensed that they expressed something she desired in art and life. A certain sensuality. She was not sure how to proceed. Would Knight's work sell? She asked Stein. He said, "The work is modest but honest and authentic, and that's not to be sneezed at. A young painter to watch. Will we be looking at her three years from now? Odds look good. For now, her timing is just right. Lyricism is in and will hang in for at least a couple of seasons. And sexiness, if you know what I mean?"

"I certainly do." *Even if Knight fades in four years, I'll come out ahead. Her painting does speak to me.*

* * *

Loeb invited Knight to lunch. After the appetizers, she said, "Herbert Stein, you know him, the curator at the Met, recommended your work. I saw it at the Tanager and admire it too. I'd like you to join my gallery. You haven't made a name yet, so we'll have to keep prices low to begin with. But I'll do the best I can. What do you say?"

"I'll have to let you know."

"What's holding you back?"

"I'm not sure I'd like it uptown."

Loeb was charmed by Knight's innocence. She knew that the young painter's Tanager friends would advise her to accept Loeb's offer, and they did.

* * *

Loeb looked at Knight's paintings, choosing which ones to show. She didn't even glance at the assemblages.

Loeb asked, "Are your paintings about sex?"

Diane looked flustered. "I never thought about that. Let's say they're sensual."

"They sure are. That's why your paintings spoke to me

the first time I saw them."

They went out for coffee. Loeb asked, "Tell me, Diane, do you still see Peter?"

"Rarely. We run into each other at openings, or at the Club. We just say hello and smile. Our affair was over a long time ago."

"Yeah, I know. After that, you and Neil Johnson became an item."

"That's over too, thank God."

"Were you in love with Peter? Do you still have, how shall I put it, the hots for him?"

"Oh no, not any more."

"What was it like living with him?"

"We weren't exactly living together. We would meet every now and then, have a meal, and go to bed. We used one another in a nice way. I was his lost youth. He introduced me into the art world. I was very fond of Peter, but it couldn't last. Then Neil came along."

"What was sex like with Peter?"

"Great. Why do you ask?"

"Curiosity, I guess."

"Good sex has more to do with me than what the guy does. I mean, if I like the guy and feel good about my myself and my art, sex is just fine. I admired Peter and in the beginning my work was going well. Then we found our attitudes on art and life too incompatible and it came to an end. Sex with Neil was okay. He was good technically, but emotionally, something was missing. Then he began to bad-mouth my work in a really destructive way. Even then it was okay, until the bastard beat me. But weren't you and

Peter going together?"

Loeb looked away, pensively. "Yes. Unfortunately, that's over. I think that I can trust you. I need someone to confide in. I'm still in love with Peter. It's kind of an obsession. I can't get him out of my system."

"What happened? Why did you break up?"

"He went out with me at first because he was doing his friend a favor, wanted me to be his dealer. His friend's painting was okay."

"Little Mike?"

"Yeah, but I hated him, and I began to stall. Peter and I were getting along so well that I got cocky and figured I might not have to show his friend. What a stupid move, so goddamn stupid. Then Peter gave me an ultimatum, and I gave in, but his friend turned me down, and Peter gave me the boot. I've been trying to make up with him ever since. I gave him my all. God, he turned me on. I did things with him that I never did with a man before, things that used to disgust me. He enjoyed it. I could see that. But love? What am I kidding myself for? He'll never love me. I should just forget him. Yeah, yeah. Forget him. But the bastard is rarely out of my mind for long. If he only knew how much I love him. How can I get him to understand? There must be something else I can do. Well at least there's no other woman. As far as I know. But what if one appears?"

Then she began to cry. She stopped suddenly in despair. "Sometimes, I wish he was far away, too far away for me to think of him, or dead. It's crazy. I love him, and I want him dead."

Knight took Loeb's hand in hers. "I don't know what to

say, except that I know how you feel. It's doing bad things to your mind. You can't go on like this. Something's gotta give."

"I know, I know. Here I'm talking to you like my best friend, and I hardly even know you. God I hated you when you were with Peter. I could've torn your hair out. Even my shrink wasn't able to help."

Knight said softly, "Then you don't need my advice. Just a soft shoulder."

"Yes, someone to talk to. Thank you."

* * *

Loeb sent Nichols to Knight's studio to look at her work. He looked hard at both the art and the artist, and bought a middle-sized one. Then he took her to lunch. The more they talked, the more sympathetic he found her. He said, "You know, back in your studio, I could barely hold myself back from making a pass. I'd still like to. What d'ya say."

"That's sweet of you, Morton, but I don't want to."

"I could help your career."

"I don't want to make it that way."

"Awright. You must think I'm vulgar."

"Only when you make silly propositions."

"A lot of people think I'm vulgar. But I'm really not."

"Look, Morton, I like you. You remind me of the Marine Corps guys I grew up with. They were good guys, diamonds in the rough, but I would never call them vulgar."

"I try not to be crude. But I can't help it, or at least, not much. Never went to college, you know, except to the school of hard knocks. Had to make my way in the world—and my world was rough—from the age of fourteen on. But any vulgarity I might have is only on the surface. Deep down, there's another Morton Nichols, the Nichols who loves art and culture, the Nichols with taste."

"I sensed that."

"I never talked like this to anyone, even my wife—particularly my wife—who did go to college and puts on airs."

"You do like the life of art, the openings, the parties."

"Not really. I love the art but I'd rather play pinochle with my old pals. To be honest, I hate snot-noses like Neil Johnson. I'm in the art world because of the art. I get to rub my collection in their stuck-up faces. They've got to accept me. And that proves that I'm cultured. But I hate the snots. I shouldn't be telling you this."

"It's okay, Morton. We come from the same background. I understand."

"You're a terrific artist and a terrific person, and I want to be your friend."

"You are."

CHAPTER 12: Neil Johnson
(August 14, 1959)

Johnson was on top of Loeb, thrusting, when he suddenly stopped. She said, "What's the matter?"

"Oh, sorry, but I just thought of something."

"What?"

"Oh, it's nothing. It's crazy at a time like this to think that I've got twenty paintings in the studio. It's on my mind."

Johnson began to thrust again.

As they lay in bed, he said, "I'm sorry about that lapse in the middle. It just jumped into mind."

"Yes, it's a tough time." *Nice try, Neil. I may shed a tear or two.*

As he was dressing, he said, "How about setting a date for a show? My new pictures will knock them dead."

Loeb looked away.

He said, "Huh, something wrong? You're not showing much enthusiasm."

"I'm not sure this is a good time for a show."

"What do you mean? I've got the work."

"With your market what it is, with no one buying, and

your collectors selling, it may be best to wait for a better moment."

"What are you trying to do? Break my balls? Did Burgh say something to you?"

"Burgh? What's Peter got to do with this? Now come off it. Look Neil, you're smart about business. You tell me. What's the purpose of a show if I don't sell and the critics murder you? Maybe its time to take a breather, and then hit them with something new and big."

"Something new? So you don't like what I'm painting? Is that it?"

"You know better. Something in the art world has been changing. I don't quite know what, but it's clobbering your generation. Even the likes of Beth Morgan are having a tough time, and the Milton Silvermans, fuggedaboudit. You want a show? I'll give you one. But don't come crying to me if nothing happens."

Johnson finished tying his shoes. With his studied swagger, he made for the circular staircase. Turning back, he said, "I think I've had it with this outhouse you call your gallery." Looking her body up and down, he added, "And best of all, I won't have to look at your sagging udders anymore."

* * *

Johnson had drained his second double scotch when he was overcome with a wave of self-pity mixed with self-disgust. *Nobody. I've got nobody. No dealer, no collectors, no critics, no curators, no friends worth anything. Nobody. I'm screwed. Gotta do something. Try to make up with Peter again. Yeah, write him a letter.*

He ripped a sheet off a pad of drawing paper, chose a pen from a jar, and wrote:

Dear Peter,
    I've done you a terrible disservice. And I want to sort things out. But first, let me explain. When I said that I influenced you, I had only one picture of yours in mind—that almost all orange vertical. It reminded me of the green picture I called *Swampwater.* Do you remember it, the one I had painted a few months earlier? That's all I said, and I am sorry, deeply sorry that it was misinterpreted. You are one of the better things to happen to me in my life in art—a model of the artist that I aspire to be, the father that I always dreamed of. I know I haven't really found myself, not yet. I tried to be up-to-date, and it worked for a time. Now however, I've got to dig into myself and find my image. And I'll do it, just as you have done. But that's not what I'm writing to you about. I want to apologize and hope that we can see one another again.
    Your son,

Johnson rubbed out "son" and substituted "friend." He reread the letter and tore it up. *That's that. I sure could use a broad tonight.*

He found his address book and began to leaf through it.

* * *

Johnson sat in his loft facing a bare canvas but not really seeing it. *If all my old pals are out to cut my throat, to hell with them. I'll find some new ones. Perhaps now's the time to call Hill. First I'll do some Hill-type paintings to take the SOB in. Problem is, how to keep clear of those no-talents he's promoting, Larry Martin and Nelson Karl. Let's see. Martin is organic. Karl is geometric. What's my move?*

He riffled through old issues of *Art News*, found reproductions of works by Martin and Karl, and tacked them to his painting wall. It didn't take him long to solve his problem. *I'll pick up on Renoir. Of course, Renoir's volume. What Martin and Karl don't have. I'm the fat-assed Abstract Impressionist. I'll paint bulky shapes in real thin paint, soak it into the canvas, stain them, like Hill likes. Thick and thin. Bulk and transparency. Stroke of genius. And I'll paint them better than those Hillites ever could. Then, we'll see what our almighty eye has to say.*

* * *

Neil painted ten new canvases and phoned Hill.

"Hi, Mr. Hill. Neil Johnson here. I've got some paintings I think you might like to take a look at. I've been thinking a lot about what you told me, and I think you'll be interested in what I've come up with. Do you have any time?"

"I can make some." *He's in trouble. I might as well take another look.* "Let's see, kid, kind of jammed up next week. What about eleven o'clock the following Monday?"

"Sounds good to me."

* * *

Thinking about Hill's visit once again pitched Johnson into a state of anxiety, a state he had never felt as intensely before. *Cool it. Hill isn't that important. Yes, but that phony actually is. It's now or never. Damn, that SOB has my future in his clammy hands.*

Much as he tried, Johnson could not shake his dread. And a week was a long time to wait.

* * *

Hill sauntered into Johnson's loft, said hello, acknowledged the painter's greeting with a nod, and slowly removed his coat. Johnson took it, hung it up, and said, "Would you like a drink?"

"Perhaps later. Let's see some work."

Hill looked at the ten paintings without saying a word. *Shrewd bastard. He's painted these pictures for me. But they're not bad, not bad at all.*

"I must admit that I didn't expect you to come up with anything this interesting, but you've surprised me. I haven't seen this kind of volume in modernist painting before. You know that when I visit a studio I say exactly what I think and feel. And if I believe I can improve an artist's work, I'll come right out with it. Hold on to the volume. You might think of painting some square canvases, say six-footers, for openers. It'll enhance the sense of mass. Your color is good. I gotta go now, but call me anytime."

At the door, Hill turned and said, "Key up the color."

"I sure will think about it, Marshall. I want to thank you." *I've thought about it. So, I passed your test, big prick. And you did say to call you anytime. How many six footers should I have Mike Pearson build?*

*   *   *

Celia Loeb bowed slightly and gushed, "Yes, Mr. Hill, I've read your art criticism. It is awesome, truly awesome. You know I've been following your writing for much of my life, and I've loved it all, adored it, and learned from it. It's awesome."

"Why thank you Celia." *Awesome. Adored. God they rear them vulgar in the Bronx.*

"What may I show you?"

Hill responded, "I've come to talk business. What interests me now is this Color-Field painting I've been writing about, you know, and especially these new guys, Larry Martin and Nelson Karl. They figured out how to use Pollock's pour and Newman's field by putting them together. They've got galleries. But a number of newer up-and-comers today are taking their cues from them, and they're the best young artists of our time. Their market is catching on and starting to climb, and it's only the beginning. Emmerich has a few of the painters but there are others, real talents, like Charles Redman, who don't have first-class dealers. I believe that you've got the taste and marketing skills to represent some of them. And I think I can persuade a few to join your gallery, if you're interested."

"I certainly am. I've been tracking your artists. They're quality."

"One of the artists I'd recommend is Redman. Another is an artist you know, Neil Johnson."

"Johnson? Not on my walls!"

"I hear you've had trouble with him before, but he's changed, you'll see. And he'll behave. I guarantee that.

Besides, let's forget personalities. It's business, and you'll make a mint on him and the other artists I recommend. I guarantee that too."

"Okay, I'll take you at your word."

Hill turned to go. At the door he said, "By the way, Celia, you ought to upgrade your stable by dropping that Knight woman."

"I've done quite well by her, Mr. Hill."

"It's not a matter of money but taste. Your gallery will now be associated with my name, and Knight is not up to my standards. Now what'll it be."

"If that's what it takes, Marshall, I'll seriously consider it." *I'll give you a try. You're supposed to have a stable of collectors. Them, I could use. We'll see.*

Hill twitched slightly at the use of his first name. "Shall I have Neil call you?"

"By all means."

As Hill left the gallery, he glanced back. *Nice bod, Miss Loeb. We'll have to do some of our business in bed.*

Loeb called her secretary in and said, "I'm expecting a call from Diane. Tell her I'll get back to her." *Hate to do this to you, good friend, but business is business.*

* * *

Two days later, Loeb returned Knight's phone call, told her that her show would have to be postponed, and that she would get back to her later. Knight sensed that their relationship had changed, but could not tell why.

* * *

Hill phoned Johnson. "The Loeb matter is settled. She'll represent you. But there has been some bad blood between you in the past. You're going to have to cool it. If not, pull out now, and we'll figure out something else. I won't put up with head games that'll screw up my plans."

"I'll be fine."

"Incidentally, Neil, I've got a blank wall in my apartment. I'd love to hang one of your paintings there. A lot of art world big-guns pass through my place."

"I'd love to *give* you a painting. Shall I have it sent up?"

"No, you wouldn't mind if I chose one myself?"

* * *

Hill quickly persuaded four collectors to buy Johnson's paintings. He said to Loeb smugly, "This is just the beginning. You'll see."

Loeb was shrewd enough to realize that the sales were to Hill's "kept" collectors, like Solly Newton, who even struck her as crass. She shuddered at the thought of him. The owner of a small chain of laundromats in New Jersey, Newton bought what Hill told him to so that he and his wife could cavort in the art world playpen, go to Museum of Modern Art openings, and rub shoulders with the Rockefellers. But when Loeb made a pitch to Ricky Black, who was on the board of the Whitney, using Hill's name, he answered, "Yeah, I know Marshall likes Johnson's work, and I take him at his word when he says it has quality, but it doesn't turn me on. You know what I mean?"

Loeb knew. A few days later, Hill called and told her to

take on Sammy Schort—and had she dropped Knight?

"Sammy Schort?" *He's a loser. So, Mister Hill, you want me to turn my gallery into the garbage heap of third-raters you use to puff up Martin and Karl. No way.*

"Yes, Sammy Schort. The new work he's doing is first-rate."

"I'm sure it is, but I don't care for his work, and I wouldn't know how to market it."

"Just leave that to me."

"I don't think so, Marshall. I'll represent Neil and Redman, but I won't take on Schort. If I don't like an artist, I won't show him or her. As for Knight, I'm still mulling it over."

Hill hung up.

* * *

Three days later Hill called Loeb. "I'm very disappointed in you, but as I said, business is business. Okay, forget Sammy Schort. I hope you come to your senses about Knight. From now on, you've got to trust my eye."

"I will, definitely, but as I've said, I've got to like the work to show it. By the way, I'm meeting Neil to make arrangements for his show."

* * *

The next day, she phoned Knight. "I've sorted out my schedule. There's a spot at the beginning of January for your show. Can you be ready?"

"Sure can."

Johnson greeted Loeb warmly as she walked into his loft, as if their squabble had never occurred.

"Would you like some coffee or wine or something stronger, Celia?"

"No, thank you." *So, you've curbed your old arrogance and turned on the Yalie charm. But have you really changed, you bastard? I'll put you through your paces.*

He brought out a picture and propped it on the painting wall. She paced ten steps up to it and with a provocative twitch of her ass, pivoted, and paced ten steps back. She said, "Next," and waited.

He said, "This is the one Marshall really liked." *This is my punishment. I guess I had it coming. Hill has given her the list of what to show, but I'll let her have her revenge.*

After Johnson had shown her the projected dozen works for the show, Loeb said, "They're okay. There's a free slot in March. It's a good time to show. I'll send down for the yellow picture over here and that smaller green one to put in the Christmas show and begin to drum up some interest. Drop into the gallery next Tuesday afternoon at three, and we'll get some contracts signed."

"My word's good. You know that."

"Since you left, things have changed, such as better accounting, and that goes for all my artists."

"Well, okay." *Forgot how tempting that ass is. But no opening to make a pass. Maybe later on.*

* * *

As Johnson signed the contracts, Loeb was on the phone with her back to him, making arrangements to deliver a Diebenkorn she had just sold. After the last signature, she turned, and, forcing a smile, shook his hand. "I'll do the best I can for you, I hope as good as I have for Knight."

"I know you will."

She turned away. As he put his copies in a folder, he said, "One more thing Celia, I don't want to mix in your business, but I am curious. Do you really think that keeping Knight in your gallery is such a good idea? I mean her work really has nothing new to say, not to mention no edge and no class. You know that Marshall doesn't think much of her work either."

Without looking at him, she said coldly, "I know. He told me." *Uh oh, the old Neil rears his arrogant head. Finally.* She pivoted to face him and feigned a puzzled look. "I don't understand. What d'ya mean, nothing new?"

"It looks too much like Hofmann."

"Which Hofmann? Early, middle, late? Thick, thin?"

"You know. That vulgar German color."

"Whatever that means. I may be blind and you may be right. It doesn't matter. The bottom line is that I like her work, it's my gallery, and I'll show anyone I goddamn please. And you can tell those who don't like it to blow it out their asses. Besides, doesn't the idea of having two of your conquests—dealer and artist—in the same gallery amuse you, even though neither of us will ever fuck you again?"

"Oh, you needn't get huffy. I was just curious."

"Yeah, yeah. I've got a client coming. Bye, bye."

* * *

It didn't take Johnson long to figure out the pecking order in Hill's côterie. Hill was "the kingmaker" in every way. His word brooked no challenge or contradiction. First in line came Felice Hardy, a leftover from Abstract Expressionism, who was the high priestess, blessed be her name. Next in line was Morris Louis, followed by Martin and Karl; critics and curators, who parroted Hill's line while professing to be independent; collectors, who were kowtowed to, but subtly patronized; and, at the bottom of the heap, sweaty toadies who looked to Hill for advice on how to paint. Elbowing each other to get close to "the kingmaker," they hoped he'd tell them what to paint and hype their work. Johnson had been number five, but he had recently been promoted to number four.

* * *

Hill's côterie met for drinks every other Sunday evening at his apartment. There were only a few pieces of modern furniture so as not to block the view of the walls, which were covered with the paintings of his acolytes. The pieces would change from week to week. Most of the guests would sit on the floor and listen eagerly to their leader's analysis, but what really interested them was the placement of the paintings. This told them more about Hill's pecking order than anything he might say. Johnson looked on with approval as, from week to week, his picture was displayed more prominently, but never with the pride of place as those of Karl or Martin. And as the sales of his work increased, he recognized that collectors and curators were paying attention to the changing display on Hill's walls. He had survived the Burgh fiasco.

Sunday conversations would range from what was good in art and what was bad—mostly what was bad—to the analysis of everybody's neuroses, to the latest hip night club and "in" restaurants. Johnson's accounts of Burgh's vices were highly popular. At one point in the evening, Hill would single out some artist or one of the guests and berate him, or more often her, for some misdeed in art or life, of which the accused was generally unaware. The others would join in the sadistic roast.

"So, Selma, Karl tells me you saw the Mitchell show and liked it."

"It had a certain zip."

"Zippier than de Kooning?"

"No, de Kooning is better."

"Better at what, zipping?"

Selma Hudson, a relative newcomer to the group, looked around, flustered, for some help. "You know what I mean. I don't particularly like it, but it's got a certain energy."

Karl piped up, "Energy? Why, because of all those brush strokes? All I saw was mush."

Hudson retorted weakly, "That's kinda hard."

"But no hard-on. But then, you wouldn't know, would you, Selma old girl?"

She was close to tears. "Look, its no big deal."

Martin added, "No big deal? You should zap the zip, Selma."

Karl turned to Hudson and, smiling, said, "Yeah, time

to zipper it, Selma. Mitchell's squishy, shitty muck is even gooier than de Kooning and slushier than Burgh."

"Slop doth a Mitchell make. Quoth William Shakespeare."

"Nah. Not slop, but sloth. Big Bill saith sloth. As in, Burgh is a sloth machine."

"Wouldn't you say, Selma, old girl?"

Johnson spoke up, "Isn't this Selma roast getting kinda rough?"

Karl said, "We all thought you had gotten Burgh out of your system. But obviously not yet."

Hill interjected, "You know, Neil, you need an art enema. Purge your system of Burgh's feces."

Johnson reddened and was about to object, but only said mildly, "You're right, Marshall, I'll zip it." *Now I'm the butt. Yeah. I'll zip it, Marshall, as long as you're making me a bundle.*

* * *

A week later, Hill dropped into the Loeb Gallery. He said, "You sold quite a few of Redman's paintings, quite a few. That and my support has gotten him in a position to move to another level, get a new class of collectors to buy. A picture in the Met's collection will help do it, and Solly Newton is prepared to give them one. I hear that Herbert Stein is a buddy of yours. Give him a call."

"Can do, but don't expect anything to come of it, unless he really likes the work, and I have a feeling he doesn't. The Met is Stein's church."

"Sure, sure, but I'm counting on you."

Loeb phoned Stein. "A collector of mine, Solly Newton, would like to donate a major painting by Redman to the Met. You saw his work in my gallery and there's a real buzz about him."

"Oh, is he your new Johnson? No can do."

"Why are you so ungenerous? I really believe in this artist. Why not lend a helping hand to this really talented painter?"

"Talented? I can think of more suitable adjectives."

"It's not just me that thinks Redman is a comer. There's also Hill."

"Why am I not impressed?"

"I know you don't like Hill, but you've got to separate the man from his taste, and his taste is first-rate, proven time and time again."

"Okay, Celia, I'll give it to you straight. The Met acquires a Redman and his prices go up, right? Solly Newton's got how many, three, four Redmans? He generously donates one out of the goodness of his heart, the other two, three jump in price, and he comes out ahead. Hill accepts gifts of paintings and sells them on the sly. He wins as well. You're Redman's dealer and his sales climb. All of you stand to gain. But it's the Met's reputation that suffers, and I get insomnia. Tell Hill you tried, and that he can go peddle his second-rate wares some place else. He once told me that it would be to my advantage to kiss his ass. He also tells people that I have no eye. Really, Celia, you should be ashamed of yourself. "

"Oh, come off it Herbert. We all know how the art world works."

"This time it's off track. But Celia, old girl, I still love you. End of conversation."

* * *

Hill continued to bad-mouth Knight. Loeb said, "It took me time, but I've thought it over and I think you're right. Knight goes, but I'll give her one more show."

Hill grunted.

Five paintings sold, but Loeb took Knight aside and said, "It's hard for me to say this but, even though the show was a success, I'm asking you to leave the gallery."

"I'm not surprised. I sensed it."

"How? I didn't say anything."

"There were signals. And Hill is a loudmouth, and you are relying more and more on him."

"Then you understand."

"Look Celia, you did okay by me. I can't say that I'm not a little hurt, but I'm not innocent any more. And I'll survive."

"I'm so relieved to hear that. Can we remain friends?"

"Sure. How long do you suppose it'll take until Hill dumps you?"

* * *

Stein and Burgh talked up Knight to Stanley Jones, and he decided to pay her a visit. He complimented her on her paintings but spent more time looking at her collages. *She's on to something. Rauschenberg hasn't closed things off. He's opened them up. Diane is different. She's into her autobiography.*

Knight put another painting up. Jones glanced at it and turned back to the collage. "This is something fresh. I like it."

"Really? I have a hard time thinking of it as art. I just enjoy making it."

"Well, it is art, damned interesting art. My gut tells me that. The art world will put you down at first. But it'll come around. What if I asked to show the collages, would you agree?"

She hesitated. "I'm not going to say no to Stanley Jones. But I'll be put down as Neo-Dada, and my seriousness as a painter will be called into question. I'd lose all my friends."

"And you'll make some interesting new ones. As a painter and collagist, you'll give the art world a double whammy."

"My painting comes first."

"Sure it does. But these paste-ups are also you. And Herbert will speak up for them. We could use a critic. I'll bet Sawyer will love them. He's a good old boy and your southern girlhood will turn him on. Then there's John Cage. You just go on being a painter and making your collages for your amusement. Leave the rest to me."

CHAPTER 13: Peter Burgh
(November 6, 1962)

Burgh knew he was growing more depressed, but he could not determine why. Was the cause hereditary? Was he taking after his father, whose depression had led to suicide? Memories of his father's death kept recurring with increasing frequency. What of Frankie? Or Frenhofer? Perhaps with Existentialism in mind, he was reacting to the absurdity of life in the face of inevitable death, or the world's rot and misery. Whatever it was, he recognized that it had been slowly poisoning his life and art. He could still paint, in fact, he painted more than he ever had before, at times for fourteen, even fifteen, hours at a stretch, with short fitful naps and breaks for another drink. He barely ate and hardly bathed. His pictures struck him as more and more despondent. Still, he went on painting them, obsessively, one after the other, putting them aside only when he was too drained to continue.

Didn't Ad Reinhardt title a series, Ultimate Paintings? *I'll title these* Terminal Paintings: Homage to Balzac.

* * *

Burgh was always aware of the gulf between his aspirations as an artist and those of his dealer (even one as supportive as Stanley Jones). He tried not to think of the differences, but couldn't help it. On one of his recent visits to Burgh's loft, Jones said to him, "The stylistic jump you're making is too big. The art world won't be able to follow it. It would help to lighten up."

"Help? Help what? Help who? Lighten up? Why?"

"You know what I mean. There's a real world out there, Peter. You know, flesh and blood collectors with their own tastes. I'm only trying to be helpful."

* * *

Burgh sat in a cavernous room in the Santini Brothers Warehouse looking dejectedly at his pictures, placed stretcher to stretcher, leaning against the walls. In just over a month, a dozen of them would be installed in the Jones Gallery. His dealer had been unenthusiastic, to say the least, but had reluctantly agreed to the show. Now Burgh wanted Sawyer's opinion. He had invited his young friend to see them and was waiting for him to arrive.

Sawyer entered the room, walked toward Burgh, and shook his hand. Pivoting in place, he looked around and paled. He said in a choked voice, "Peter, this is something completely new. This darkness. Truly unexpected."

He walked slowly around the space, scanning the work. He suddenly stopped, looked at the floor, and with his head bowed, turned to Burgh. "These are real shockers. You know how I admire your work, but I don't know what to make of these. They are so different from what you've done before."

"It was time to start afresh. But I can see that you don't like them."

Sawyer hesitated, "I'll need more time."

"What will the art world think?"

"You want an honest opinion? This work won't wash today. Lyricism is in. Beauty has made a comeback. And it isn't that grim grey. I don't think that even your comrades will get it."

"What about your generation?"

"Do you mean, Color-Field or Hard-Edge painters? They won't look twice. And the Pop artists? Or Frank Stella and his friends? Peter, you've got to face it, it's the 1960s. It's another art world out there, and your painting is going against the grain—about as far against it as it can go. All that gloom. It's a non-starter."

"I see. Out of fashion, am I? I needed an outside opinion. That's why I invited you here."

"I hesitate giving you any advice, but as a friend, I'd have to say, don't show these paintings now. Cancel the exhibition. They'll only hurt your reputation."

"But this is what I'm painting now. I've never worried about my reputation before."

Sawyer looked uncomfortable. Burgh noticed and said, "Well, time to get back to the drawing board. Thanks for coming Joseph and thanks for telling it straight."

That evening, at the opening of the David Smith show at the Jones Gallery, Herbert Stein was chatting with William Seitz, a curator at the Museum of Modern Art. Stein overheard Sawyer saying fervently to Beth Morgan, "They were all a drab gray, a weepy gray mess. The show will be a disaster."

Stein turned to Sawyer, "What'll be?"

"Peter Burgh's new canvases. I just saw them at the warehouse. You won't believe what's happened to his painting. I've supported the earlier works, wrote an article on them. But this new stuff is something else."

Morgan interjected, "How bad? Even worse than the earlier pictures?"

Stein asked, "Where'd you see them?"

"At the Santini Brothers Warehouse."

Looking at Morgan, Stein said, "If they've made that strong of an impression on Joseph, I think they're worth a look."

She responded, "It's your time to waste."

* * *

Stein phoned Burgh the next morning and asked if he could see the new paintings. Burgh said that he had planned to be at the warehouse that afternoon, and if Stein was free, he could join him there. Stein entered the storage room, said hello to Burgh, looked around, and stood motionless. Burgh waited…and waited.

Shaken, Stein said, "They're the saddest, most hopeless pictures I've ever seen. Like a black hole that's sucked out all the light."

"But do you like them?"

"'Like' is hardly the word I would use. I'm deeply moved.

You've painted the bottomless pit of despair."

"I think you mean that. Thanks."

"No. I thank you. What do I know about despair? When did I experience it?" Stein lowered his head in thought and said quietly, "My uncle Saul, beautiful man, died suddenly in our house. He lay down on the couch and never woke up. I was only a child and didn't really understand it, but I sensed what had happened and couldn't stop crying. You've painted what that moment felt like."

Burgh responded, "Strange to say, but I find that very reassuring. I really can't talk about these paintings. They are miserable, I know that, but they're the most honest paintings I've ever made. What's the sorrow in them about? Is it mine alone or the world's as well? Am I foisting my private anguish on the world? Or am I exposing how life feels, really feels?" He paused. "How do you think the work will be received? Were you at the Smith opening the other night? Rothko told me that he overheard Sawyer saying that he saw my paintings and they were awful."

"They really shook Joseph up. And the passion of his rejection made me want to see them. Peter, if you show these canvases, prepare yourself for a blood bath. Even if the time was ripe for a tragic art—and it's not—even then, these paintings are too sad. If art world opinion matters to you, you'll end up being unhappier than you are now. Even your friends will turn away. In my opinion, these are great, great paintings and they ought to be exhibited. There'll be people out there, like me, who will appreciate them—and who need them—but I doubt you'll find many at this time."

"I was thinking of canceling the show, but not anymore."

The door of Burgh's storage room was open. As Stein was about to leave, he caught a glimpse of a geometric abstraction propped up against the far wall. He stopped. "Is that one of yours from the 1930s? I didn't think you painted abstract pictures then. It looks terrific."

"It isn't mine. It was painted by a friend, you remember him, Michael Pearson."

"I remember meeting him with my professor. He was looped. I don't know his painting."

"He's the best kept secret in the art world."

"I'm curating a show of American abstraction and would like to include him. How can I reach him?"

"You can't. He's disappeared. But I've got about two dozen of his works. Take your pick."

"Can you lend them?"

"Pearson gave them to me, but he says I bought them, and I did give him money, so I guess they're mine. It would be nice to see them at the Met, for his sake."

"Are they all about that size?"

"More or less. We preferred to paint big pictures then, murals for the masses, but we did paint easel paintings for the bourgeoisie, like these."

"Can I borrow six?"

"Help yourself."

Burgh pulled the Pearsons out of the rack. Stein said, "They're very good." He made a quick selection. "I'll have Art Movers pick these up. Thanks again for showing me your work and introducing me to Pearson."

* * *

Burgh had always disliked openings of his shows. He knew that they were not only about displaying the paintings, but also about showing off the artist. As usual, the guests stood with their backs to the works on the walls, gossiping with each other. Recognizing that his new pictures would not be acceptable to the art world, he thought that this opening would be more uncomfortable than usual. And it was. He had hoped that Jones would stand by him and help him greet the visitors, but Jones was in his office. Hiding, Burgh thought.

Sawyer and Stein were right. Burgh's friends gave him the customary compliments and sympathetic nods, but he knew most didn't mean it. When he looked directly at them, they averted their eyes, as if to hide their dishonesty. Worse still, a few seemed to pity him. Conversations would suddenly stop when he came within earshot. His unsuccessful artist acquaintances, sensing his eclipse, suddenly became avuncular, which Burgh recognized as patronizing. At the dinner after the opening, Jones seated him at one end and himself at the other. The guests conversed brightly but mainly with each other—not with him and not about the work, except for the composer Morty Feldman. He said to Burgh, "The night of the soul. Did you really have to go there?"

"How could I not?"

"But why? Your earlier works were so wonderful. Now, it's all misery. Why?"

"Maybe you really didn't understand the early ones either."

"Peter, I always thought I was one of your close friends, close enough to be honest with you. There's gotta be more to art and life than what you've just given us."

"Not to me."

That night, Burgh paced his studio, unable to sleep.

* * *

A few days after the opening, a burly sculptor, sporting cowboy garb with a hand-rolled cigarette hanging from the corner of his mouth, staggered up to Burgh at the Cedar and bellowed drunkenly, "Everyone says you've lost it. I say you never had it."

Burgh replied sneeringly, "Behold the shitkicking Wild West welder doing the Jackson Pollock schtick. Are we really supposed to take a pathetic hayseed like you seriously?"

"You will when I beat the crap out of you."

Burgh stared at him, "Be my guest, big macho man. Beth over there has more balls in her left tit than you'll ever have."

"I don't hit old people."

"Yes, that's sweet of you, you yellow-livered phony."

Herman Wilson came over and said sheepishly, "You're drunk Sam. Let me take you home."

Burgh suddenly lost his temper, turned on Wilson, and shouted, "You agree with this frigging shitkicker. If you couldn't make believe you were my friend, you'd be a zero. Creeping around parroting 'me and Peter, me and Peter,' like a fucking broken record. That's all you ever had going for you, you no-talent jerk. Whose ass will you kiss now?"

John, who was tending bar, came over and said, "Peter,

you're bugging the guys. Please, cool it. If you don't, I'll have to ask you to leave."

Burgh turned to protest, but said quietly, "Alright Sarge, I'm on my way out."

At the door, Burgh turned and shouted at Morgan. "I only meant to put down Paul Bunyan over there and his ass-kissing playmate—not to say anything nice about your left tit. You're a frigging bitch. Sure, you can paint, unlike Herman here, but your stuff is second-hand and second-rate, and you know it. Put it up against a de Kooning and it fades into the wall."

* * *

The art world's growing fascination with assemblage and Pop Art further fueled Burgh's anger and depression. He took it as a betrayal of all he stood for, and despised it. And this fake art was commanding art world attention at the expense of real art. His kind of art. He felt that Pop Art glorified the growing commercialization of art. Burgh was unable to control his anger. He had had rages before, but they were rare and generally aimed at people he believed were wasting his time. Now, let anyone have a good word to say about Andy Warhol or Roy Lichtenstein, and he erupted into a cursing tantrum. When, with an effort, he calmed himself, he wondered where the fury had come from, the madness.

* * *

On a visit to Burgh's studio, Nichols said, "I hate to say this, but I much prefer your earlier painting. These are so gloomy. You know, collectors won't buy them—too depressing."

"I'm not painting them with selling in mind."

"Sure, sure, I understand Peter, but…" Nichols shook his head sadly.

Burgh turned to Nichols and blurted, "Mort, I've heard that you've bought a Warhol."

"Yeah, and a Lichtenstein. Their stuff is new and kinda exciting. Don't get me wrong. Those popsters aren't in the class of you old guys, but it's different and, like I said, kinda interesting. Very now."

"Interesting? Comic strips? You can't be serious. You don't see illustrations of Campbell's soup as a rejection of what our painting stands for? Our values, our dreams?"

"No, not at all. It's just something different. You do your thing, they do theirs. Different takes, different styles, you know."

"I can't believe you're saying that. What about our vision of painting the human condition? Our aspirations to high art? Our enemy was kitsch and hucksterism. And that's what Pop Art is, glorified commercial art. Can you really hang a Warhol next to a de Kooning, a Guston, a Rothko, or, for that matter, a Burgh?" *If Nichols' idea that Pop Art is the relevant art of our time, am I and my guys passé, history?*

He felt the anger rising in him. "Yeah, *you* can. Finally reverted to your true nature—the schmattas in the soul of Morton Nichols. You talk about art as if you love it, but what you are really after is to be trendy and make a couple of bucks."

"Hey, cool it. I'm your friend, remember?"

"Not anymore."

Burgh lost control and began to shout, "Get the fuck out of my studio!"

Later, when he had calmed down, he felt guilty. Not because he had insulted Nichols, but because once again he had lost his temper. Why the anger? He sensed that the cause was only partly Pop Art. The main source was deep within him.

* * *

Burgh did not feel like going to the opening of the belated Franz Kline memorial show at the Whitney. There was no one there he wanted to see. But Kline had been a good friend, so Burgh reluctantly shaved and put on a suit and tie. At the museum, he nodded at acquaintances but soon became engrossed in looking at Kline's work. Then he heard a voice behind him. "Mr. Burgh?"

He turned. It was Warhol and Simon Copperton, the Modern's trendy curator. Warhol said, "Um, Mr. Burgh, I love your work."

"I wish I could say the same about yours"

"Um, I know you and your friends don't like it. I wish I knew why."

"Come off it. You must know why. Painting soup cans. How dumb can you get?"

"Um, but I love Campbell's soup."

"Better than my painting, or what? Are you for real, or

are you putting on an act?"

Copperton spoke up, "Andy paints what he likes, and what America likes. America likes Campbell's soup. What's wrong with that?"

"He may as well paint money."

"He has."

"And he considers that high art? You can't be serious. I can't believe you mean that."

Warhol's expression did not change. "But I do."

Copperton interjected, "And so does the art world. We're in a big generational divide here. Andy just wanted to tell you that he likes your painting. That's all."

"He said 'love.' But what does he love about them? Can he treat art as a business and copy soup cans and love my work at the same time?"

"Sure he can. Why are you so hostile?"

"Hostile? I've been perfectly civil. Yeah, we are in a generation disconnect. I know Duchamp's work—and Duchamp, for that matter. He has an interesting mind but was a lousy painter, so he thought up the Readymades. Produce art without making it. It was a smart idea—a long, long time ago. But it's come back to haunt us with the likes of soup cans. Am I supposed to be impressed?"

"Yeah, soup cans. That's exactly what makes Warhol different from Duchamp."

"We worked our asses off to make new art, avant-garde art, with a profound message about our time."

"Warhol's work speaks to our life in America today."

"The America I hate. His stuff copies what already exists. It isn't new. And what's worse, it's kitsch."

"There isn't anything like it in art. It's original. Face it."

"Face it? Never. But I'm about to blow my top, so I'd better be off. Good day to you, Mr. Andy Warhol and Mr. Simon Copperton."

As Burgh walked away, he glanced back and saw Warhol and Copperton looking after him quizzically. *Can Warhol really believe he's like me because we're both painters? If he manufactures pictures of soup cans that sell, and I paint abstractions that sell, does that make us both business artists? Birds of a feather? Is he putting me on? He must be. Even so, why was I so bitchy to them? They must think I'm nuts. Maybe I am. Fuck 'em.*

* * *

Burgh began to spend more time at museums. Looking at old and modern masters was alternatively comforting and unnerving. At the Met, he would always check the room in which Pollock's *Autumn Rhythm* and his own *Elegy* were installed. Unfortunately, he had to listen to remarks of other visitors.

Once, Burgh encountered two couples standing in front of *Autumn Rhythm*. The fat man scowled, "It's scribble-scrabble. Your five-year-old could do it better. What are we looking at this shit for?"

Fat woman, evidently his wife, answered. "I read in *Life* that the museum paid thirty thousand for this painting. They say he's a great artist."

Thin man, belligerent, "Who says?"

Thin woman, placatingly, "Critics and curators, I guess."

Thin man, smirking, "Bunch of phonies, I'll bet."

Fat woman, thoughtful, "This picture, it's called *Elegy*, looks kinda sad."

Fat man, scoffing, "Another critic heard from. You mean sad, like in tragic, or sad, like in lousy?"

Thin man, jeering, "She means sad, like this asshole here can't paint."

The fat woman shook her head resignedly.

Fat man, taunting, "You really think this isn't just crap?"

Thin man, derisive, "Better get her out of here or she'll want to buy one. We can hang it in the toilet."

Thin woman, edgy, "That's not funny." Turning to Burgh, she asked, "What do you make of this? What do you think it's supposed to mean?"

Burgh responded, "How does it make you feel?"

Thin man, snorting, "Like getting the hell out of here."

"Then why don't you?"

Thin man, hostile, "You trying to be smart?"

"Why are you so angry? Is it because something in the work is reaching you and you won't accept it, or because the work doesn't look like what you expect art to look like?"

Thin man, angry, "It looks like shit and it ain't art."

"But why look at it if it bothers you?"

Thin man, his voice rising, "Bothers me? Makes me want to puke. Let's get the fuck outta here."

As they left, the fat woman glanced sympathetically at Burgh. He smiled back. *What a farce! But something's gotten across to one of them. How much can we expect from the great American public? But the audience for our work is growing. And we now hang at the Met.*

Burgh left quickly, feeling even more hopeless than when he came.

* * *

Burgh's show at the Jones Gallery had come down months ago. Nothing had sold and the works had been returned to the studio. The critics had ignored it. Much as he had prepared himself for misunderstanding and rejection, when it occurred, it rankled him more than he had expected. *I can understand the public not liking it, but the art world? That hurts.*

As he smoked a cigarette and sipped a scotch, he looked at one of his canvases. *It's sad. Is Stein the only one who can see what I'm after, that I have to reveal my life, my sorry life? He suddenly thought of Pearson and their last discussion. I had called his slashed paintings nihilist. What is my work now? What's left to paint? Am I painted out? Dead in the water? Does it matter? I've got to get a handle on myself. Take a break, get out of town, smell some flowers. Or I'll flip out and end up like Frenhofer.*

* * *

Going away proved to be too much of an effort. Burgh stayed in New York, trying to paint with growing frustration.

* * *

After Burgh's show, the Jones Gallery mounted a show that "established" Pop Art in the art world. When he found out,

Burgh phoned Rothko and the other Abstract Expressionists represented by Jones. They were as furious as he was and were planning to leave the gallery. Burgh called Jones in a rage. "How could you show Warhol and those other creeps? How could you?"

"Calm down, Peter. Showing Pop Art doesn't change how I feel about your work. It may even help me sell it. Proximity to new art keeps the gallery alive. Hip. Know what I mean?"

"Bullshit, you're using our work to give cachet to that crap. We're now being used to promote the enemy. You've sold us out. I always thought you understood our vision, that you were one of us. I was wrong. You're just a lousy money grubber, like the corrupt kitsch you're now peddling."

"Easy, Peter, try to see it my way."

He calmed down and said sadly, "I thought you were different, Stan, that you believed in what we were painting, but I was wrong. What's the use of talking? Just send my stuff back to the studio."

* * *

Burgh stopped going to the Cedar, the Club, exhibition openings, and the lofts of friends (who did not seem to miss him, since few called). At first, the loneliness was painful. He would console himself by thinking that he was in what Harold Rosenberg termed "an interior exile," and that it was the situation of the authentic contemporary artist—solitude and despair. Then, he would pour himself another scotch and soon it didn't matter.

Burgh sat in his studio studying the latest of his finished dark paintings. He looked at it impassively. *Can't do another homage to Frenhofer. Nothing more to say. Give it all up or try something else? But what?*

He replaced the painting on the wall with one from 1954 and began to reproduce it, brush dab by brush dab. After six hours, he was exhausted. He stepped back to take it all in. He thought, not bad, not bad at all. Actually, it's quite good. He sat down. *Reduced to forging my own work.*

He scraped down the canvas. Unable to obliterate the ghosts, he grabbed a knife, and angrily scraping it, cut a gash in the canvas.

* * *

The more Burgh tried to paint, the more despairing he became, and the more he drank—until he would become too benumbed to think. Frenhofer would involuntarily come to mind. *Poor bastard, works ten years on a painting. It was going to be the ultimate painting.*

He found the Balzac novel and leafed through the pages. *Who is it that Frenhofer is talking to? Yes, here it is, Poussin and Pourbus. He tells them, "My painting is not painting; it is a feeling, a passion." Poussin tells him that all he can make out is "a confused mess of colors held in place by strange lines which form a wall of painting." What would Poussin say if he saw my painting, all that gray muck? Then Frenhofer kicks his friends out of the* studio. He thinks that all of his long and hard labor has yielded "Nothing! Nothing," and he trashes the work and he dies. Do I, Peter also have a screw loose? I need another drink.

CHAPTER 14: Neil Johnson
(December 7, 1962)

The dinner after Richard Diebenkorn's opening at the Celia Loeb Gallery was hosted by Nichols. Johnson and Knight were invited. They had been together at other art world events and had kept their distance. But that night, her cool began to rile him. As the person who had first told Loeb about Diebenkorn, Stein was also a guest, and his presence further annoyed Johnson. Johnson was still angry at Nichols for auctioning his paintings, and his resentment worsened when he found out that his host had bought two Diebenkorns. The final irritant was Diebenkorn's work—its painterly quality intimidated Johnson.

He quickly gulped a double scotch and walked over to Diebenkorn, who greeted him cordially, but Johnson regarded this as condescending. He said, "Your painting is okay, but I can't help thinking you take an academic figure and fuck it up with academic action painting. Two kinds of passé academicism."

Diebenkorn smiled and said softly, "Could be," and walked away.

Johnson started after him but turned to the bar, ordered

another double scotch and stood by himself, drinking and glowering. He knew he ought to leave but went to the dinner nonetheless. During the meal, the conversation turned to the topic of Burgh's last show.

Johnson poured himself a glass of red wine, downed it, and said drunkenly, "The creep's lost it. Marshall Hill says he never had it."

Knight responded quietly, "What do you mean lost it? I found the new paintings very dark. I'd say tragic."

Belligerently, "Tragic?" Mockingly, "Oh, woe is us, woe is us. Is that the Diane who screwed Peter talking?"

Coolly, "You owe your career to him. You should be grateful."

Angrily, "Owe him what? For turning the art world against me? I'll never forgive that bastard, never, and I'll get back at him."

Sawyer turned to Nichols. "The repartee tonight has a certain sparkle, wouldn't you say?"

"You know, Neil," said Nichols, trying to establish some decorum, "Burgh never bad-mouthed you, even after your *Art News* interview."

Knight added, "He had other things to think about, like painting great pictures."

Stein flashed a "well done" smile at her. *You're a smart one and a good artist and beautiful. I'll phone.*

Johnson caught Stein's signal and turned on him. "I hear you're also a Burgh fan. Someone as blind as you would have to be."

Smiling, Stein said, "It's not only me who likes Burgh. It's my seeing-eye dog. He cued me in. Great nose for a great art, that pooch. And he sniffs it out without Hill as his pointer."

"Think that's funny, you shit. You tried to fuck me up at the Met. Did Burgh put you up to that?"

"But we ended up by taking your work, even with me still against it. Do you expect everyone to love your work?"

"I ought to kick your ass. What am I even doing here with you losers. I'm outtahere." He stood up.

"Please, not on my account," said Stein.

Johnson sat down and snarled, "Nah, I'm not ready to go, not yet. I'm not done with you, asshole."

Loeb spoke up harshly, "Oh, yes you are. This is Diebenkorn's party. You're finished here. Now leave this instant."

Johnson looked angrily at his dealer. She stared back stonily and said, "Now!" He quickly calmed down, saying plaintively, "I didn't mean to make a scene or insult any-one. It was just the liquor. Excuse me." He turned to Diebenkorn. "Forget my putdown of your work. I really do think it's okay." To Nichols, "Thanks for the dinner." Johnson staggered out.

* * *

Two days later, Stein invited Knight to lunch. They arranged to meet at the Tanager Gallery's Christmas show. It consisted of a hundred small works—a cross-section of the art world. Stein and Knight looked at the work in a leisurely fashion, commenting on their likes and dislikes. Standing in front of Knight's painting, Stein said, "It may be small, but it's the best painting of yours that I've seen. It struts."

"Thank you." Pointing to the de Kooning, Knight said, "How does it hold up against that?"

"Apples and oranges. Bill has been at it for a little longer than you. And the content is different."

"How about the Burgh?"

"Same as with Bill. I've only come around to Burgh recently. I now think he's a great painter."

Over lunch at the Cedar, Diane said, "Talk about greatness, the Tanager is in my neighborhood and I look in on it a lot. I know that my work holds its own quite nicely, but I keep looking back and forth from my picture to Bill's and to Peter's and back. They may have been working longer than I have, like you say, but I know that I'll never paint with that kind of originality, big vision, and authority. Never, no matter how much time I have." Knight suddenly looked distraught. "I've thought a lot about it. I paint what's me. It's small stuff."

"Bonnard's vision was no bigger than yours. And neither was Vuillard's."

"I still keep thinking I'll never be first-best. Will that make me quit? No way. But people will keep looking at Peter's paintings—and Bill's and Guston's—at the Modern while mine are buried in the storage bins of provincial museums, if I'm lucky. Sometimes I think, how can I justify my life as an also-ran, if that?"

They sat silent for a while. Then Stein said, "That's not for you to decide. If you could figure out some better way to spend your life than painting, then you should go with it, but I don't think you will. So, as lawyers say, the point is moot. We're living through a great period in art. Our guys are the best in the world. And you're one of them. Let the future take care of itself. Besides, as Groucho Marx once said, 'What's the future ever done for me?' Maybe, your destiny is in the collages. Your dealer is doing a real PR job for you. He's convinced an important sector of the art world that you are a double threat. You can choose one medium or go with both."

"I'm not ready to decide yet. I can't give up painting, but maybe my future is with the paste-ups."

"Hey, you don't have to make up your mind yet. You're still a kid artist, you know."

Knight laughed and looked seductively at Stein.

He caught her look and responded with a warm smile. *We're on the same wavelength. Yeah!*

She said, "It occurs to me that we never mentioned Neil's moronic behavior the other day."

"You put that halfwit in his place, but good. Nothing more to say. Still, he's an interesting case study. Lurching from de Kooning to Burgh to Hill, like a drunken groupie. Hill made him second fiddle, just below Martin and Karl. He's just using Johnson to boost his two favorites, but when he can inveigle another promising painter to play second fiddle, he'll demote Johnson, let him hang around as window dressing, sell some of his work, but not do much more for him. I wonder what Johnson will do then. I won't hold my breath, but I'm curious."

"I guess I should let bygones be bygones, but I still wish him the worst."

* * *

Stein phoned Knight and invited her to join him at an opening of Hofmann's paintings at the Met. Later, they had a snack at the Cookery and he took her home. She invited him in for a nightcap. As they sat on her couch, he said, "The more we meet, the more attractive you become. I think I may be falling in love, corny as that sounds."

"Ditto."

They both burst out laughing. Without another word, she stood and began to undress. He followed suit. They stood naked looking at each other. She led him into the bedroom. "I'm ready," she said, "I want you inside." She lay on the bed, spread her legs, and guided his penis inside her. As his body pounded against hers, she came, shuddering and moaning. He kept thrusting, every thrust eliciting a laugh that seemed to well up from her depths. "Yes, yes, I love it, yes, yes." Her delight was infectious. She began to gyrate in abandon. Then he came with a low moan. They lay together.

"You're still throbbing inside me."

"I hope it never stops."

"Is it love?

"What else? My love loves me, and my love can fuck."

"Our drinks have gotten watery. Let me refill them."

She turned on the radio. Mozart.

They lay propped up in her bed, sipping their drinks and listening.

He said, "You have the most stunning ass and tits. Just looking at you turns me on."

"So I see. Eros is rising. I think I'll give it a little nudge."

Over breakfast, she asked, "Whose place do we live in, mine or yours?"

"Both. One week you commute uptown, one week, I'll commute downtown. Best of both possible worlds."

* * *

Hill looked at Johnson's paintings one by one. The second time around, he stopped at the seventh and exhaled loudly. "That's it. That's the way you ought to go."

Hill soon left. Johnson tacked up a fresh canvas, but as he began to follow Hill's dictate, he saw other interesting possibilities and began to explore them instead. The more he worked, the more excited he became about these new ideas. He worked with a passion he hadn't felt for some time.

When he had completed ten canvases, he phoned Hill. "Hey, Marshall, you've got to see these new babies of mine."

Hill studied the pictures. He said coldly, "Nah, nah, they're no good, no good at all."

"But, I've poured all of myself into them."

"So you get an 'E' for Effort and an 'R' for Rotten. I know I'm right, but just in case, I'll ask Martin and Karl to take a look and see what they think."

It didn't take any imagination on Johnson's part to predict what they would say.

* * *

A week later, at a gathering of Hill's côterie at his apartment, Johnson noted that his picture had been banished to the hall. Hill turned to Martin and asked, "What did you think of Neil's new pictures?"

"Just like you said, Marshall, in a word, crapola."

Hill said sarcastically, "That's not nice. You know that Neil gave them his all."

Johnson bristled at Martin, "What's wrong with them?"

Hill interjected, "You poured your soul into the works, like you said, *o sole mio*, and painted with your brush up your ass."

A roar of laughter from the Hillites.

"But there's more. Your work doesn't add a thing to the future of modernist painting, not a goddamn thing. It's a cop-out. What about it, Karl?"

"I think that Neil ought to do the history of art a favor and junk the whole shitty mess. And if he can't paint better pictures, he ought to quit."

"That, Karl, is a very judicious suggestion. If it's shit, down the toilet with it."

More laughter from the Hillites. Johnson had been witness to such bullying of other Hillites in the past, and he sat silent.

* * *

Johnson phoned Hill the following day and said that he had looked very hard at his new paintings with Hill's criticism in mind, and had decided that Hill's "eye" had been vindicated again. The work was inferior and he would destroy it. *Like hell, I will. But I did kiss the sadist's corrupt ass. Never again.*

Hill said curtly, "Just do like I suggested and call me when you have."

Johnson debated whether to show up at Hill's next Sunday night or phone to see whether he should come. He decided to go and suffer the verbal flogging for his disobedience. Hill ignored him, Martin and Karl patronized him, and, worst of all, Sammy Schort solemnly offered advice. Johnson said, "Yeah, interesting. I see what you mean. Yeah, Yeah." *You pompous punk-ass shit, Sammy Schort. Unbelievable. Advising me how to paint, that fucking bottom-of-the-Hillite. But, I've really fallen into deep shit. Still, as long as Marshall sells me, I'll grin and bear it. But I won't forget.*

* * *

Johnson stored away the pictures put down by Hill. He began again to paint as the critic's brush. After he had completed fifteen pictures, he mailed a note to Hill suggesting a visit to his loft. Six weeks later, Hill stopped by.

* * *

Hill said, "Now that's better, Neil, and you are certainly ready for a show. But there is a small problem. Celia doesn't think she can do any more for you. She's sold your work to all of her collectors, and her market's dried up. Besides, she hasn't forgiven you for your Diebenkorn tantrum. At any rate, it's time to move to fresh pastures. The Wheatley Gallery people are interested, and I would advise you to accept their offer."

"Why not Emmerich?"

"Nah, he doesn't like your work."

"Couldn't you talk to him?"

"Nah, nah, It won't help. He's too much of his own man. You know that."

"I don't know about Wheatley. His stable isn't the greatest. I'm a little short of cash. Will Wheatley buy a couple of my works?"

"I'll see what I can do. I think I can make him understand that you'll upgrade his gallery."

* * *

Johnson sat at the Cedar dejectedly twirling the ice in his scotch. *Well, at least Wheatley is buying my paintings. Marshall is a fucking sadist, but he wouldn't wreck the market he created for me, and he does own nine of my paintings. But I won't play third fiddle to Martin and Karl. Or second for that matter. No more. Where do I go from here? What are my options?*

In one of his increasingly rare appearances, Burgh walked in and sat down at the bar. Johnson's face flushed. He walked up to Burgh, shook his fist at him, and said angrily, "Loeb, that bitch dropped me." Burgh looked startled, "Sorry."

"What do you mean, 'sorry,' you son of a bitch? You did it, you got her to kick me out."

"That's crazy."

"Crazy, huh? Think I'm blind? You've been stabbing me in the back since that interview in *Art News*. But you've gone too far now, you son of a bitch."

"That's weirdo paranoid. You're the last thing on my mind."

Johnson lunged at Burgh, knocking him off his stool, and jumped on him. Burgh jabbed up and hit him in the mouth, causing Johnson to fall back.

John raced around the bar, grabbed Johnson, and shoved him out the door.

"None of that in my bar. Now go home and cool off."

Johnson shouted through the door at Burgh. "You haven't heard the last of me. I'm gonna pay you back for fucking up my life!"

Burgh got up, brushed himself off, and said to John. "Poor bastard is out of his mind."

* * *

The next day, as Johnson was discarding some old mail, he saw a letter that had come a week earlier offering him an associate professorship at South Colorado University. He had thought then, me? Teach? Across the Hudson? *Getouddahere.*

Now, re-reading the letter, he thought this job might be his ticket out. *Out! Outta Burgh, outta Hill, outta New York, at least for a while. I can see it now. "Big-Time New York Hotshot Brings Enlightenment to the Boondocks." Pay's good. A studio's part of the deal. Okay, pardner, pack your bags, saddle up. Go west, young man. Professor Neil is on the trail. You lucky corn-fed nookies.* Suddenly Neil felt light-hearted and physically lightened, as if a heavy burden had been lifted from his mind. That night he went to sleep without thinking about Burgh.

CHAPTER 15: Peter Burgh
(February 4, 1963)

Pearson rang Burgh's doorbell. No answer. The door was unlocked, and he entered. The window shades had been drawn and the studio was dark. He heard Burgh's voice, more like a croak, "Whoever the fuck you are, fuck off." Pearson found the light switch and flicked it on. Burgh, in his underwear, was lying on the couch facing the wall. The floor was littered with empty and half-full scotch bottles, cigarette butts, half-eaten donuts, and rotting sandwiches.

"Christ, Peter, it's two-thirty. You look awful and smell even worse. This place is a god-forsaken shit hole. What have you been doing, peeing in your pants or on the floor? When did you last bathe or change your clothes?"

Pearson released the shades and threw open a window.

"I heard about the art world response to your last show, and I thought you might need my help. And when I couldn't get through by phone, I thought I'd better check on you. But I didn't think you'd be this far gone. I've been away for ten months and look at you. You've been on a binge all that time, haven't you? Yeah, you really need my help."

Burgh looked up, shielding his eyes from the light.

Blearily he said, "Oh, it's you." Composing himself somewhat, he added, "Do you really think a pathetic drunk like you can help me?"

"Pathetic drunk? Past history."

Burgh peered up at Pearson, "Shaved, cut your hair, got clean pants and shirt. A brand new Little Mike. I don't want your help. Bug off."

His slashed canvas caught Pearson's eye. Pointing at it he said, "Pretty artful cut there, Peter. I see that I've inspired you. What'll you title it, 'Homage to Little Mike'?"

"Who the fuck do you think you are? The frigging Good Fairy?"

"Well, at least you're *compos mentis*."

"Why don't you just scram?"

"I may do just that, but not until after we've talked. I owe you, Peter. Payback for when you took care of me when I was down and out. You saved my no-good life. Fuck gratitude. We go further back than either of us cares to remember, so far back that I bet I'm the only friend you can really talk to. Just remember, I've been where you are. Hell, I'm the world's foremost authority."

"You're about to be a frigging ex-friend."

"When did you eat last? I'm going to the store. If you lock me out, I'll break down your goddamn door. For old time's sake, try to get up, take a shower, put on some clean clothes, even shave."

When Pearson left, Burgh did get up, showered, changed, and brewed a pot of coffee. He picked up the empty bottles and half-eaten food and pitched them into a garbage bag. Pearson returned with a large paper container and washed some glasses, cups, dishes, and knives. He poured orange juice, cut two bagels, smeared them with cream cheese, and slapped slabs of smoked salmon on them. Burgh looked at them with distaste but began to nibble on one.

"Now Peter, we've got to talk—old buddy to old buddy."

Burgh stared at Pearson, "What in the hell have you done with yourself? Where'd you get the new suit? Steal it?"

"Yeah, yeah, I'll tell you my saga later. First, we talk about you."

"I need a drink."

"All right, I'll pour you one. Then we talk. You're too weak to push me out of here. Call the cops, if you like."

Pearson picked up a quarter-full bottle of scotch, poured some in a glass, handed it to Peter, and said, "First, a little homemade therapy. You're a depressive and so am I. It takes one to know one. And you have whopping personal problems. But your art was always the real thing, and it still is. You are always pushing beyond, God knows to what, and never satisfied. That in itself can be depressing. Well, now you've gotten to the end of the line, looking at the End with a capital 'E' in the eye. You can't stomach it, you can't back away, and you can't go on. Am I right?"

"Terrific, you're a deep, deep thinker Dr. Siggy. Your analysis is too frigging long-winded and full of crap. You want the thirty-second version? I can't paint. And if I can't paint, I drink, period."

"It's killing you."

"Big frigging deal."

"Peter, you can't decide once and for all that you can't

paint. You've had a helluva run, and you've run out of steam. You've got to give yourself a break. Take some time off, a year maybe. Pull yourself together. You've got the dough to do it. Go to a clinic and dry out. That's what I did. Then maybe visit your ex-wife and daughter, if only to see your kid. Then start anew. Fiddle around with a pencil on paper. Just do it."

"I can't just fiddle around. The only thing worthwhile in my life is my painting. That's who I am. If I lose that, what remains is nothingness. Non-being. And you want me to *fiddle* around?"

"To get you started, change your life, it can help."

"Change to what?"

"Come on Peter, ease up on the melodrama. I saw a reproduction of a recent painting of yours. It seemed profoundly moving. Really tragic—at death's door. Maybe you can press further. Or find a way back. You might even find redemption. God. Who knows? Whichever way, it'll take genius. Well, you've got a bucket full of that."

"I'm very inspired by your little homily, Father Little Sartre. Now what's your story?"

"I'll reveal all, but first, let's get out of this dump, go someplace decent, and get a good meal."

Seated at a table at the Jumble Shop, Pearson said, "I'm going to give you the long version of my saga. Saga? It'll sound more like a soap opera. Why tell you? Because you're the only one I can tell, and it may even be of some use to you."

He paused and looked questioningly at Burgh. Burgh said, "Go on." Relieved to see that his friend was interested,

Little Mike continued.

"Okay, I took a teaching gig in the boonies. Used some of the money you gave me to pay my studio rent. Out there in the middle of nowhere I decided to face up to myself and try to get a life. I knew it was then or never. We last talked when I slashed some earlier work—not that much of it, thank God, but some. Strange as it may sound, the cuts were very arty and the pictures still looked good. One even sold. Can't get art out of my fingers. So I was receptive to those phony revolutionaries on the Bowery. Besides, they liked my slashed canvases. How dumb can you get? But it made me feel young again, like reliving my proletarian past. And with my new comrades, I railed against the assholes who controlled the art world, even though I knew that it was mostly bull. Then, my radical buddies began to go at each other's throats over who was ideologically correct, just like we did in the old days. Remember, one day you would be a hero of the working class, the next day, a social fascist. But their arguments were even more stupid than ours. I tried to tell those kids how dumb they were, and I got accused of all sorts of counter-revolutionary crap, so I dumped them.

"And then there was my work. I was never original, but I was a damn good painter, and for most of my career, an honest one. I was off to a good start with my Social Realism, but I gave it up when it struck me as phony. I really believed in the geometric stuff I did next, really did, but it went out of fashion and no one wanted it. On top of that, my vision of a brave new, totally rational world struck me as a fraud. So I loosened up the geometry, and began to introduce irrationality into my work. I tried to do the best I could. Slashing it was the end. Now, I've gone back to geometry, the new hard-edge kind, you know, like Ellsworth Kelly and Al Held. I'm still not original, but my paintings are fresh and good, damn good, and they're mine, and I love painting them.

"Out there in the sticks, I decided that I'd had enough of self-pity. So I looked up a shrink, joined Alcoholics Anonymous, and became a new man. Looked up the wife. She wouldn't let me see the kids at first. So I waited across the street from her house for half a day. She came out to chase me away but when she saw how I had changed, she relented and let me take them out for ice cream. She's done a decent job with them, no thanks to me. But at least they know their dad is no bum. Not anymore."

"Back to you now, Peter. I know that my stuff is good, but yours is great, always has been. Whatever you decide to paint, it will still be great. And it's worth your life trying to. Damn, this preaching is a bitch."

He said, with anguish in his voice "Peter, if you don't get yourself together you're going to kill yourself, I mean really die. Please, please, face it."

Burgh sat silent for a long time. Then he said simply, "Okay, now what?"

"I don't think Alcoholics Anonymous will work for you. Too spiritual. I've got the name of a clinic upstate. My shrink told me about it, just in case I needed it. Says it's decent. Will you try it? I'll rent a car and drive you up there myself."

"Okay, I'll give therapy a try. Give me a couple of days to sort things out. I really don't think a shrink will help. This painter's block is different. I've had them in the past, more than I like to remember. Sitting in front of a bare canvas for days at a time, or after weeks of painting, waking up one morning and seeing that it was all false—self-indulgence, self-deception—and had to be destroyed. How often have I thought, terror-stricken, that I could never paint again? That I wouldn't even know how to begin. But I really knew I would. The kind of block I now have is new. It's a total paralysis and a constant torment. It's a sickness—not any old mental kind—but a sickness of the soul, whatever that is, and it has destroyed me. I can't even bear to look at my paintings anymore, or any other art. I went to the Modern a few times and got out as fast as I could. The Met was no better. Imagine, running away from Rembrandt. And then I have these weird recurring nightmares about being lost in some wilderness and encountering some shadowy fig-ure, a walking corpse, with a rifle who shoots me between the eyes, like in a horror movie. And I wake up sweating with scary heartburn and anxiety attacks that take my breath away—the physical signs of heartache. The dead in my past are rising from their graves to haunt me in my dreams. There's no going back or getting around whatever it is that's eating me. Drink is the only consolation. All those words, what a crazy roll."

"I understand. I'm not going to bug you anymore today. One more thing. In Kansas U's library, I picked up an *Art News* and saw a reproduction of a picture of mine being shown at the Met. It was one you bought. I couldn't believe it. Some critic—name of Sawyer—Thomas Sawyer, no, Joseph Sawyer, raved about it. Then a story ran in the *Times* about this unknown artist. You're quoted. I phoned Herbert Stein. He says that collectors want to buy some paintings. You did that for me. See, like I told you, I'd be famous and you'd be rich. You and I know the work's good but not great." Pearson went on to say, "Peter, if an asshole like me can clean up his act, so can you. Give it a shot."

"Your act's not completely clean, not until you stop whining about being a mediocrity. It's getting on my nerves, so just cut it out. You're a terrific painter. And maybe you've discovered what to paint. And stop trying to be a great artist, like you seem to think I am. Just paint it. My bill for that advice will be in the mail."

"Good advice. Now take it yourself."

* * *

Pearson drove Burgh to the clinic. On the way, Burgh gave him a sealed envelope and said ominously. "I gave you a duplicate of this folder some time ago. It's a kind of will. If anything happens to me, open it and follow the instructions."

Pearson walked with Burgh to the door of the clinic. As they parted, Burgh said, "Well, wish me luck. Maybe the shrinks here will have some answers."

* * *

The room at the clinic consisted of a single bed, table, chair, bureau, closet, and a small alcove with toilet and sink. But, Burgh noted, no lock on the door. On the wall was a picture of flowers. The antiseptic smell was off-putting, but the sparseness of the room was comforting, particularly after Burgh removed the picture. He soon wanted a drink, needed a drink. A doctor who looked in on him immediately recognized his plight and gave him pills to lessen the desire. "You do understand, Mr. Burgh, that you're in for a rough ride. If it get's too bad, pull the cord by the bed. Someone will try to help you."

"Thanks, I'm going to fight it." *Kick the habit. Take control.*

At ten o'clock the next morning, Dr. Saul Mannheim, the psychoanalyst who was assigned to treat Burgh, walked into his room. Mannheim was a Freudian who went strictly by the book; he even sported a Freud-like beard. He said, "Good morning. Mr. Burgh, follow me, please." He ushered Burgh into his consulting room and beckoned to a couch along one wall. Peter lay down on it. The doctor settled in a chair behind him and said, "I hear you didn't even ask for a drink last night. That was commendable. You may be on your way to getting the better of your alcoholism. To begin with, what do you know about psychoanalysis?"

"I've read some Freud and Jung. In the art world, psychoanalysis is the second biggest topic of conversation, just below art. And a number of my friends are going to shrinks and talk a lot about it."

"Then you have some idea about our procedure. You don't sound as if you believe in it."

"I'm not against it."

"Now, tell me what you think is troubling you."

"Above all, not being able to paint. Then, drinking too much. And what's happening in the art world and the real world, my ex-wife who I can't get out of my head. On top of it all, I get this recurring nightmare about a Marine in my outfit, name of Frankie, who was killed in the Pacific. And he's kind of mixed up with my father who shot himself."

Dr. Mannheim interjected. "You do know that your dreams are critical. How does your father appear in yours?"

"The dead Frankie in his Marine uniform has my father's face with a bullet hole in it."

"Tell me about your father. Let your thoughts wander."

In the following six weeks, Dr. Mannheim focused on Burgh's childhood. Burgh knew that his dreams and early life were the basis of Freudian therapy but, lying on the couch, he became increasingly frustrated. He couldn't make himself care about his childhood. What engaged him in the past were his paintings, the Cold War, politics, and his marriage.

Burgh said to Dr. Mannheim, "You want to deal with my childhood as the root of my problems, but I just don't think that's important." Then Burgh challenged, "When will we deal with my life as an artist, which is what most of my life has been devoted to. And how will you deal with it? What really disturbs me is the sorry state of the world, the Cold War that can turn hot and trigger an atomic holocaust. My concern with politics obsessed me in my youth and in my painting then, and it still does. My private life didn't matter all that much to me back in the thirties. The revolution did, and my life's work was in its service. And so was my art. That's what mattered most. And it still does. I wonder whether my solution is not to find myself but to find my work again."

"Can you find your work without finding yourself? Like Freud said, I would suggest that for now we keep politics and art apart, and concentrate on your unconscious motivations."

In the next session, Burgh said, "Let me tell you about a fictitious artist I identify with and think a lot about. His name was Frenhofer and his ambition was to paint the greatest masterpiece ever. He worked ten years at it, decided he had failed, and committed suicide. Would Freud have had a label for Frenhofer's ambition? It's more significant than some childhood trauma. The ambition to paint works as great as Rembrandt or Piero. All artists share this dream to some degree and, for many, it makes life worth living."

"You mentioned suicide. Have you over considered it?"

"I don't think I could do it. But nothing in my life is as important to me as my art. I understand Frenhofer and empathize with him."

"Does your imaginary artist have other meanings for you? Think of your father's suicide."

Burgh was disturbed by Dr. Mannheim's comment, but he still felt that Freudian therapy was not working for him. His analysis was over. But he had stopped drinking and had begun to review his life. *To save myself, I have to paint. But what? It doesn't matter. Just be in the studio, pick up a brush, like a worker, nine to five. And stay off the booze.*

Burgh checked out of the clinic.

* * *

Upon his return to New York, Burgh stretched a canvas, tacked it to the wall, sat down, and waited for an idea. Nothing. He squeezed some cerulean blue in an old can, thinned it with turpentine, and hurled the pigment onto the canvas. *My homage to Pollock.* He tried to coax images out of the mess, and this got him working again. He now painted spontaneously, literally without thinking. The abstract images that emerged in his canvases were depressing, even more than those in his last show. Without exactly knowing why, he would decide to remove a canvas from the wall, stretch it on the floor to dry, and tack another to the wall. He often seemed to be in some kind of daze, but he painted.

Looking intently at his latest canvas, Burgh decided enough. *Enough gloom. Paint something that is totally different. Why not this chair? Yes, a portrait of a chair.* As he painted, he became increasingly fascinated by it, its "thingness." *No angst in a chair. It's just what it is, an object. Nothing subjective, nothing romantic.* This was comforting. Then he thought, was he supposed to believe in a piece of furniture? He recalled criticizing Knight for depicting a vase, demanding to know why she bothered painting it. But the chair was as real as the vase. Why paint it? Burgh put the canvas aside.

* * *

A phone call from Harvey Ravin. "Peter, long time no see. How's the superannuated action painter?"

"Still schmeering but no masterpieces."

"How about a studio visit?"

"Why not?"

When they met, Burgh said to Ravin, "Remember when I told you that no artist painted the kind of totally spontaneous gesture paintings you called for? Well, I was wrong. I've recently become your kind of painter, no ideas, no pre-conception of form, no thought of anybody's art, my own included. No thinking. No nothing. It's pure improvisation with some emotion I hope. What do you make of that?"

"Well, it's about time."

Burgh brought out three of his new works and placed them along one wall. Ravin sat on a chair and stared at them. After what seemed to him to be a long time, Burgh asked, "What do you think?"

"I came here because Little Mike said you were in a bad way and that I might be of help. You know what came to mind as I looked at them? Auschwitz, the tragic mood. I don't talk about it, but my family survived the Holocaust. I can't say more, except that this is your private genocide. If any work captures the death camp experience, the mood of it, this is it. Adorno said that you can't make art after Auschwitz. If it is possible, you have. I'd keep this to yourself. You'll be accused of cheapening the Holocaust."

"Thank you, my friend."

"What next?"

"There really is no next."

"Can't move on from your private hell?"

"That's about it."

"You know, you've got to step back. You're at the brink and about to fall in. It can kill you."

"I know that, but I don't know what to do about it. It has

to do with the dystopia we're living in."

"Aha, the total reverse of your old commie belief in a future utopia. Nothing seems worth doing. Little Mike said you tried psychoanalysis."

"Yes, but it didn't work."

"Look, life may be shit. But there are things worth doing. You know that. I want you to call me if things get too bad. Promise?"

"Oh, sure. Why not?"

"Let's lighten up. I'll tell you a Jewish joke, even though you're not Jewish, you poor thing. There's this black man on a subway reading a Yiddish newspaper. A Jewish man next to him finally couldn't contain his curiosity and said, 'Tell me, sir, are you Jewish?' The black man answered, '*Dos noch feylt mir*?' Translation: 'This too I'm missing?'"

Burgh laughed and Ravin said, "That's a step in the right direction. Treat tragedy as comedy. I've got a message for you that might take your mind off your misery. There's this newish critic—she's brilliant and droolingly beautiful—who has a crush on your art and wants to meet you. If you're lucky, she may have designs on your body, geriatric though it may be. She may give you a new lease on life. Her name is Marcia Dayson. She wants to write an article on you for *Political Review*. I asked her why a fan of Pop Art would be interested in you. She accused me of pigeonholing her. *PoliRev* with a Dayson article will reach a broad audience of intellectuals you pal around with but don't really love. She's the darling of the literati and their missionary to the avant-garde, even got the cover of *Time*."

"You mean use an affair as therapy?"

"Why not? As a distraction. It can't hurt."

"Yeah, I read a few of her articles. I need to get out of this frigging studio, out into the world. Bring her on."

* * *

Awaiting Dayson's visit, Burgh removed the new canvas from the wall and replaced it with an old one. As she entered the studio, he was stunned by her green eyes and straw-blonde hair that almost reached down to her waist. Tall, slim but with full breasts and ample hips.

He smiled and said, "I won't tell you that you're too beautiful for someone as smart as you."

"But you just did. You're forgiven." She added with a tinkling laugh, "I've got a thing for pretty over-the-hill men, and you're as pretty as they come, for a kid your age, that is. And I am tickled that I find your painting pretty as well. I think we ought to deal with this animal thing first of all. Would you like to fuck me?"

"Can I get back to you on that?"

She again laughed her little laugh. "Certainly, take your time."

"Judiciously contemplating the issue from every perspective, I'd answer in the affirmative. Have you been told that you have a very sexy laugh?"

Sex. Her hair was an erotic turn-on. But the sex was without passion. Dayson was distanced. She barely moved. Later, he asked her if she had had an orgasm. She told him she would in time, but he did not believe her.

Burgh said to Dayson, "Try to convince me that Pop Art

has any validity. And if you love Warhol, how can you admire my painting as well? I would have thought pee and oil don't mix, or is it apples and bananas?"

"As I see it, you and Andy may seem very different but, underneath it all, you are more alike than you think."

"Me and that huckster?"

"He's a gay artist into ironic camp; you're a life-and-death existentialist, weighed down with the high seriousness of purpose. So, how are you and Andy linked? You both comment on your time. Your art is rooted in the hot and cold wars of the forties and fifties. Andy is the high priest of today's consumer culture. He paints its icons."

"Supermarket reliquaries. If there's a Macy's heaven, Warhol is the God or the Son. Who's the Holy Ghost? Nelson Rockefeller?"

"And, you're both tragic artists."

"Campbell's Soup? Tragic? Even your *PoliRev* rhetoric won't persuade me of that."

"Think of Andy's car crashes, race riots, Mona Lisas, and Marilyns. His commodities, too, are pervaded with the aura of death."

"Death of art, if you ask me."

"Maybe that too, but I'm talking about the human condition. Okay, take the soup cans. On the one hand, they represent consumerism and seem to glorify it. But they signify other things as well."

"I can't wait to hear."

"The send-up of consumerism, the shallowness of shopping. This is a profound social commentary in the guise of camp."

"Profound? To duplicate tin cans is profound? Your *Poli-Rev* reviewing sounds more and more like PR. If you do write an article on my work, I hope you keep Andy out of it. Camp? Isn't it supposed to make the serious frivolous? I try to make the serious even more serious. If you team me with Warhol, you would make my art frivolous and his art serious. Let's face it, Warhol's stuff is just kitsch, nothing more. You won't link us, will you?"

"Probably not. But first of all, I need to know more about your art. That's the reason I'm here, that is, aside from ravishing your bod. Talk to me about that picture. How would you characterize the existential situation that it exemplifies?"

"It's a painting. What you're talking about is content. That's all intellectuals seem to experience. What about the painting? Painting is its own thing."

"I know that, Peter, and I will deal with the sensuous dimension above all."

"I wonder."

* * *

That evening after Dayson left, Burgh replaced the old canvas with the new one and began to paint half-heartedly. He was suddenly overcome with the old feeling of confidence in his powers. Poring over the surface, he saw what he had been about semi-consciously. What could he consciously do with it? He would see. He glanced at the dozens of canvases in the rack and thought that he would repaint them.

* * *

Burgh and Dayson saw each other twice or so a week for the next two months. She took him into her world of the *PoliRev* intelligentsia. He showed her his scene, the Cedar, the Club, openings, and parties.

* * *

Dayson did write an essay, which focused on the formal dimension of the paintings in Burgh's last show. Then she introduced Warhol's works and compared them favorably with Burgh's. Much as Burgh admired her cleverness, he was enraged. Above all, he felt betrayed, and when she phoned, he told her that, no, he wasn't really angry, but that they had exhausted their conversation—at least for the time being—and ought to take a breather from their affair. But it wasn't the article that caused him to call it off. Her indifference to sex had begun to curb his desire. It was fine, he thought, to make love to a magnificent body, and to have something to say to one another before and after, but there had to be more. There had to be passion.

* * *

Burgh began to drift back into deepening states of depression and to paint less and less. He would sit for hours looking at a canvas but hardly seeing it. Random thoughts would flit through his mind, often of his father, Frankie, the park in which he played ball as a child, the jungle on a

Pacific beach, or a beach in Coney Island. He would stare at photos in *Time* magazine of corpses in Buchenwald, charred bodies in Hiroshima, a starving child in the Sudan, a mother shot dead in a Belfast street. He would pore over reproductions of Grunewald's *Crucifixion*, Goya's disasters of war, Callot's hangings. His response was not so much of sadness but a kind of numbness. *That's the way it was. Is.*

* * *

Pearson looked in on Burgh often. Recognizing his friend's worsening state, he said, "I know the shrink at the clinic didn't work out, but another might help, not a Freudian but someone who'll deal with your situation now. You need someone to talk to."

"It won't help."

"It's worth a try, isn't it?"

Burgh sat silent. *It is not.*

Pearson continued, "What is it with us? Some of us guys are creating the best art today, some of it will even live for the ages. Yet what a miserable lot we are. Most of us are drunks. Neurotics. Many of us have tried psychoanalysis, and it didn't help. Our marriages are disasters. Then there are the suicides."

Burgh said, "Being a nutcase may be a precondition for our painting. The best of it is tragic. Maybe, too, it speaks to the agony and anxiety of our time."

Pearson countered, "And maybe that's all a big fat rationalization. Van Gogh was a loony, but his art is not, and neither is yours."

"Is it really worth anything? Worth continuing to do? I wish I could convince myself that it was."

"Bullshit. And whining doesn't suit you."

"But I am making progress. I haven't told you once to fuck off."

"That's a good sign. Your buddy, Harold Rosenberg, called American intellectuals a herd of independent minds. As for artists, we're a herd of independent crazies. You've always prided yourself on being original. Why not do something really original? Stop being a loony. Or do you really like wallowing in your shit?"

"I just can't help it. I don't know what to do."

"Well, get off the bottle, keep painting, no matter what, and maybe get a woman."

* * *

Burgh couldn't stop drinking. And he stopped painting. One morning, badly hungover, he glanced at the pile of canvases stacked haphazardly against the wall. *Shit, got to get rid of that crap.* He began to drag canvases toward the door, but the effort exhausted him and he stopped. He would do it later. *First go out for a coffee.* He had never felt this weak before.

As he left the building, he heard a plaintive voice. "Mr. Burgh."

Huddled beneath the stairs by the garbage cans was a woman. Another Bowery bum, Burgh thought. But she seemed familiar, and he looked again. It was the woman he had met in the gallery on the Bowery where Pearson's slashed canvases had been shown.

"I remember you. Sally. No Sheila. What are you doing down there?"

"Waiting for you."

"Why on earth, why?"

"I was living with BRB, you remember him, and he beat me up. So I ran away. I didn't know what to do. I looked you up in the phone book. I don't know why I came here. Maybe because you seemed like a nice man."

"Like a father."

"Not like my father, I hope. Or, for that matter, my mother."

"You must be hungry."

"Yes."

"Well, let's get some breakfast."

Sheila climbed the stairs. Her hair was disheveled, her jacket ripped, and her jeans grimy. Dirt barely covered the bruised spots on her face.

He said, "We can't go into any cafeteria with you looking like this. Better come up to my studio. Take a shower and clean up."

In the studio, he said, pointing, "The bathroom's over there. There are clean towels in the hamper."

"Thanks. I managed to pick up some clean clothes as I ran away. They're in this bag."

Sheila came out of the shower looking like a different person. Her dress was clean and her hair artfully combed to hide the bruises. Burgh looked appreciatively at her legs.

"Now, we can get some breakfast."

She wolfed down orange juice, two eggs, bacon, fried potatoes, and two orders of toast.

"Okay, now tell me what the problem is."

"My life, that's what."

"What about it?"

"It's a mess."

"Let's begin at the end. What do you think you want to do with your life?"

"Be an artist, I guess."

"You can't guess about that. You either are or are not. There's no in-between."

"I know. That's my problem."

"Now, begin at the beginning."

"My father was a brute. He beat me. My mother looked the other way. I got outta there as soon as I could. Had some rough times but got by modeling for Hans Hofmann and trying to learn how to paint. Then I fell in with BRB's crowd. I liked being with them because they hated the establishment."

"I've got the picture. Now that you're here, now what?"

"I don't know."

"Do you need money?"

"I'm broke."

"Okay, I'll hire you to do some work for me."

They went back to the studio. Burgh said to Sheila, "See that pile of rolled canvases? Load them neatly into that walk-in closet over there."

Burgh's mood lightened as he watched Sheila lug his canvases. She was thin, probably undernourished, yet shapely. He reached for a bottle of scotch, then changed his mind. No, he would stay sober. When she had finished that chore, he found more work for her to clean up. Then he took her out to lunch. He was surprised at the quantity of food she managed to put away.

Dinner time. They ordered in Chinese.

Sheila said, "Can I stay here with you tonight?"

"Just this once."

They had sex. He said without thinking, "This will probably be the last time for me." But she was asleep.

Sheila was on the phone when Burgh awoke. She was crying. "O.K., BRB. I'll come back but only if you promise not to hit me, because if you break your promise again, I'll be out of your life forever."

Peter gave her three ten-dollar bills.

"Can I have some more?"

"That's three times more than I pay my helpers."

"But you don't fuck them, do you? Or get as good a fuck?"

Burgh said sadly. "Did you do it for the money?"

"Maybe not yesterday. But today is today."

"Yes, life is tough."

He handed her two more tens.

She left quickly. He found his watch missing. He smiled to himself.

Burgh remembered Harvey Ravin's remark about the tragic quality of his imagery. *A real representation of my feeling, tragic passion. Can I paint the consummate picture? It would be my masterpiece. Frenhofer tried it and it killed him. Or rather, he killed himself when he failed. Well I'm killing myself with booze. His way sounds more interesting. I'll give it a go. For six months.*

Burgh understood that there were no guidelines. He would have to begin with improvisation, and who knew where it would go. He kept the picture hidden, even from Pearson. On the last day of the six months, he invited his friend to his studio, sat him on a chair facing the back of the canvas and quickly turned it around. Pearson looked stunned and, after studying it, remarked, "I don't get it. I need more time."

Burgh had failed. He told Pearson that he wanted to be alone. Sensing his disappointment, Pearson said, "I wish I had loved it, but I had to tell you the truth. It has real possibilities. Give it another shot."

"No," said Burgh. "It's finished." *And I'm finished.*

* * *

Pearson began to visit Burgh daily, bringing him food, which he barely touched, making him shower, and cleaning the loft. Pearson tried to talk to Burgh, but his friend's responses were increasingly garbled and incoherent. Pearson found it painful to witness Burgh's mental and physical deterioration, but he continued to visit him, even when it became unbearable.

* * *

Burgh's condition so oppressed Pearson that he felt he had to talk to someone, but who? Burgh rarely talked about friends he felt intimate with. Then Pearson remembered Knight and phoned her. "Diane, Peter's in a really bad way and I don't know what to do. Can we meet and talk? At the Cedar?"

"I'm free now."

The Cedar was empty when Pearson arrived. He sat down in a booth, ordered a cup of coffee, and was soon joined by Knight.

He said, "I don't know why I'm laying this on you. I can't imagine what you can do about it. But will you please hear me out?"

"Of course, go on."

"I got Peter to check in at a clinic but he only lasted a couple of months. He stayed off the bottle for a time but now he's drinking again, worse than ever. Blackout after blackout."

Pearson removed an envelope from his coat pocket and drew out pieces of paper. "Know what these are? Letters Peter wrote. You wouldn't believe to whom. This one's to Rubens. Let me read it to you. 'Dear Peter Paul—you don't mind me calling you by your first name—your painting stinks. All that meat and no potatoes. What do you imagine the crucified Jesus in your painting would think when he looks around him? The poor bugger's up there dying, and what do you do? You make show biz of it. If there is a heaven, and you and I get to it, I'll kick your phony ass. Cordially.' Here's a letter to God, berating him for making life so miserable and then ending it in death. He also proposes to kick God's ass. Then there are the really, really crazy letters, in which Peter yearns for death, so that he can go to heaven and kick a lot more ass. Then there was the time, after I nursed him through yet another one of his alcohol-fueled manias, I poured all his scotch down the sink. First chance he got, he drank rubbing alcohol.

I rushed him more dead than alive to Bellevue. They suspected suicide and wanted to keep him there. He begged them to discharge him. I still see his look of panic in my nightmares. I made up some cockamamie story about his misreading the label on the bottle. They didn't believe me, but with all they've got to do, they let him go. In the taxi home, he kept moaning, 'Better dead, better dead.' When he calmed down, I said, 'Peter, next time, they'll lock you up in the loony bin, and no one will be able to save you. Do you understand?' He said that he knew and that I was his best pal and that he wanted to die. He began to cry. And I began to cry. Each of us wallowing in self-pity, blubbering. There's much more to tell. Do you want to hear it?"

"No, I've heard enough."

She sat silently, her head bowed, deep in thought.

"What do you think I can do?"

"I don't know. Any ideas?"

"None. Peter obviously wants to die."

"Yes."

Knight suddenly began to sob, quietly but uncontrollably. Pearson was touched by her tears. "Please stop, or I'll begin to cry myself. Please stop."

She calmed down, and sniffling, said, "Knowing Peter, nothing is going to stop him. Not you, not me. No one."

"Yes."

"What are you going to do?"

"Take care of him as best I can. You can't be of any help. I knew that before I phoned you. Thanks, though, for listening."

* * *

Loeb phoned Burgh. "Please, Peter, don't hang up. Grapevine has it that you are ill and depressed. Won't go out or see anyone. I want to help you. Can I come over? Or at least talk?"

"Don't you dare come here. And I have nothing more to say. Goodbye."

"Wait, Peter, please listen, just for a moment. I love you. You know that. I'll do anything for you. Just ask, anything."

"I don't need anything. Goodbye."

"But I do. Please don't be cruel. Can't we just talk?"

"We just did. *Finis*."

CHAPTER 16: Joseph Sawyer

(January 10, 1963)

Having seen Burgh's latest work, Joseph Sawyer recognized that he could not continue writing his book on the artist. This upset him. So did the likelihood that his investment in the Burgh market was anything but secure. Sawyer's misfortune soon took a worse turn. He received a phone call from Patricia Milton, an old friend of his mother's in Athens, Georgia.

"Your mama has had a stroke. She's alright at the moment but we don't know whether she'll recover, or if she does, what her condition will be."

"Oh, my God! I'll come as soon as I can."

Sawyer's mother had not been in contact with him for two years, but with his father dead, he was her only close relative. He'd have to take care of her. She had hardly any money, just a small pension and no savings. There would be medical bills. He had to get his money back from Nichols and Loeb.

Sawyer phoned Nichols. "Mort, my mother in Georgia had a stroke and I must go to her. I need the money I gave you. It's not much. You and Celia can buy me out."

"Sorry Joseph," said Nichols, "I haven't got the cash. I'm way overextended, and my business has fallen off. You know that in order to buy those Burghs, I went heavily into debt. And that investment seems pretty shaky now that fucking Peter killed his career."

Nichols hung up abruptly.

Loeb told him much the same story as Nichols had, but with a twist. "The word on the street is that the Burgh market is really in trouble and might even collapse. That goes for the old works as well as the new. I don't see how I can help you now. I stand to lose enough money without taking you off the hook. I've got a client waiting, have to hang up."

* * *

And then disaster. That very evening, an early Burgh came up for auction at Sothebys. Nichols and Sawyer were in the audience. Nichols was relieved to see major collectors of contemporary art in attendance. He waited for a bid. No takers. His bid was the first—and the last.

Nichols was too distraught to notice Herbert Stein sitting some three rows behind him, but Stein saw his ashen face. He also observed Sawyer make his way to Nichols looking frantic. Nichols turned away from him.

* * *

In a panic, Sawyer called Nichols again. The secretary said that Nichols would call him back. He did not. Sawyer called again and hysterically announced that he was desperate and might do something crazy if he was not put through to Nichols. He was.

"Don't do this to me, Mort. I've got to go to my mother now and need some cash fast. I haven't even got the fare. Tomorrow will be too late."

"No can do. Not after last night's auction. End of conversation."

"Not quite. I know everything about your operation. I want the cash by tomorrow or I'll call *Art News*. Hess will love it."

"Are you blackmailing me?"

"Call it what you will."

"You'll lose your share, asshole. And your reputation."

"I don't care about the future. I need the money now."

"Listen to me, you little shit. You know better than to mess with me."

"I can always kill myself and leave a tell-all confession."

"Awright, lets cut the melodrama. Never say that Morton Nichols doesn't have a soft heart. I'll give you two, that's minus a thou for my trouble. If the Burgh market comes back, I may give you the one back, but don't hold your breath. Be at my office at four o'clock with the contract we signed, and I'll write you a check."

"Make it a money order."

"Don't you trust me, you insulting twerp?"

"With my life, Mort, but not with my money."

* * *

As Nichols gave Sawyer the money order, he said, "Now get this straight. One word out of you about the Burgh business, and....Remember, your career is also on the line."

* * *

Within minutes of Sawyer's departure, Nichols received a phone call that made his stomach ache. "Word has it that our investment in what's-his-name's art is shaky. You said that our fifty G's would yield a hunnerd. That's what you owe us. Unnerstand?"

"Awright, but we agreed that I'd have two years to pay up. And I will make good."

"I'm sure you will, but two years is now six months. Unnerstand?"

Then Nichols heard a click and the dial tone.

* * *

Upon his return to Athens, Sawyer found his mother in better health than he expected. Her friends in the Daughters of the Confederacy had paid her medical bills and provided for a nurse. She wanted her son to stay close to her but couldn't deny him trips to Atlanta.

Visiting a gallery, a painting struck him and he arranged to meet the artist. Word got around that a big-time New York art critic had moved into the area, and he soon had a dozen invitations. The respect he received was extremely gratifying. He also liked the cordial attitude of the artists to each other. They kept recommending that he visit their friends.

Impressed by what he saw, Sawyer phoned Tom Hess and asked if he could write a "Letter from Atlanta" for *Art News*. Hess agreed. Sawyer's article further enhanced his reputation. One of the artists included in the article, Stuart Dalton, the Dean of Studio Arts at the University of Georgia, invited him to teach a course on modern art. Atlanta's not-for-profit art space, AtlantArt, asked him to write catalog introductions. When the director suddenly took ill and had to retire, Sawyer replaced him. The art shown at AtlantArt was not on par with the best in New York, but it was creditable. What Sawyer found most to his liking was the community formed by the artists, the kind of community he yearned for in New York. He had found a home.

Sawyer also found a companion, Adam Meade, an associate professor of art history at the University of Georgia, whom he met at AtlantArt.

Sawyer confided in Meade. "In New York, even when I saw a show I liked, it was distanced from me. Down here, it's different. A lot of the art I see seems to speak to me personally. I can't quite put my finger on it. But it has something to do with this region, growing up in the South. Am I sounding corny?"

"Not really. In literature, we have a Southern School. Maybe there's a counterpart in art."

"I'm going to look for it. I may have to create it."

Sawyer noted that one of the older local artists with forty years of painting behind him had been depicting Confederate paraphernalia in an abstract "action" style. Another artist, three years out of art school, was introducing commercial art imagery that referred ambiguously to the civil rights movement—just enough to mildly shock his fellow white Atlantans. A third was painting landscapes—swamps, cotton fields, one-room churches, and the like. And a fourth had been inspired by local outsider art. None of the artists had had, or would ever have, shows in Manhattan. Then, Sawyer had an epiphany and found his mission. *This work, all of it, was southern—not New York, but southern. Put these good old boys together, and what? A regional school. By God, a regional school. Outside of New York. Give it a name. Southern Outsiders…Outriders…Outliers…Outlaws…Outreach…Southern Outreach…outside of what? New York! On the edge of New York, the Southern Edge. That was it. The Southern Edge.* Then he recalled another painter who used ads with a peculiar southern cast as subjects. That made five. Their group show at AtlantArt did not make news in New York, not yet, but word filtered through the art-conscious Southland.

At a dinner party one evening, a guest wearing a bolo tie strung through a silver bull's head, said to Sawyer, "Name's Billy Cranston, son, from Amarillo. I don't much care for your modern art. I collect cowboy pictures and sculptures myself. But I hear your kind of modern art is southern and could give the goddamn Yankees a run for their money. They tell me you call it Southern Edge. I like what I hear about you."

"I would love to kick some Yankee butt—pardon my language, Mr. Cranston—with regional art from Texas and Florida to Virginia, but I can't make it happen yet, not the way I want to, not yet."

"Why not?"

"I don't want to have to limit myself to Georgia. There's a lot happening all over the South. Good old boys are sending me photos of the most terrific art, really terrific, yeah, and a bunch of it is from your state. But I can't take the next step."

"What's stopping you?"

"Money. I've got to see the work. That'll take travel money, and I haven't got it. I would need to visit Houston and Savannah, for starters. There's an artist in Charleston, name of Jamie Forrest, I'd like to see, and I know there are others."

Cranston cocked his head and gave Joseph a slit-eyed look for which he was famous in Amarillo. "I like you, son, and I think I can trust you. I'll give you some money. How much will you need?"

"I don't know. I'll put some figures together."

"Tell you what. I'll do twenty-five grand. Give it to AtlantArt for your travel and a southern show, like you call it—Southern Edge—that you'll curate."

The slit-eyed look again. "And I'll take a tax write-off."

Sawyer put his thumb in the air. "I can do a lot of Yankee butt-kicking for twenty-five."

CHAPTER 17: Peter Burgh
(September 30, 1963)

On September 30, 1963, at five minutes after ten P.M., Peter Burgh died from a bullet wound to his chest. Pearson called the police. Opening the envelope Burgh had given him, he learned that he was the executor of the artist's estate and his primary heir. Pearson phoned Gilbert Truson, vice president of the Art Dealer's Association, who had been Burgh's lawyer. He told Truson that he would like him to represent the Burgh estate. He also remarked that he didn't think Burgh would have wanted a public funeral, just a private one with his closest friends at Campbell's Funeral Parlor. And a cremation. Truson said, "The art world will expect a public memorial at a later date. If you'd like me to, I'll arrange it. I think I can count on Herbert Stein to get us the Met's auditorium."

Pearson responded, "Please do it."

CHAPTER 18: Herbert Stein
(January 7, 1964)

In a memo to James Canning, Stein wrote, "Now that Peter Burgh is dead and his market has hit rock bottom, I think we ought to buy another of his paintings, perhaps two or even three. There is a lot of controversy about the last body of work. I think it is far more significant than current art world opinion allows. The pieces are selling for very little. We might also think of mounting a memorial show. He is, after all, a first generation Abstract Expressionist and if he doesn't have the reputation of Pollock, de Kooning, or Rothko, I believe he soon will. I'd like to curate the show."

Stein's memo was returned with Canning's scrawl, "Agreed on all requests. Buy what you can up to twenty thousand dollars."

* * *

Stein phoned Mike Pearson and introduced himself.

"Oh, you're the Met curator who salvaged me from the garbage heap of history. I'm not sure if I ever thanked you properly, but my life has been out of kilter."

"We exhibited your paintings because they deserved it. But I'm calling you on another matter. I hear that you are the executor of Peter Burgh's estate and I'd like to buy a few for the Met."

"I'm kind of new at this. Haven't figured out the market."

"I've got twenty thousand dollars. At today's prices, that ought to get me four or five Burghs. I'd like three of the middle fifties and two late ones."

"Let me check it out with our estate attorney, and if he agrees on what the market is today, the Met will have itself a deal."

"Might I inquire who'll you be asking for advice?"

"Peter's lawyer, Gilbert Truson."

"Makes sense. He's a straight shooter."

"I know that the Met would be on the top on Peter's list of museums. And I think we can do business." *Did I say that? Am I becoming a bourgeois fink? They're the enemy, remember? Have the fat cats gotten to me?*

* * *

Stein phoned Sandy Jones and was told that Burgh had severed his connection with the gallery before he died and that his pictures had been sold or returned to Burgh. "Try Celia Loeb. She bought a bunch recently."

Jones also said that he had sold many Burghs to a new gallery in Paris called Galerie Global, cash up front. "I made a pretty penny and so did Peter. I asked Celia to send me the address of the gallery."

"May I have it?"

"She wouldn't give it to me. I wanted to write the Galerie Global asking for the names of the collectors. It didn't have a phone either."

"Can I have an inventory of the paintings you sold her?"

"Of course. I'll have a copy in the mail. Interesting you should ask. Some time back, Joseph Sawyer also wanted the list."

* * *

After Jones's letter arrived, Stein asked a fellow curator at the Louvre about the gallery. She had never heard of it.

* * *

Stein called Tom Hess and asked for Sawyer's number and address in Georgia. A woman's voice answered, "Yes, he's here. Joseph, it's a Mr. Stein for you."

Stein said, "Finally located you. I didn't know you had left New York."

"My mother took ill, and I have to take care of her. I'll be here for a lengthy spell, but I spend much of my time in Atlanta. Lucky you found me here. What's up?"

"I've been trying to track down some twenty paintings by Burgh. They've vanished in Paris. Sandy Jones gave me the list and said he had also given it to you. Did you locate any of them by chance? The Met wants to acquire a few."

A long pause. "Pictures sold abroad? Let me see. That was when I was thinking of doing a book on Peter, but I dropped the project. No, I didn't get too far."

"Too bad." *You're a lousy liar. What are you covering up?* "I've begun to write on Burgh. He gave you material that may be of help to me. Will you mail it to me? In case I need to reach you again, can I have your address and phone number?"

Again a pause, and an uncertain, "Sure. You'd best try me in Atlanta."

* * *

Stein phoned Loeb and asked about the Burghs she bought from Jones. She said, "I sold them."

"To whom?"

"Can't say. That information is confidential."

"Would the owners lend any for my show at the Met? Might they give or sell one or two to us?"

"I'll have to check."

"Come on Celia, this is your heart-throb Herbert you're talking to. And I'm representing the Metropolitan Museum. Why the mystery?"

"Look, it wasn't my idea to keep this information confidential. It was a condition of the sale."

"Do you think your collectors would turn down an artist's retrospective at the Met?"

"I doubt it, but I really don't know."

"How strange. Well, see what you can do."

* * *

Stein kept poring over the list Jones had sent him without knowing why but with a growing suspicion that he was missing something, but what? Then one of Burgh's titles, *Lament,* called to mind the picture. Hadn't he seen it somewhere? But where? Taking a piece of paper, he made a quick sketch of his mental image. Was there actually such a picture? Was his mind playing tricks? No, he had seen the painting reproduced. But where? He tried to remember everything he had read or looked at over the past year without success. Better let it rest. It would come to him. He couldn't put it out of mind, but he had to. There was an acquisitions committee meeting early in the after-noon and he had to make a presentation. Just as he finished making his recommendation for the acquisition of a combine painting by Rauschenberg, he saw the Burgh in his mind's eye. It was reproduced in the catalog of a show at the Cincinnati College Gallery of Art. After the meeting, he went to Met's library and found the catalog. There it was, "*Lament,* 1955, Private Collection."

Stein knew the curator in Cincinnati. "Say, that Peter Burgh in your show. Terrific painting. I'd like to include it in a retrospective we're doing at the Met. Whose is it?"

"Oh, we got it from Morton Nichols's wife. A few of her relatives live around here, and an aunt of hers is a friend of the gallery."

"Thanks, old buddy. Do me a favor, if anyone wants to know if I asked about the Burgh, say no. I can't tell you why now, but when I can, you'll be the first to know." *Nichols? How could he buy a Burgh from a nonexistent French gallery? It gets more and more curious.*

***

What should Stein do? He phoned Gil Truson and, swearing him to secrecy, told him the story. "I hate to impose on you, but would you try to buy a Burgh from the Celia Loeb Gallery? I'm curious to see what happens."

"I'll try, and if the price is right, I may even purchase it."

Truson called Loeb. She said, "I don't have any Burghs for sale at present."

"I was told you had a few of his paintings in stock."

"I sold them to a single collector."

"Could you tell me who? I'd like to purchase one."

"I can't reveal his name, but I can contact him and inform him of your desire to buy one, although I don't think he would want to part with any of them. However, if the price is right? Hmm. Let me feel him out. And I will certainly put in a good word."

"Thank you, but keep my name to yourself. I have reasons for not disclosing it."

***

Loeb was delighted that a collector of Truson's stature would want her to help him buy a work by Burgh. Three days later she phoned him and invited him to lunch at her gallery. He agreed. She dressed her best and greeted him with her most refined and gracious air.

"My collector will sell, but the price is steep. He wants ten thou."

"That is high. Only yesterday, it seems as if Burghs were

selling at a third of that, and that was before his market collapsed. Who is this collector?"

"I can't tell you that, that is, unless you are serious about buying."

"I can't get serious about acquiring a Burgh until I know it's a first-rate painting, particularly given the price you quoted. You understand, of course."

"Yes, but I'd like to say that in a very short time you'll be able to sell the work for twice what you'll be laying out for it."

Loeb caught a slight look of annoyance on Truson's face. *Damn it Celia, wrong pitch. Cool it.*

Truson said, "If the owner wants me to keep mum, I will. You know my reputation." With an edge in his voice, he added, "But I must know whether the collector is known for his taste before this negotiation goes any further. And do something about the price. I'd hate to waste his time, or yours or mine."

"If you'll excuse me for a moment, Mr. Truson, I'll phone him." Loeb went into the next room.

Nichols said, "Yeah, tell Truson he's dealing with me. He's an old friend. And Celia, old girl, tell him that because of his services to American art, I'll sell at seven. If word gets out that Truson bought a Burgh—and I'll see that it does—his prices will shoot up. We'll have seen the bottom of the market."

Loeb returned to Truson and said, "The owner is Morton Nichols. The painting is *Melville*, dated 1956."

Truson repeated, "Morton Nichols. I know him. A fine collector. And 1956 is an excellent year for Burgh."

"Nichols says that he will cut the price to seven because of your support of American art."

"That is very good of him. But, I'll think it over and contact Mr. Nichols, informing you, of course. If you hear of any other Burghs for sale, please let me know."

"I know of another picture in Nichols' collection, titled *Golem*, that I think he will sell. Are there any other artists you might be interested in?"

"As a matter of fact, there is. A young Californian by the name of Diebenkorn. I understand you represent him."

"May I show you some of his paintings?"

* * *

Truson called Stein, "She found me two Burghs in the Morton Nichols collection, titled, *Melville* and *Golem*, both dated 1956. Nichols wanted ten for *Melville*, would settle for seven—the discount as his gift to me for my services to American art."

"I sense that the price will soon jump."

* * *

Stein slouched by the phone staring into space. *Yes,* Melville, *it was on the list of works sold to a fictitious gallery in Paris. And it ends up with Nichols. And both he and Loeb want it kept secret. Why have they bought dozens of Burghs? And how does it affect Burgh's biography and my writing of it? What's Sawyer's role in this?*

Stein sat bolt upright and said out loud, "They're speculating, even trying to corner the market."

CHAPTER 19: Michael Pearson
(January 24, 1964)

Herbert Stein met Pearson at Burgh's studio. He said, "Were you surprised by Peter's will? That he left his estate to you, except for the money he left Eileen?"

"I never expected it. I guess that in the end I was the only friend he had left—or trusted."

Stein said, "Abrams offered me a contract to write a Burgh book. The publisher wants me to get permission from the estate to go through his papers and to quote whatever I want. Also, I'll need the right to reproduce the pictures. Will that be okay?"

"Sure. Peter thought highly of you. If a book were going to be written, he would have wanted you to do it. But I've got more in mind for you. Look at those piles of paper in that bookcase over there. All that stuff—lists, inventories, photographs, and slides. Then there's those file cabinets— a lifetime of letters, articles, reviews, announcements, and catalogs. And those cardboard boxes in the corner. What a mess. I suggest that as you do your research, you organize this stuff. When you're finished, the estate will donate it to the Archives of American Art. We'll also pay them to do interviews on tape with art world people who knew Peter, particularly the oldsters before they belly up. I think you ought to be paid for your work. Could you take a year off from the Met? I also need two more trustees for the foundation. Would you serve? I'm thinking of Truson as the third guy."

"I'd like to organize this archive and serve as a trustee. I'm due for a sabbatical from the Met, but I'm not sure I can take a year off or take any money."

"We'll see. May I talk to your boss?"

"Of course."

* * *

The next morning, Pearson phoned James Canning and said, "The Burgh estate would like to donate a major painting to the Met. Can we talk?"

"Let's have lunch."

Over lunch, Pearson said, "Putting Peter's papers in order will require a lot of work. I can't do it and wouldn't have a clue as to how, but I know who can, and he works for you."

"Herbert Stein."

"Right. And he tells me he's writing a book on Peter, which Abrams has agreed to publish. Can you spare him for a year? The estate will pay his salary, of course."

"I don't see why not. He's due for a leave. And a major book will advance his career and serve the museum."

"Good, and one more thing. Can he act as a trustee of the foundation I'm setting up? It'll be not-for-profit."

"He most certainly can."

"Perfect. If it's okay with you, I'll have Stein choose the Burgh for the Met. You know that it'll be the best one."

CHAPTER 20: Marshall Hill
(March 6, 1964)

Solly Newman, the collector, visited the Celia Loeb Gallery and announced that he would like to purchase a mid-1950s painting by Peter Burgh.

"We don't have any in the gallery, but if you would like to choose from photographs, I can provide some."

"Okay."

Newman looked through the file and pointed to one. "I like this one. How much?"

"I've been asking ten."

"Get serious. I'll pay four."

"Let's settle for eight. That's as low as I'll go."

"I hate to say this, but it's a deal."

"Where shall I have it delivered?"

"My apartment, 43 Sutton Place."

"It will be delivered tomorrow."

He went for it. Newman wouldn't buy without the advice of Marshall Hill. He never had any use for Burgh. I wonder what he has in mind?

Loeb phoned Nichols to tell him of the sale.

He responded, "If another Hillite wants a Burgh, charge him twelve, sell at ten. The next one, fourteen. Then we'll really jack up the price."

"Are you sure?"

"Trust me. Or rather, my instincts. It's our time to cash in big."

That afternoon, Loeb sold two more Burghs to collectors advised by Hill. They complained loudly about the new prices, but paid up. Then a new name wanted to buy one and when Loeb told him it would cost him twenty, he said, "You're out of your mind. I won't even pay you eight."

"You must understand, Mr. Selkirk, that Burgh is suddenly hot. And it's about time that the market recognizes his genius. Twenty's the price. I won't accept less."

Selkirk paid up.

A short article by Marshall Hill in *Art News* stunned the New York art world. It read:

> I don't like being wrong about art, but I am occasionally. And when I am, I publicly admit it. I confess that I was wrong about Peter Burgh's late pictures. On first viewing them, I thought they were just bad paintings. On prolonged viewing, my eye tells me that a number of them—not all—are of the highest quality.
>
> Moreover, I now believe that Burgh's late work constitutes a formal breakthrough in modernist art. It replaces stained Color-Field painting, which has run its course. All of the problems that stain painting posed for formalist artists have been solved. To be sure, artists like Nelson Karl and Larry Martin continue to paint

masterpieces. Nonetheless, a new move in modernist art is called for and, much to my surprise, it has already been made, not by an acknowledged formalist painter, as I would have thought, but by Peter Burgh. Such are the unanticipated developments in art. Burgh perceived the problem and solved it by carrying thin field painting into the thickly painted surface, and he did so in brush-work so alive and persuasive that painting will no longer be the same. Burgh synthesized the thinly painted, open Color-Field of Barnett Newman with the fat facture of Hans Hofmann, and created an advanced and original style. Burgh's painting opens up to the future. Indeed, the destiny of contemporary art today depends on the awareness of his painting by today's artists.

Gray is the predominant color in Burgh's late paintings, and I use the word "color" advisedly, because he succeeded in making what is generally thought of as a "non-color" richly chromatic.

Burgh's painting looks crude, even clumsy and ugly. But then, truly radical art has always muscled into work that was considered inartistic, at least, at first. But more importantly, the crudeness of Burgh's painting is the result of his conviction, the intensity of which calls to mind Cézanne's still lifes and Pollock's poured abstractions. I should add, that conviction is a rare quality in today's art, too much of which chases novelty.

I have changed my opinion not only of Burgh's late canvases, but also of a number of his works from the 1950s as well. I now believe that they will rank with the most accomplished modernist paintings.

* * *

Loeb phoned Nichols and said, "Now Mort, I've done something that will get you angry, but I had no choice. I had to sell a Burgh for ten to Mrs. Goldsmith because she's my most devoted client, buys most anything I recommend."

Nichols responded, "I'm not going to have a fit, but our Burgh business has nothing to do with your gallery business, bloody nothing at all. This is the last time you're going to do anything this stupid, because I'm taking over the sale of our Burghs. You haven't got the balls to do this kind of selling. Besides, I'm a great salesman, been flogging schmattas before you were born. Send the photos of the Burghs to my office and send anyone who wants to buy a Burgh my way."

* * *

Herbert Stein phoned Hill and congratulated him on his review. He then told him he was writing a book on Burgh and asked if they could talk. Hill invited Stein to his apartment, which was a sign that Hill considered him special.

Stein said, "Try to recall when you changed your mind about Burgh's painting. What prompted such a radical reversal? Was it only your eye that did it?"

"Not quite. I had been feeling uneasy about Color-Field abstraction for some time. There was too much of it around and, except for Karl and Martin, none of it was on a par with their work. So I was on the lookout for what art needed to stay vital—and there was Burgh."

Stein hesitated, then said, "From your essay, it appears that his late work is now your new agenda."

Hill retorted with an edge in his voice. "That's crap. I have no agenda. I'm open to every kind of art. But I've got an instinct for what's fresh and what's stale, and above all what has quality. And Burgh has it all."

"But you do dismiss artists who work in styles you don't approve of? I'm thinking of Rauschenberg and Warhol."

"You're not going to tell me that those losers are in the same class as Karl and Martin. Your eye can't be that deficient, or is it? It's the difference between authentic modernist and phony novelty art—here today, gone tomorrow. Face it, history shows us that there is a mainstream in modernist art, and there are only one or two artists in a generation who recognize it and have the genius to advance it. Look, take Abstract Expressionism. Who aside from Pollock and Newman is truly great? And don't give me de Kooning and Guston."

"Why did it take you so long to single out Burgh?" *Yeah, I was way ahead of you.*

"It wasn't long. The last works did it." Hill stood up. "Time's up. Let me show you some of the paintings on my walls."

As he accompanied Stein to the door, he said, "You really ought to rethink art of the last half-century, and when you do, give me a call."

* * *

Stein phoned Pearson and reported his conversation with Hill. "I think he was trying to recruit me into his clique. I failed the test. But he's invited me to call again, the lure of my job at the Met, I guess. How can we use him?"

Pearson responded quietly. "Our problem is, how will he try to use us? Better be careful."

* * *

Within months of Hill's review, Burgh's late painting had spawned a school of painters slathering pigment. Or as Stein said to Knight, "A new Hill cottage-industry—impasto art—Pasta Art."

"Fat Art."

It did not take long for a Burgh painting to be sold at auction for fifty-five thousand dollars, a price that would soon be considered "the bargain of 1964." Nor did it take long for Stein to learn via the grapevine, that Hill had bought two Burghs from Nichols on the sly, with the proviso that the sale be kept secret. But, like most everything in the art world, it wasn't.

* * *

Soon after his meeting with Stein, Hill met Pearson at an opening and invited him for a drink at a nearby bar. Over a scotch for Hill and a Coke for Pearson, Hill said, "I understand that you are nicknamed Little Mike, after Big Mike. Mind if I call you that?"

"Not at all."

"I think you know how much I admire Burgh's painting and all I've done for his reputation and, as I've been told, for his market. I can do more. But to be up front with you, I've got to live, which means that there has to be something in it for me. You understand."

"Yes, I appreciate your support of Burgh, but I don't know what we can do. The estate is giving most of the works to museums. There is some small income from the sale of his work, most of which goes to a modest salary for me and Herbert Stein."

"I don't want money, but I would like a painting to hang on my wall, even a small one."

"No can do. But if you write an article, we'll pay for it on the condition that we can announce that the estate is the sponsor."

"You could be using me better than that. Think it over."

"I certainly will." *Fat chance.*

CHAPTER 21: Michael Pearson
(April 4, 1964)

Looking through Burgh's paintings in the Santini Warehouse, Pearson said to Stein, "Did you hear what a Burgh sold for at the Christie's auction the other night? Seventy-five grand. Would you believe it? Hill's article was partly responsible and we should be thankful. Of course, Peter would have been furious with Hill's turning him into commodity and a formalist."

Stein said, "Maybe not. Peter believed that you couldn't begin painting as a formalist, but art history would turn you into one. That's what Hill's done to him."

Pearson pointed to a small piece of paper tacked to the back of one painting. He said, "What's that? I missed it. It's written in Peter's scrawl." Stein read it out loud:

> "Strange regions there are, strange minds, strange realms of the spirit, lofty and spare. [Where] criminals of the dream...brood...where solitary and rebellious artists, inwardly consumed, hungry and proud, wrestle in a fog of cigarette smoke with devastating ultimate ideals. Here is the end: ice, chastity, null. Here is valid no compromise,

no concession, no half-way....Here reigns defiance and iron consistency, the ego supreme amid despair; here freedom, madness, and death hold sway."

Later, in his research, Stein tracked down the source. It was from Thomas Mann's 1904 short story, "At the Prophets."

* * *

Stein phoned Eileen, "I'm writing a book on Peter and would like to talk to you about him."

"There's nothing much to say. I fell in love with him because he was a great artist. And probably as important to me at first, was that he was a war hero. That doesn't sound like much today, but back then, to have seen Peter in his captain's uniform with his medals was a real turn-on. On top of that, he was about the most beautiful thing I had ever laid eyes on. Sure, he couldn't keep his fly zipped and I couldn't live with his sleeping around, but in the early years, our marriage was glorious. If you think it'll help, we can talk. But meanwhile, I'll ship you his letters and other stuff I saved. When you're done, turn them over to the Archives of American Art with the proviso that they keep them on hold for a couple of decades. And you must promise to get my approval for any personal material you use in your book. After all, I have a daughter and a husband to protect. I also own early work that you could photograph and maybe find a museum to donate it to."

Stein replied, "Thanks for your offer. I'll mail you a

notarized letter that says you have complete control over what you send me."

* * *

As Stein examined the letters and notes, he became increasingly aware of the complexity of Peter's life and art. He went from optimistic communist to gung-ho Marine to tragic existentialist. His art shifted from Social Realist to Surrealist to Abstract Expressionist. A typical monograph would be inadequate. He would need to deal with Peter's biography and the changing social situation in the United States. He would need to interview not only Eileen and Little Mike, but also Burgh's Abstract Expressionist friends and acquaintances: de Kooning, Guston, Rothko, Motherwell, and Newman, as well as Jones, Loeb, Nichols, and Sawyer, and also old friends and acquaintances—before they were dead.

What might prove most difficult was the treatment of Burgh's late depression and suicide. In discussing the book with Pearson, he broached the subject of Burgh's death.

Pearson related, "I witnessed Peter's depression as no one else had, days, weeks, and months. I won't give you the details. He had this revolver, a thirty-eight. Then, the day he died, he begged me with whatever wits he had left to use it. And he begged me in a whine—proud Peter begged me in a whine that broke my heart—to kill him with it. I wonder if I could have saved him." He stopped. Then he said, "The truth is I tried. Okay, here's what really happened. When I saw Peter nursing the gun, I shouted, 'Wait,

I want to tell you something!' He hesitated, which enabled me to move close to him and lunge at the gun. I grabbed it and tried to take it away. Then it went off. Who pulled the trigger, him or me? I'll never know. There, that's the whole story."

Pearson added, "Strangest thing. When I first came into the studio, Peter said, 'Is that you Frankie?' He had never mentioned any Frankie to me. I thought you might try to track Frankie down, I mean for your book, but it would probably end up like the quest for Citizen Kane's 'Rosebud.'"

* * *

Pearson phoned Gilbert Truson. "Thanks for setting up the Peter Burgh Foundation. I think it will help further his reputation. But a bunch of Peter's paintings are still in the hands of Nichols and Loeb, worth a fortune. I want to sue the bastards to get them back."

"That will be very difficult. You could consider what they did hanky-panky but there was nothing really illegal."

"But didn't they conspire to corner the market? Wouldn't that be restraint of trade or something? Aren't there anti-monopoly laws?"

"That will be very hard to prove, if not impossible."

"I've been doing some hard thinking about this issue. Does the collector have total control over a painting just because it's his property? After all, he didn't create it. Doesn't the artist retain certain residual rights to it? Does the public have an interest? Peter's work is art history, American art history. I mean, a collector can't just destroy a work he bought just because he owns it, or can he? After all, a piece of art is more than a piece of furniture. Can't we claim that it is more like a pet—a dog or a cat—and there are laws against cruelty to animals?"

"The artist's and the public's residual rights have not been defined by the courts."

"Well, maybe it's about time they are. I refuse to accept that the Nichols-Loeb cabal have the right to do what they want with the work of a great artist, what the Japanese would call a "national treasure," just because they own it and that after their shenanigans, they'll make a mint. I won't let the bastards get away with all of it, not if I can help it."

"Litigation costs money."

"There's enough money in the estate, and I think it ought to be used to reclaim some of Peter's work from those money-grubbers. Peter would have liked that. Besides, it'll cost them too—not only in money, but in reputation, especially now that Nichols is on the board of the American Federation of Art and still angling for the Met. Lawyers' costs will make them think twice. Will you help me sue the bastards?"

"Love to. Peter deserves his day in court. I'll prepare the papers. But I'm troubled that the sensation about a court fight over Burgh's work might detract attention from the art. You know what I mean. I think I may be able to tie up the Nichols-Loeb holdings for a long time. That'll give them pause for thought. It might be better for all of us to sit down and work something out. Like, we don't blow the whistle if Nichols and Loeb donate a part of their stash to your foundation, say half of the Burgh's they still own? Two-thirds? That'll make them look good, and with the tax write-off and the Burghs they have left, they'll still make a bundle, too much of a bundle in my opinion. Also, remember that the estate has legal control over reproduction and copyright. If they don't play ball, they won't get a penny of that."

Nichols and Loeb were easily persuaded to settle for a fifty-fifty split.

* * *

Sawyer visited Pearson to arrange his retrospective show in Atlanta. Pearson had reservations about showing the slashed canvases, but Sawyer talked him into taking the risk. "Let it all hang out. No self-censorship. I'll deal with it in the catalog."

The mayor of Atlanta attended the opening and spoke. "I was told that Michael Pearson's nickname is Little Mike and that he was named after Michelangelo. He may not get as much coverage in the art history books as the Renaissance master, but just to be coupled with his illustrious predecessor is honor enough. And this about a painter of the American Southland, who brings glory to the culture of our great region. Thank you Little Mike."

Pearson responded, "Thank you, Mayor Briggs, I'm proud to be here and to show in this beautiful museum."

* * *

The next day, as Pearson was entering the museum, he heard a voice saying, "Little Mike, that you?" He turned and saw an African-American man who looked vaguely familiar. When he raised a clenched fist, Pearson shouted, "It's Boomer Bowman. Is that really you? It can't be. The man I knew had no pot belly."

"I can say the same for you, Little Mike. You've become so bourgeois I scarcely recognized you."

"You've come to see my show and pay homage?"

"I saw it yesterday before the opening and it sure looks good, really good. But today I've come to see you on another matter."

"What's up? You still painting?"

"How could I not? But only when I'm not loading trucks. Painting on nights and weekends it is. You still got a social conscience or has the bourgeoisie housebroken you? That suit and tie makes it hard to tell."

"I've been tamed but I still hate the bastards like I used to."

"Well, I'm glad you've still got a bit of the old-time lefty religion. I've got something to ask of you. There's a dozen black artists here in Atlanta. We go on making art and rarely showing or selling it. Poor black folk can't afford to buy. The new rich black lawyers and doctors buy what's safe, meaning white. We want to be recognized, finally. But they haven't come to terms down here with this new age—black liberation. Down here too many whites still use the 'n-word.' You're a honcho now and can get the word out where it'll help, we hope. Maybe get us a show in this museum or even an alternative space? Talk to what's-his-name, Joseph Sawyer. Could you find time to check my guys out?"

"Right on. When? I don't know how long I can stay down here."

"How about tonight? The guys get off from their day jobs around six."

"I've got a dinner I gotta go to. Sawyer will be there. Maybe he can come along. It'll last to around ten."

"Ten's okay with us, but it'll be a long night."

"Pick me up at the Holiday Inn."

"Right on."

As they moved from studio to studio, Pearson said little, except in front of the painting by Jeb Jackson. He then became animated and said to him, "This is terrific. It's new and it's yours."

They finished the visits around two A.M. Over a drink and a snack prepared by Bowman's half-asleep wife, Pearson said, "You know, the work on the whole ain't great, except for yours and that Jackson fellow, but it's as good as the best of what I've seen around here. And, come to think of it, it would look creditable in New York. It's really worth a show. I'm only a visitor here, but I'll see what I can do."

"But not only for myself and Jackson. The support we give each other has kept us going. And we don't want the idea of winners and losers messing us up. We'll only show as a group, call us the Russell Square Painters. Russell Square, that's ghetto territory."

"Can you get me some slides of the work?"

"It just so happens that I've got a packet of them right here. I knew in my gut that the muck-a-mucks couldn't totally co-opt you."

Later Pearson recalled that Sawyer had said very little during the entire visit.

* * *

Pearson met Sawyer the next day.

"What did you think about last night? They really deserve a show. They're good old boys too, you know."

"Wrong color. It won't fly, not in this part of the South. Not even in Atlanta. A show of black artists wouldn't get past the museum trustees or even the board of my alternative space."

"Even though the attitudes are changing?"

"It's too soon. It hasn't really penetrated down here."

"Would you try?"

"It's no use."

"I would have thought that you of all people would extend yourself for your fellow pariahs."

"What do you mean by that?"

"Race discrimination, sex discrimination, six of one, half a dozen of the other. Would you at least go so far as to arrange a lunch with me and one or two more liberal museum trustees? You must have some as buddies."

Sawyer phoned. "I've arranged lunch at the museum tomorrow at one with Manny Woodman, a trustee. And I'll be there."

* * *

Woodman brought a fellow trustee, Richard Overton. They listened closely to Pearson. Overton said, "Well, this is a show that's overdue. Can you get slides?"

"I have them here."

"Look, can you arrange studio visits, say tomorrow? That's Sunday afternoon."

"Let's meet at my hotel. What time?"

"Two P.M."

* * *

Pearson and Bowman met Woodman and Overton. Bowman offered a ride in his old Ford but Overton suggested his station wagon with a smile, "Mine's larger."

Bowman's studio was the last they visited.

Woodman said, "This is your home."

"Yes."

"Where's your family and the families of the other artists we looked in on?"

"They've all gone to the movies or the park to play it safe. My wife's afraid my six-year-old grandson, a charming but rambunctious kid, would say the wrong thing. I don't have to tell you, sir, how important your visit is to us."

"I don't mean to pry, but I'm curious about your lives."

"What can I say? Mine is much like most other artists. I wanted—needed—to be an artist and created a life with that in mind. I work loading and unloading trucks. From my boyhood on, my family needed my paychecks, so I couldn't take the time for much schooling. My wife could. She was able to earn a masters degree in education and teaches high school. We've got two of our kids in black colleges, luckily on scholarships. I do read a lot."

As they parted, Woodman said, "You know we can't promise you anything, but we'll try."

* * *

Woodman quickly set up a lunch meeting the following day with the museum trustees and invited Pearson and Sawyer. The meeting was short. Woodman and Overton reported on their studio visits, showed the slides and recommended a show of the Russell Square Painters. Timothy Perkins objected. "Is now the time? Do we really want to get mixed up in the politics of race? A lot of people are going to be mighty mad. There's still the Klan. May even bomb the museum. Can't we just stick to art?" The vote was five to two. Martin Stone, the board president, said, "Well, the matter's settled. I think it's about time."

"Well, our racists won't think so."

Pearson spoke up. "You'll need funds to do this show properly."

Woodman said, "I'll raise the money."

Pearson added, "If you need more, my foundation will chip in. Pay for a really first-rate catalog dedicated to Peter Burgh. And Joseph Sawyer here can curate the show."

* * *

Pearson took Sawyer aside and said, "You came through in the end, but deep down in your soul, there's still a reservoir of Jim Crow."

"I'll make up for it by organizing a sensational show and catalog."

"For openers. There's still your Southern Edge and no black face to be seen in it. Or female face for that matter."

"You're asking too much, too fast. I know the world down here and it'll take time. The white artists won't go for it, and if they pull out, the Southern Edge will go belly up. I have to proceed carefully, but I will try."

"There may be less of a negative reaction than you think. Times are changing, you know. But it's up to you, not me. And a person in your minority ought to extend himself more for other minorities."

"Okay, Little Mike, I'll do whatever I can. I mean that. I'm not just putting you off. Your show at the museum is the first step. And let's see how it plays out."

* * *

Pearson decided to stay in Atlanta for a few more days, not so much to bask in his success, but to study his work in order to see or feel what his next moves might be. He also closely watched the people who visited the gallery, trying to fathom what they were experiencing. He would sometimes follow them, listening in on their conversations. He found one woman particularly interesting to watch. She looked intently at every painting, one at a time, totally engrossed, at times moving back to a painting she had already looked at. Little Mike stood beside her. He said, "Forgive me for disturbing you but, when you turn back to a painting, what are you looking for?"

She looked startled for a moment and said, "Do I know you?"

"No, I don't mean to intrude. I'm just curious."

"I wondered about the different ways this artist used shapes and colors and what he might have had in mind. The pictures strike me as very satisfying."

"Satisfying? That's curious. Are you an artist?"

"No, and I don't know much except I enjoy looking at art. I am very moved by these pictures. Don't ask me why."

"Too bad, because I'd like to know why."

Pearson sized her up. A faded southern belle in her late forties or early fifties. Spinster. Thin but nicely put together. Still handsome in a patrician way, antebellum South. Primly dressed and wearing sensible shoes. *School teacher, I'll bet.*

She said, "What do you think?"

"May I try to tell you over lunch?"

She smiled and said flirtatiously, "A pick-up at my age? Lordy, lordy."

He said sternly, "I'll have you know that I'm a proper southern gentleman."

She rolled her eyes.

"And I should tell you, I'm the artist."

"I sensed that. You're Michael Pearson. My name is Anne Beaufort."

"Friends call me Little Mike."

"Aren't you rather un-little for that nickname?"

"I'll recite my narrative over lunch."

That was the beginning of their romance.

*** * * ***

Upon his return to New York, Pearson called his phone service. A message from Stein.

"Nichols is in trouble. Listen to this headline on the front page of the *New York Times*. 'Big-Time Collector Charged with Tax Evasion.' The article says that Mort has broken tax laws to make huge profits on his paintings. Mort wants us to tell the *Times* about his generous gift of paintings to the foundation."

"Well, we'll just give them the facts."

* * *

While investigating Nichols, the IRS discovered that he hadn't declared the money he made on the sale of Burgh's paintings on his latest tax return. They decided to make an example out of him.

At the hearing, the judge ruled that Nichols had to pay the back taxes and in addition, subsidize art classes in a ghetto high school. This was the beginning of the Morton Nichols Program for the Advancement of Art Appreciation in Public Schools.

CHAPTER 22: Knight & Stein
(August 14, 1964)

Stein and Knight had drunk too much cheap wine at the Whitney opening of Burgh's thirties drawings. They then went to her apartment. Resting after sex, he said, "Let's look into the future. What's in store for us, I mean, for all of our acquaintances?"

"You tell me."

"I'll be the Director of the Institute of Contemporary Art in Philadelphia or Boston. End up at the Hirshhorn or Whitney, maybe even the Modern, if I'm lucky. You'll go on being the painter and collagist you are today, becoming better and better, and slowly getting more recognition. A retrospective at the Whitney, perhaps even MoMA."

"I'll settle for all of that. In the future, we'll have a new suffragette movement, and I'll be rehabilitated as a great lady painter who paints as good as a man, almost."

"Don't hold your breath. What about Neil?"

"Neil? I can't remember when I've last thought of him."

"I got word from the boonies. He's become a big-shot professor, lectures his students about the good old hey-day of American art, when he palled around with Pollock and de Kooning and showed Burgh how to paint. And how, when Marshall Hill and greedy dealers like Celia Loeb corrupted the New York art world, he escaped into America where he could uphold the great tradition of Western Art, with a capital 'W' and a capital 'A'. Pontificates that he wouldn't allow his painting ever again to be sullied by a show in a New York fleshpot. As for the future, he'll knock up some corn-fed graduate student and have to marry her. Womanize on the side. Have a big retrospective organized by his university museum—what's the name of the state he teaches in? The show will travel to the Art Museum of Anal Falls, Arkansas and other such distinguished venues. *American Artist* will list it in the 'Summer Shows to See.' Then the College Art Association will award Neil its great teacher award. That'll be the high point of his career."

Knight shook a finger at Stein. "Bitchy, bitchy, bitchy. And Hill? What about Hill?"

"Neil will get back at Hill in his speech at the CAA. Hill will be sent up as a vampire who sucks the blood of artists for his own fame and money—and that'll be for openers. The creep is already the grand old man of art criticism. As alcohol eats his brain, he'll write less and less. And the less he writes, the greater his fame. Don't ask me why."

"What about Sawyer?"

"He'll remain the spokesman of the new Southern Edge in the great Southland. It'll fall apart over the issue of accepting African Americans and women. He'll get to run the Georgia Institute of Modern Art and teach on the side, or the other way around. He'll also curate occasional museum shows of southern artists. Share an apartment with a professor. Male, of course. He'll attack New York as the art world Sodom, but his envy will show through his hatred. He'll be featured in *Art in America*, once, and in the Sunday *New York Times*, once. Then, the Southern Edge will edge out of the art world's picture, and so will he. But Sawyer will be revived every four and a half years to do another show of artists below the Mason Dixon Line and write a book on them, which will become a kind of bible for Americanists."

"Little Mike?"

"He's having a comeback as an old master of geometric abstraction and an early practitioner of Hard-Edge abstraction, a minor master but a master nonetheless. And he'll make the history books of American art. His rehabilitation is well under way. Little Mike told me that Schumacher came to interview him the other day and even wanted to talk about *his* work as well as Peter's. Thomas Moran, you know, that new curator at the Whitney, offered Mike a retrospective, and wants to acquire several of the pictures. The show will travel to good venues. Respectful reviews. But he will also be remembered as Peter's closest friend. And Little Mike has found a new woman, a handsome southern matron who'll keep him out of trouble, and he's in love."

Knight said, "Then there's Nichols. He'll turn the crime of screwing New York taxpayers into a public service. He's already used his efforts on behalf of art in ghetto schools and parlayed it into winning the Mayor's Medal for Community Service. I always thought he'd wind up in jail or in the East River clad in cement shoes. How wrong I was."

Stein added, "A thirty thousand dollar donation to the Mayor's campaign for re-election helped. He'll never be considered for the Met's board, but he'll keep pushing."

Knight said, "I guess I wish him well. He was the first to buy my work. The Loeb Gallery will peter out. Celia will flog art out of her apartment to Bronx and Brooklyn nouveau riche. Become an art advisor. And make a name of sorts as an interior decorator."

Stein added, "As for us, you and I'll get married and have two-point-four kids and a station wagon and live happily ever after."

CHAPTER 23: Peter Burgh
(September 28, 1964)

Burgh would have been astonished at the turnout at his memorial. Pearson was. Standing just inside the door of the Metropolitan's auditorium as the crowd surged in, he wondered who they were. He nodded to a few of the oldsters and recognized some dealers he had pestered and a few museum people. But who were the hundreds of young people, some in paint-smeared jeans? Celia Loeb stopped and said hello sweetly. He returned her greeting solemnly.

Gilbert Truson stopped and greeted Pearson.

Pearson said, "Who are all these people?"

"It's an art world ingathering of the tribe to celebrate a great artist, and to be seen doing so. Memorials are major social occasions."

Rothko's talk was short. Looking down, he spoke in a strained voice that was barely audible.

"First Arshile, then Jackson, then Bradley and Franz, and now Peter—all of them painting great pictures to the end. God has not been kind to American artists. Too many have died young, but they inaugurated a great period in world art. It is dying with them, but their pictures will live on. Not everyone will appreciate them. But those who dare confront the tragic aspect of life will need them." Rothko broke down. Harold Rosenberg helped him from the podium.

Guston, his great head bowed, stood silent for a moment. "I want to talk about commitment. Commitment to what? Good painting, some would say. Sure, good painting. But about what? One's truth, some would say. But what truth? Peter's answer would have been, 'a personal truth that is more than personal.' Peter spent his entire life in search of this truth. Did he find it? Look at his paintings and decide for yourselves. Was it worth a life? What other kind of life is worth more? Like Mark says, Peter's paintings will live on. But will the example of his commitment to high art? It ought to be a beacon for all of us. I hope it will be."

Schapiro orated in his high-pitched voice, as he did no matter what the occasion.

"Marcel Duchamp thought all painters were dumb by nature. As in most everything else, he was wrong. I've met my share of great artists and they all were smart, every one of them. Peter was the smartest. He was a true intellectual. Now there are many in our world who think that brains are the enemy of emotion. I say this results in brainless art. Art, if it's to have any relevance, has to be critical, and that takes intellect. And in this sense, Peter was a profound thinker. This is why he recognized what painting needed in order to be relevant in our time. Peter wouldn't base his art on ideas in which he no longer believed. And that's why his canvases speak to us today as powerfully as they do."

Ravin raised his eyes upward and nodded sadly.

"Now Peter Burgh too is dead. Gone is a master painter. Gone too is my friend whose intelligence, warmth, and spontaneity was a delight, not only for me but for the many others who knew him. Gone too is a role model for American artists. No, not only artists, but the American people as well. What did Peter teach us? To cultivate our unique vision and aspire to creative excellence, and at a time in American art when both were sorely lacking. Yes, Peter was the exemplar of the nonconformist American who utterly rejected mass culture. He made extraordinary artistic demands on himself, and many times I had witnessed his profound anguish. But he had another side. And standing here and looking back, I see in my mind's eye the smiling Peter Burgh, whose camaraderie those of us who knew and cherished him will not forget."

Then, William Rayburn, the chairman of the Trustees of the Museum of Modern Art, walked to the podium and intoned.

"I met Mr. Peter Burgh only once, at a dinner party at my mother's home, and was impressed by his culture. This didn't surprise me, because on my bedroom wall there is a handsome, small painting by Burgh, which I cherish. The picture is a beautiful abstraction of nature and makes me feel good every time I look at it. Although it is an abstract, it is in the grand tradition of American landscape painting. With his death, we have lost a great American painter, and he shall be missed. We at the Modern are proud to own three paintings by Burgh. They are now hanging in the lobby in his memory."

Pearson winced at just about every word that Rayburn said. He was the last speaker.

"I'd like to begin by saying that I owe Peter a personal debt. A few years back, he kept me alive by buying my work, which was his way of giving me money in order to save me the indignity of accepting charity. He literally kept me alive when I was down and out. In fact, he was my only patron, and I am grateful, more than I can say.

It's nice to hear Peter Burgh eulogized as a national treasure, a beacon of American art, a model for young painters, and a painter of beautiful pictures. None of these represented a critical side of the Peter Burgh I knew, and I knew him longer and better than anyone here. My Peter Burgh was a rebel, an artistic and social rebel. We met in the 1930s when we were both on the Federal Art Project, barely keeping body and soul together. There was this cafeteria that served free hot water and had ketchup bottles on the table. Peter and I would make tomato soup by mixing the water with the ketchup. We were not only poor, but we identified with the poor, and both of us were members of radical organizations intent on overthrowing or reforming the capitalist system that had impoverished America. But our own poverty could not curb our need for art, and we kept on painting. When the reactionaries closed down the Federal Art Project, we went hungry, but by then, Peter and I had gone to war against fascism. He earned medals for bravery.

After the war, he resumed his painting, working even in the dead of winter, when he had no heat. He could have painted what was fashionable. That is, he could have sold out, but he wouldn't. When our government did take notice of Peter, it was to condemn his abstract art as subversive, degenerate, and un-American. He is now recognized by the establishment, and he would have been grateful for this small favor, even though he is often acclaimed for the wrong reasons.

Peter hoped that there would be an end to man's inhumanity to man. There wasn't and he knew there wouldn't be. So in the name of truth, his work was tragic. The late work has the aura of death, the stink of rotting bodies, the unholy waste—the misery of it all.

Most of all, these paintings speak to our wretched time, and that makes him the relevant artist that he is."

END

Irving Sandler's career began with a fortuitous encounter with Franz Kline's, *Chief,* in the Museum of Modern Art in New York around 1952, a painting that moved him deeply and as he said, changed his life. He began to meet artists and soon became immersed in the then-small avant-garde New York art world, becoming the manager of the Tenth Street Tanager Gallery, the first artist cooperative, and running the Artists Club (founded by first-generation Abstract Expressionists) between 1955 and 1962. By 1956, Sandler had begun to write art criticism for *Art News,* and subsequently for other major art journals, as well as a weekly art column for the *New York Post.* He came to know and to interview so many artists and in such depth that he was called the "recording angel" of the New York art world (by Carter Ratcliff in *New York Magazine* in 1978, and the "balayeur des artistes," the sweeper-up of artists (by Frank O'Hara in a poem of 1964). On behalf of contemporary artists, he co-founded Artists Space (1972), now the longest running non-profit exhibition space in New York. He was also instrumental in the development of the program of the Marie Walsh Sharpe Foundation, which provides studio space in New York to artists (now the Sharpe-Walentas Studios) and served on its advisory committee.

During the time when the events in this novel took place, Sandler himself lived on Second Avenue between Ninth and Tenth Street. Sandler (B.A., Temple University, M.A., University of Pennsylvania, Ph.D., New York University) was Professor Emeritus of Art History at Purchase College, State

University of New York, where, in addition to teaching generations of art students, he also served for a short time as the director of the Neuberger Museum. His numerous publications include four surveys of art since World War II: *The Triumph of American Painting: A History of Abstract Expressionism* (1970); *The New York School: Painters and Sculptors of the 1950s* (1978); *American Art of the 1960s* (1988); and *Art of the Postmodern Era: From the late 1960s to the Early 1990s* (1996). He also wrote *A Sweeper-Up After Artists: A Memoir* (2003); *From Avant-Garde to Pluralism: An On-The-Spot History* (2006); *Abstract Expressionism and the American Experience* (2009); a second memoir, *Swept Up by Art, An Art Critic in the Post-Avant-Garde Era* (2015); and monographs on Alex Katz, Al Held, Philip Pearlstein, and Mark di Suvero (all artists whose early exhibitions took place in Tenth Street galleries), among others. He was a former president and board member of the American Section of the International Association of Art Critics. He was the recipient of a John Simon Guggenheim Fellowship in 1964, and in 2008, he received the Lifetime Achievement Award in Art Criticism from the International Association of Art Critics. Irving Sandler passed away in New York City on June 2, 2018.

OTHER BOOKS *by* IRVING SANDLER

Art of the Postmodern Era:
From the Late 1960s to the Early 1990s
Icon Editions, Harper Collins Publishers

The Fields of David Smith
Thames & Hudson

Abstract Expressionism:
The Triumph of American Painting
Routledge

The Collector as Patron in the Twentieth Century
Knoedler & Company

American Vanguards:
Graham, Davis, Gorky, de Kooning, and Their Circle, 1927-1942
Yale University Press

Richard Bellamy Mark Di Suvero
Storm King Art Center

Dan Budnik: Picturing Artists, 1950s-1960s
Knoedler & Company

At the Crossroads
University of Pennsylvania, Institute of Contemporary Art

Swept Up by Art:
An Art Critic in the Post-Avant-Garde Era
Brooklyn Rail

Polly Apfelbaum
University of Pennsylvania, Institute of Contemporary Art

Esteban Vicente: The Aristocratic Eye
Ameringer Yohe Fine Art

Abstract Expressionism and the American Experience:
A Reevaluation
Hudson Hills Press LLC

Judy Pfaff
Hudson Hills Press LLC

Al Held
Hudson Hills Press LLC

Al Held: Paintings from the Years 1954-1959
Robert Miller Gallery

Natvar Bhavsar
Rizzoli International Publications, Incorporated

Hans Hofmann: Circa 1950
Brandeis University, Rose Art Museum

A Sweeper-Up After Artists: A Memoir
Thames & Hudson

American Art of the 1960's
Icon Editions, HarperCollins Publishers

Alex Katz
Abrams, Inc.

Natvar Bhavsar: Painting and the Reality of Color
Gordon & Breach Publishing Group

Mark Di Suvero at Storm King Art Center
Abrams, Inc.

Defining Modern Art: Selected Writings of Alfred H. Barr, Jr.
Abrams, Inc.

From Avant-Garde to Pluralism: An On-The-Spot History
Hard Press Editions

Seymour Lipton: An American Sculptor
Hudson Hills Press LLC

20 Artists: Yale School of Art, 1950 to 1970
Yale University Art Gallery

Antonakos
Hudson Hills Press LLC

Beverly McIver: Invisible Me
Kent Gallery

The New York School: The Painters and Sculptors of the Fifties
Routledge

CPSIA information can be obtained
at www.ICGtesting.com
Printed in the USA
FSHW021748070419
57040FS